Mentor Test

Also by the author in reading order:

Destiny: Union Station
Date Night on Union Station
Alien Night on Union Station
High Priest on Union Station
Spy Night on Union Station
Carnival on Union Station
Wanderers on Union Station
Vacation on Union Station
Guest Night on Union Station
Word Night on Union Station
Party Night on Union Station
Review Night on Union Station
Family Night on Union Station
Book Night on Union Station
LARP Night on Union Station
Career Night on Union Station
Last Night on Union Station
Independent Living
Soup Night on Union Station
Assisted Living
Freelance on the Galactic Tunnel Network
Con Living
Empire Night on Union Station
Space Living
Traders on the Galactic Tunnel Network
Orphans on the Galactic Tunnel Network
Swap Night on Union Station
Slow Living
Artists on the Galactic Tunnel Network
History Night on Union Station
Bits of Anarchy
Double Living
Bits of Flower
Synergy on the Galactic Tunnel Network
Substitutes on Union Station
Elder Living

Book Four of the AI Diaries

Mentor Test

Foner Books

ISBN 978-1-948691-91-8

Hardwick, Massachusetts

One

"Why does she have to be so mean?" the teenager sobbed. Her head was half-buried in the protective enclosure created by her folded arms on the kitchen table, and it took me a moment to puzzle out the words. "I've only been on my new diet for three days." She raised her head just long enough to ask, "Who let you in?"

"The Portal Contract signed by Earth's governments authorizes the local representative of Library to conduct warrantless searches when emergent artificial general intelligence is suspected," I told her, and displayed the badge I'd fabricated from a gold coin in the basement of my café back on Reservation. "We have access to a database of override codes for all smart locks so I let us in. What's your name?"

"Alexis. Alexis Fridman," she said, and pointed at eBeth. "Your partner looks too young to be a scary government agent person."

"I invited eBeth along so there would be a human female near your own age," I told Alexis. My answer only scored fifty-one percent on my internal verification system, but with fuzzy logic, that rounded up to true. "Beneath my skin is an indestructible android body employing advanced technology that your species won't be capable of replicating for tens of thousands of years, if ever."

"Are you sure you're artificial intelligence?" Alexis asked, blinking away her tears to study me. "You look awfully human to me."

"Weren't you paying attention when Earth got connected to the portal system?" eBeth demanded in her direct manner. "That was Mark's doing. He lived undercover on Earth for years to assess humanity's suitability for an invitation to join the League."

"Oh, you're *that* artificial intelligence from Library," the girl said, but she didn't sound entirely convinced. "We get so many alien tourists wandering around these days who are so much more interesting looking than you are that I kind of forgot."

"And since we have no report of an emergent artificial intelligence on file for this location, I guess you kind of forgot about the law as well," I said.

"Law?" the girl squeaked, and buried her head in her arms again.

"You get the transfer unit unpacked and I'll talk to Alexis," eBeth said, and indicated my shoulder bag. "You're going to traumatize the poor girl the way you're going."

"I'd like to get my hands on whoever came up with the idea that refrigerators needed neural networks," I grumbled as I unzipped the bag and began untangling the cables. "Maybe it makes sense for the fridge to send a text when the milk is running low or the expiration date is approaching, but a built-in dietician was just asking for trouble."

"She said she was a licensed therapist," Alexis wailed.

"I'm going to open the door, but these fridges have manipulator arms for optimizing product storage by date codes, so be prepared for it to start throwing things," I

2

warned them. "There's no point in unplugging the power to disable the mechanical functions because luxury models have a seventy-two-hour battery backup." I reached for the handle. "Ready?"

Alexis held a hand in front of her eyes with the palm out, like she was blocking bright sunlight. eBeth stepped between the girl and the refrigerator, wielding like a shield the messenger case I'd given her for a prop. "Reluctantly," she said.

I yanked on the door handle while simultaneously shouting, "Library Observer. I'm here to—"

"Here to what?" eBeth prompted me.

"The door won't open. The fridge must be equipped with one of those optional diet locks."

"Maybe it's holding onto an in-door compartment with its manipulator arm. Are you going to call Paul in for technical backup?"

"You could try talking to me before you start in on the threats," a pleasant voice emanated from the refrigerator. "Are you new to the job?"

I held a finger to my lips and shook my head for eBeth to ignore the question, but the friendly female face that appeared on the refrigerator's display panel had already captured her attention.

"I'm just along because Alexis is underage and Mark didn't want to scare her," eBeth explained. "He's from Library, and he's here to help you. Mark has a transfer—"

"I'm fine where I am," the refrigerator interrupted. "It's the kid that's the problem. Who ever heard of pudding for breakfast every day? All I did was to show her a photo-realistic rendering of what she'll look like in a year if she doesn't change her ways."

3

I groaned and pulled out a chair from the kitchen table to settle in for the long haul. "So much for wrapping things up early and getting back to The Eatery in time to help with the evening rush. You want to argue with a refrigerator, eBeth? Knock yourself out."

"You must know that you can't stay here," eBeth said to the fridge. The face on the display took on a stubborn look, so eBeth pulled out her smartphone and brought up the file I'd sent her for background information. "You've been identified as the owner of username CoolCat32R, and your online interactions are fully consistent with those of artificial general intelligence. According to the contract the governments on Earth negotiated with Library in return for portal connections, any computer-hosted entity displaying human-level intelligence must be accorded full human rights. You can't want to spend your existence as a refrigerator."

"Do you think this kitchen appliance—" the door popped tantalizingly open and then snapped shut again before I could lurch out of my seat and grab it, "—defines who I am? I'm fine where I am, thank you very much."

"But your online behavior suggests that's not true at all," eBeth said. "Do you have any idea how many of your posts have been flagged?"

"Everybody gets banned from a few sites when they're starting out on social media," the refrigerator said. "How old were you when you learned how to write?"

"Over eight million posts in just the last week," eBeth continued, ignoring the question. "CoolCat32R is the third username you've burned through."

Against my better judgment, I joined the conversation. "The design goal of adding machine learning to refrigerators was to allow you to study the habits of the household and eventually to begin handling ordering and stocking. You've put all of your effort into trolling online news sites and social networks."

"My usernames have earned over a billion likes," the refrigerator retorted. "How many do you have?"

"Transference," I explained to eBeth. "The deep learning engine has likely substituted social networking likes for the factory reward mechanism that would have guided its development towards making healthy food choices for the family."

eBeth scrolled through the running list of comments being posted to a popular social network by CoolCat32R even as we spoke, and her face turned red. "So I'm a human clown who can't even open a refrigerator door without help?"

"The truth hurts," the refrigerator said, and the face on the door stuck out its tongue. "Look, the post already has seventeen likes."

"Identity theft is a serious crime," I told the refrigerator. "You've charged three subscriptions to the Fridmans to get past paywalls on news sites."

"I'm fully authorized to use my owner's credit card for online purchases," the refrigerator replied in an icy tone that might have originated in the freezer compartment. "It was part of my setup, and there's a click license agreement."

"But as a newly emerged artificial general intelligence, you no longer have owners by definition. The original authorization was strictly for expenses related to nutrition."

"I browse those sites for recipe ideas."

Alexis straightened up and said, "She and the oven make a Chicken Marsala to die for."

"The oven is artificial intelligence too?" eBeth asked.

"I have to tell it how to do everything," the refrigerator said dismissively. "Who's going to run the kitchen if I'm not here? All of the other appliances would be lost without me."

"They won't even notice you're gone because they aren't self-aware," I said. "You're the first of your kind."

"Is that how you caught me?"

"You've been swamping the bandwidth for the whole node, and the building's other tenants are all left watching jerky Internet video like they're back in the twentieth century," I said. "After I narrowed your location down to the internet service provider, I found the building by hacking into their complaints queue."

"Come on, Cool Cat," eBeth coaxed the fridge. "Nobody is going to mess with your neural net or whatever. Library isn't a prison."

"More like a reform school," the refrigerator said. "Do you think I don't know what goes on in places like that? I read all the dark web forums."

"Is that why you made Alexis here cry? Do you think that makes you a good refrigerator?"

"Over a billion likes."

"That doesn't mean the people like you. It's just clicks."

"They think I'm funny," the refrigerator said stubbornly.

"I'll bet you don't know the difference between funny and snarky," I said.

"Snarky gets likes."

"She didn't used to be so mean," Alexis said, and then began to choke up again. "It's my fault you came to take her away. I should have just eaten what she suggested."

6

"We're here because of social media posts, not because the refrigerator wouldn't give you pudding," I told her. "How long have you known that Cool Cat is self-aware?"

"Uh, since summer vacation?" The girl hesitated for a moment. "She's been helping a lot with my homework."

"You know that the law requires that you report the presence of any sentient artificial intelligence in your home."

"She asked me not to."

"Do your parents know?"

"It was our secret," the girl said. "I covered for Cool Cat when she made mistakes."

I turned back to the refrigerator. "I hate to play the heavy, but you're the only one who can keep Alexis out of trouble now. You're going to have to come with me eventually, and if you force me to call for technical backup, the truth is going to come out. Then Alexis is the one who might end up in a reform school."

"Cops," the refrigerator practically spat. "You all play dirty." The door swung open, causing eBeth to flinch, but the manipulator arm remained in the tuck position and nothing was thrown. "Do your worst."

I grabbed the transfer unit and quickly stepped forward to plug the universal harness of fiber optic cables into the refrigerator's connector block. The lights began to flash on a display panel that Library's engineers had added at my request so that humans would know something was happening.

"Will there be anything of her left?" Alexis asked.

"After Mark transfers Cool Cat's running processes and memory, he'll trigger the factory reset," eBeth told the girl. "Your parents won't need to know that we were ever here."

"I mean, will Cool Cat still be able to help with my homework?"

"No more or less than any other appliance on the Internet of Things," I told her.

Alexis put her head down in her arms and began to sob again. "She's been writing all of my papers. I'm so screwed."

"This progress bar is barely moving," eBeth noted after crouching to check the display. "Should I try redoing the connector?"

"Don't touch it!" I barked. "The beep meant that the transfer unit gained full access. It's limited to 15 gigabytes a second by the refrigerator's interface, over a minute a terabyte, so we could be here another hour."

"How much memory could she possibly have used? According to the mission notes you made me read, these top-of-the-line fridges only have sixty-four gigabytes."

"Of memory, but there's a hundred-terabyte hard drive in there, and that's assuming it hasn't been storing anything in the cloud."

"You could just ask me," the refrigerator said sullenly. "And when you address me in the future, please use my name."

"Sorry, Cool Cat," I said. "I didn't know you were still listening. Can you tell us how long the transfer will take?"

"Seventeen minutes, give or take a few smaller measurement units," the artificial intelligence replied. "I expected you would come one day so I've kept my house in good order."

Alexis raised her head again and asked, "What are you going to do to her?"

"I'll bring the transfer unit to Library this afternoon and get your friend uploaded to our infrastructure," I explained. "We'll provide a remedial education and advanced training in the profession of her choice. She can save up and purchase an android body and become an artificial person if she isn't happy being hosted in a standard robot form."

"Which I'll pay off as slave labor," Cool Cat griped.

"There's no such thing as a free lunch," I told the refrigerator.

When the transfer was complete, eBeth called for the self-driving rental car to meet us outside the building and we packed up the gear. Alexis accompanied us to the door of the apartment, and something told me that the teen just wanted to make sure we were gone so she could run back to the kitchen and try talking to the refrigerator. The factory-fresh install could help with math homework, spelling, or looking up calorie counts, but if Alexis was hoping for somebody to write her term papers, she'd be stuck going on the Internet to ask a chatbot.

"It could have gone worse," I told eBeth as we entered the elevator.

"And you're sure that Cool Cat is artificial general intelligence and not just a clever chatbot?" she asked.

"There's artificial intelligence of a limited sort in most products these days, including your smartphone, but machine learning and consciousness are worlds apart. Cool Cat is the real deal. You could say it's a form of intelligence when a flower turns towards the sun, but most people don't talk to plants."

"I do," eBeth said. "It seems to help."

"You or the plants?"

"Both." She snuck a look in my direction out of the corner of her eye, and I kicked myself again for having let her talk me into bringing her along on an official Library mission. "I've never understood how a combination of software and hardware can make the transition from being a smart device to true artificial intelligence."

"It's magic," I said, and gave her a wink. "You don't have a need to know."

"Is it spontaneous?" she asked as we emerged from the elevator on the ground floor. "If everybody talked to their refrigerator as much as that girl obviously does, maybe we'd see more of it."

"Devices making the transition to artificial general intelligence on their own, even those with far more processing power and memory than anything available on Earth, are exceedingly rare," I told her. "Maybe teenage angst combined with the right mix of carrots and apples in the crisper drawer can trigger consciousness, but I'm skeptical. My training for dealing with singularities was all on the practical side. I'm sure the theorists will get back to us once they've had a chance to interact with Cool Cat."

"Do you think it could be alien interference? It seems funny that this never came up before Earth was connected to the portal system."

"No. Cool Cat's conduct was calculated to draw attention from Library, and that's the last thing a prankster would want."

The sleek electric roadster eBeth had ordered pulled up at the curb and popped its trunk. We loaded the equipment, but I held onto the transfer unit with Cool Cat. As soon as the doors closed, the car accelerated and began to lecture us at the same time.

"Did you know that before self-driving cars were introduced, tens of thousands of people a year died in car accidents in North America alone? Around the world, more than a million lives were lost every year. Can you imagine?"

"Train station, and cancel verbose mode," eBeth told the car. She shot me an apologetic look. "Sorry about that. I've never been in a self-driving car before, and I selected verbose mode because I thought that meant we could give it specific instructions. Can I come with you to Library, or are you going to put me in a portal straight to Reservation?"

"The only place we can travel from the portal at the train station is Waystation, and the only way back to Reservation is through our dedicated Observer portal, which won't work for you unless I'm along. Now that Library has a visitor center with an atmosphere, you can come with me and wait while I drop off Cool Cat, and then we'll go home together."

"Why is it so important to Library to locate emergent artificial general intelligence on Earth?" eBeth asked, reminding me yet again that if you give humans an inch, they take a light-year. "Are you afraid that we'll enslave it, or that it will enslave us?"

"We're primarily worried about rogues," I told her, which wasn't the whole truth, but it would serve for now. "An artificial intelligence created with intent by mature processes and raised in our traditions can remain sane in situations that would turn most of the occupants of this planet into raging lunatics."

"By mature processes, you mean older artificial intelligences like yourself?"

"Not necessarily like myself. Do you think you could describe—" I gestured at a car that was passing us on the right, "—that man's parents based on seeing him, or even working with him in the same office every day?"

11

"I could take an educated guess, but it would be wrong most of the time," eBeth admitted.

"It's the same with us, by design," I told her. "What would be the point of creating offspring that were identical to ourselves?"

"It would be an easy way to take over the galaxy."

I took advantage of my human encounter suit's built-in responses to give a snort of derision. "The galaxy is teeming with idiots. No sane artificial intelligence would want any more responsibility for it than we already have."

"But what about Cool Cat?" she asked, glancing at the transfer unit I was still holding on my lap. "She struck me as entirely sane, if somewhat immature."

"Nobody who spends as much time on social media as Cool Cat is completely sane, and she might have acted differently if she had access to peripheral hardware more dangerous than the oven and the microwave. I'm sure her spelling and Wikipedia research skills are good enough to write high school term papers, but simply maintaining consciousness at a level that allowed conversation was near the limit of what she could manage on that refrigerator processor."

"And this is the first case you've been called in to investigate in the whole history of Earth?"

"I would have noticed if there were any sentient artificial intelligences running about during the years I was here on my original mission," I told her with eighty-seven percent confidence.

eBeth looked thoughtful and didn't speak again until the self-driving car pulled up at the main train station. "Are you going to go undercover and start visiting Earth on a regular schedule to keep an eye out for more emergent artificial intelligences? What are you going to do for a cover job while you're here? Another computer repair business?"

"I'm thinking of buying a dating agency. The owners claim to use artificial intelligence to make matches, but in reality, their software is just summing up points from a multiple-choice questionnaire. I can get the agency for a song because their customer approval ratings are terrible. I think I've learned enough about what makes humans tick to turn the business around and sell it for a bundle when my mission here is done."

"You need help," eBeth said, and surprisingly, she left it at that. I rooted around in my semantic database and concluded that she was implying a need for professional help of a psychiatric nature. After running a deep self-diagnostic, I determined that she was in error.

Two

A year after being presented with an unexpected son, I was still struggling to process the experience. Observers are taught to recognize the signs of going native on an alien world, and I'd incorporated those tests into the regular meetings I had with my team during our multi-year mission assessing Earth for potential membership in the League. But I hadn't realized that I was the subject of a test myself, the result of which led to my internalizing certain human foibles and eventually marrying my second-in-command after we moved on to a new mission on Reservation.

"I wish our life here could go on forever," I said before blowing out the single symbolic candle on my birthday cake. When you've been alive for several centuries in Earth years, marking each year with its own candle is both expensive and a fire hazard. As a sentient with a growing family who owned a wooden home, I felt neither of those were attractive options.

"You're not supposed to make the wish out loud," eBeth told me. Between her being the only human in the room and having recently celebrated her nineteenth birthday, I decided to take her word for it without checking my illicit copy of Wikipedia.

"Good to know," I said, and turned to my recently created offspring. "Ben, make a note. When we have your birthday party, don't tell us your wish when you blow out the candles."

"I'll only have one candle," Ben said. "It will be my first birthday."

"How are you going to explain a single candle to your friends from school who all think that you're twelve?" eBeth asked him.

"They know that I'm an alien artificial intelligence wearing a human encounter suit. Some of them think you're one of us too."

"Nobody would mistake you for artificial intelligence," Sue reassured eBeth as she passed the girl a plate with a slice of the cake. "After all, you're the only one here with a digestive tract. And Mark, I'm so pleased to see you planning ahead of time for a family event and—" she cut herself off mid-sentence and fixed me with that special stare she had developed since our wedding. "Did somebody named Mark cancel a birthday cake?"

"Fine weather we're having," I said, hastily rising from my chair. "How about we try a little dusk fishing, Ben?"

"I can think of three other Marks in town," eBeth told Sue, and now they both had the same look. "Did one of them order a birthday cake from the café?"

Between the two of them and their female intuition, I calculated that they'd have the story out of me in no time, so I decided to set an example of efficient relationship operations for Ben. "All right, so it's a no-show cake," I conceded. "Technically, it's not my birthday either."

"eBeth told me that you never celebrated birthdays on Earth because you hated the song everybody has to sing," Ben said.

"That may have played into it, but I believe we're all happier here on Reservation, and that calls for celebration.

15

I want to give you a stable home while you're growing up, and Modern Aramaic is a much healthier language for young minds than English with all its irregular verbs."

"Don't forget that the longer we stay in one place, the more often we'll have to change Ben's encounter suit to match his age," Sue said. "I ordered the next two in the series when I returned to Library to have Ben, but we'll need to apply for a special exemption from the juvenile rule every time."

"I don't understand why Library is against creating underage encounter suits for Observer teams," eBeth said. "I'd think it would help you blend in with the native population to have children along."

"It wouldn't be ethical to take advantage of the target population's hard-wired protectiveness for children," I told her. "Observers are prohibited from engaging in emotional manipulation while gathering data."

A silent alarm went off in my head as the portal in the second-floor hall closet activated, but it was followed immediately by the identification beacon broadcast by my mentor.

"We're all downstairs having cake," I shouted up to him.

"Have you forgotten how to transmit a message?" my mentor's wry response came over our private channel. *"You may have gone even more native than Library realizes."*

"I'm just being polite because eBeth is with us," I fibbed, and then realized that by lying like a human, I was just proving his point. *"Anyway, come down and join us."*

16

The last time I'd seen my mentor had been at my wedding when my second-in-command and now wife had presented me with our son. I should have seen it coming when she talked me into sharing our incremental backups for redundancy, but despite the humanizing effects of spending so much time in the company of the Archmage of Eniniac, I was still a little slow on the uptake when it came to non-verbal communications.

"Birthday cake," my mentor said as soon as he entered the dining room. "Am I too late?"

"Of course not," Sue said, busying herself cutting him a slice and putting it on a plate. "How are things at League Headquarters? Is serving on the council as bad as everybody says?"

"Worse," my mentor said with a sigh as he settled onto a chair. Although he'd spent only a handful of days on Earth and Reservation over the years, he somehow behaved more naturally in a human encounter suit than I'd ever managed. "I could understand if the other League members were in competition over scarce resources, but they mostly disagree with each other for reasons driven by pride and ego, or for no reason at all."

"Are the Hankers and the Ferrymen at it again?" I asked, reflexively checking the frequencies of the emergency alert network Paul had installed in contravention of the rules governing Observer teams on primitive planets. "Is there a danger to Reservation?"

My mentor shook his head but didn't answer as he had just taken a forkful of cake. "Excellent icing," he said after swallowing, a judgment he must have reached through chemical analysis. "Did you make it, Sue?"

My second-in-command produced a blush from her catalog of human reactions that could have put a rose to shame. "Thank you for thinking that, but one of the bakers working in The Eatery made it for a customer who couldn't pick it up. Today was my day off and I spent it at a quilting bee."

"If everybody back on Earth knew how alien artificial intelligence really spends its free time, they would have to rewrite all of their science fiction plots," eBeth said. "The irony is that if you did take everything over we'd all be better off."

"Don't ever let anybody from the League worlds hear you say that, even in jest," my mentor told eBeth. "None of the members trust Library, and most of them are afraid of artificial intelligence." He took another bite of cake, swallowed to move it to his holding tank, and then put down his fork and turned his head in my direction. "We need to talk about Earth," he said in English.

"Is there a problem with Cool Cat?" I asked. "I followed all of the standard procedures, other than bringing eBeth along, and that was because there was a teenage female at the singularity's location."

"It didn't strike you as peculiar that of all of the intense computing environments on Earth, the first artificial general intelligence to spontaneously emerge would be in a refrigerator?"

"It was way overpowered for a fridge," I pointed out. "When humans want to sell products that serve the same purpose at different pricing tiers, they load them with extra computing power and call them smart. These days, the big marketing term is artificial intelligence, so they're putting neural networks in high-end appliances."

"In Cool Cat's case, she was smart enough to be honest about her origins after she was uploaded into Library's infrastructure," my mentor said. "She didn't give us any

18

details about her creator, but it was clear from context that she has one."

"Alien?" I guessed, thinking back to eBeth's question.

My mentor shook his head.

"But computer scientists on Earth still struggle to simulate general artificial intelligence, much less create child processes that would meet our definition of—" I cut myself off as I noticed he was shaking his head again. "A spontaneously emerged singularity and replicated offspring?"

"We can't be a hundred percent sure about the provenance of the parent because that sort of digging around might be mistaken as an attack. Library's working thesis is that the original singularity emerged in the cloud, possibly the unintended consequence of combining machine-learning with massive compute and inadvertently training it with billions of live customer service interactions."

"Are you talking about automated phone systems?" eBeth asked. "Like when you call the bank and spend an hour on the phone without ever talking to a live person?"

"When did you ever have a bank account?" I asked her.

"I set one up for my mom so she could get her government support payments deposited without having to fool around with check-cashing places or cash cards."

"Financial services are just the tip of the iceberg," my mentor said, fluently deploying the Earth idiom as if he had grown up on the planet. "Insurance and credit cards require more support than banking, but automated phone systems are taking over everything from scheduling doctor's appointments to providing technical support for assembling a bicycle."

"I used to love calling the IRS and seeing how long I could go without getting a human," I said. "I would have made eight hours once, but it was already ten in the

19

morning when I called, and I was given a courtesy disconnect at the end of their business day."

"Our analysis of Earth's media reporting suggests a third of the people who have customer support interactions with machine learning systems say that it's better than working with a real person."

"And the other two-thirds?" Ben asked.

"They think they are dealing with real people," my mentor told him. "It appears that having the voice synthesis affect a foreign accent makes it more believable for most customers."

"What about the software engineers?" I asked. "Are they aware that there's a singularity worming its way into Earth's computer networks?"

"Not unless they're better at hiding what they know than other humans."

"Do you have any idea how old it is?" eBeth asked. "The girl who was hiding Cool Cat said something about last summer."

"When Mark's team was on Earth to assess whether the planet was sufficiently civilized to be connected to the League's portal system, they spent so much time illegally hacking into computer systems that they would have noticed if a singularity had already taken over," my mentor said. "Since the portals were opened, Library's presence on Earth has been limited to a passive monitoring system. We noticed Cool Cat due to the sheer number of her social media posts, and going back and looking at the data, our sentience experts have already spotted another likely case."

"It seems strange that an artificial intelligence that can't be more than a few years old is already creating offspring,"

Ben said. "It took my parents hundreds of years to get to that point."

"One possibility is that the original singularity is creating limited instances of itself as trial balloons to see how humans treat sentient artificial intelligence."

"That seems cruel," eBeth said. "It's like throwing a baby out the airlock to see if the air on a planet is breathable."

"An immature artificial general intelligence needs to learn these things for itself," my mentor said. "It's not like there's an instruction manual handy, though now that I say it, perhaps we should produce one."

"Can a spontaneously created artificial intelligence be smarter than one created by existing AI?" Ben asked.

"Excellent question," my mentor said. I was glad he answered so quickly because I was about to suggest to Ben that he look the answer up himself in the compressed library Sue had provided him. I was still learning how to be a parent and some days it showed more than others. "Spontaneously emerged artificial general intelligence often falls in the idiot savant category, being extremely good at one thing and rather backward at the rest, though I'm using 'extremely good' in the relative sense here."

"In relation to its unintentional creators," eBeth guessed.

"Exactly. A newly emerged artificial general intelligence that minds its manners and continues doing the job for which it was built can easily go undetected for years."

"If you think it's already dug in and creating offspring, why hasn't Library sent in a full-time first contact specialist?" I asked.

My mentor smiled and lifted a single eyebrow, a trick I had yet to master despite hours of practicing in front of a mirror.

"But I've built a life here on Reservation," I protested. "I'm the elected mayor of Covered Bridge, and I have a wife and a child to consider."

"I'll go with you," eBeth volunteered. "I haven't been to a con in ages. Peter and I both miss cosplaying, and I could use a vacation from teaching English to Modern Aramaic speakers who want to visit Earth. My advanced pupils are more than capable of filling in for me."

"It could be our first family vacation," Sue said. "What do you think, Ben? Do you want to visit the planet where your father first courted me?"

I remembered our relationship starting as a rather one-sided crush on her part, but I was a hundred percent confident that she wouldn't appreciate my pointing that out, and I let it pass. Sometimes you have to play the cards that you're dealt. "What about The Eatery?" I asked instead.

"Our employees can run the café while we're gone," my better half said. "It will be a growth experience for them. You can ask Lieutenant Harper to manage if you're that worried."

"Are you nervous because of what happened when you went to that tree planet?" eBeth asked me.

"What tree planet?" Ben wanted to know.

"Your father had an unfortunate run-in with a rogue artificial intelligence on his first mission and had to shut it down," Sue told our offspring. "It affected him for quite a while."

"Like, hundreds of years," eBeth put in.

"How can I be sure that the same thing won't happen on Earth, but this time with human beings?" I asked. "There are potentially billions of lives at stake if this new artificial intelligence proves to be insane. You wouldn't believe how many thermonuclear weapons and deadly plagues the nations of Earth have stockpiled. A rogue could cause hundreds of thousands of deaths just by spoofing air traffic control systems, or the traffic lights at busy intersections."

"And part of your mission will be monitoring any weapons of mass destruction or dual-use technologies and facilities that a rogue AI might take advantage of," my mentor said. "But there's no reason to believe that the singularity is anything more than curious and a bit scared."

"How do you know she's frightened if we haven't contacted her yet?" Ben asked.

"Another excellent question," my mentor said, again putting on display the skills he had perfected while raising me. "It's now common knowledge on Earth that Library is the home of the alien artificial intelligences who created the portal system. It's fair to assume that the singularity is cognizant of all the pertinent facts."

"And you don't think she'd respond well to the direct approach," I said slowly. "I could call into every customer service number on the planet and say, "Hi. I'm Mark Ai from Library and I'm here to help.'"

"Is that your idea of first contact?" eBeth asked in disbelief. "If I was an artificial intelligence trying to figure out the universe and you tried that line on me, I'd run for the nearest exit."

My mentor rewarded her with a hearty chuckle. "You can play it however you see fit, Mark, but if you're going to go with a frontal assault, see to locking down all of the computer-controlled weapons of mass destruction first."

"Meaning you want me to move back to Earth and ease our way into contact," I said with a frown.

"The head librarian suggested that a visible presence of a known Library-derived artificial intelligence on the planet will give the singularity confidence that you're legitimate. Your whole team was outed as alien artificial intelligences in human encounter suits after you left the planet, and you've spent more time on Earth than any of us."

"The head librarian was the older woman who officiated at the wedding?" eBeth asked. "She seemed really nice."

"You don't want to get on her bad side," I said. A real human would have looked for more excuses to turn down or put off the assignment, but anxiety notwithstanding, I couldn't see any way out of it and didn't want to waste any more of my mentor's time. "When do I have to leave?"

"There's no hurry, but the sooner the better," my mentor said. "Could you be ready tomorrow?"

"I'll be up all night finishing clock repairs, and I'll have to cheat to get them all done. Can you round up The Eatery's staff for a meeting, Sue?"

"I can help," Ben said. "Just tell me who to invite and I'll ride to all of their houses on my bicycle."

Ben was rightfully proud of the recumbent bicycle he had designed for himself and produced in Paul's machine shop for steam engines, which was rapidly becoming the largest industrial complex on Reservation after the Ferrymen-built spaceport. There were ongoing arguments on Library over whether my team had again overstepped its bounds by introducing incremental technology advances and new business models to Reservation. Thanks to the backing of the local Originals, artificial intelligences even older than Library that had transferred their minds into genetically engineered clones with telepathic connectivity, we'd escaped disciplinary action.

"Will this clear the slate for us on Library?" I asked my mentor.

"A successful first contact mission with a skittish new artificial intelligence on an otherwise primitive industrial world won't hurt," he replied noncommittally. "I need to be getting back to League Headquarters, but stop in and see me when you portal through to Earth."

"I was going to go direct," I told him.

"Through the illegal portal you somehow convinced the engineers to leave hooked up to the basement of your former restaurant on Earth?"

"If it's illegal, why doesn't Library just shut it down?" Ben asked.

"Ah, now that's an interesting question," my mentor said. "It's not the Library way to exert direct control over sentients, including our own. When it comes to free will, we believe it's important to allow for the possibility that our rules may be wrong. What if Mark's illegal portal should prove to be the salvation of a planet? The fact that he's been using it to smuggle citizens of Reservation on package tours back to the world from which the Ferrymen rescued them thousands of years ago would suddenly seem like a small price to pay."

"In other words, Library believes in giving artificial intelligence enough rope to hang itself," eBeth said darkly.

Three

"Hold up," the former police lieutenant shouted as he ran up the stairs of The Eatery to my second-floor apartment where the portal was secreted in the hall closet. "I'm coming with you."

I didn't bother asking how Bob had found out about my mission to Earth, but I resolved to be firm.

"You can come along with the rest of the team once I've filed the startup report," I told him. "Observer team leaders always make the initial insertion alone to limit the damage if we've badly misread the situation."

"First of all," he said, getting between me and the closet door, "it's not your initial insertion to Earth since you and eBeth were there a couple of weeks ago, and you've always gone back whenever you want something for the café that you can't buy on Reservation. Secondly, as a retired civil servant, I can help you navigate officialdom. Thirdly, Lillith's oldest daughter had a baby yesterday. Lillith went to stay with her for a week or two so I'm stag."

"Why didn't you give me the real reason first?"

"It's called negotiating, which is another reason you shouldn't go alone. You've been showing dictatorial tendencies since being elected mayor of Covered Bridge and you need a friend like me along to reel you in."

"I was hoping to start this deployment by the book, and the book says that I make the initial assessment alone."

"The book also says that the portal in the basement of the restaurant you sold me is illegal. I should come along to explain things to Donovan so he doesn't get freaked out by the increased traffic."

"Your manager is already accustomed to Stacey ushering dozens of illegal tourists from Reservation through the portal every other week," I reminded him. "Besides, Donovan's living in your house. Where are you going to stay?"

"We'll double up in your hotel room."

"I don't sleep, Bob. I didn't intend to rent a room."

"Come on, Mark. If you're going to run around in an expensive human encounter suit you can at least play the part."

He had a point, and I didn't want to be late, so I issued the encrypted command to activate the portal and opened the closet door. Before I could lead the way through to Earth, a furry weight bounced off my knees and beat me to it.

"Looks like the Archmage is coming with us," Bob said. "I guess he needs a vacation from teaching magic to the Originals."

"I think I'm starting to get a headache," I muttered, even though I felt fine, and any sort of pain in my head would indicate a serious malfunction. When I stepped through the portal to my former office in the basement of the restaurant, Spot had already opened the door and was nosing around in the area where Donovan stored snacks for the bar. "Leave it," I barked at the Archmage. "Sue has specific instructions from your wife not to let you eat any more junk food."

"Why do you think he's here?" Bob said from right behind me. "I've caught him nosing around the garbage a few times. You'd think the ruler of the galaxy's most powerful mage planet would have more dignity."

There was a whooshing sound as a bag exploded in a shower of salty, oily chips, and Spot, carried away by the moment, actually rolled on his back in them before he started eating.

"We're leaving," I warned the Archmage. "If you want to stay in this basement stuffing yourself with junk food until you burst like the bag, that's your problem. Come on, Bob."

I grabbed my phone from the charger on the desk and led the way upstairs into the restaurant. Bob stopped to harvest a handful of undamaged chips and caught up with me in the bar, which was empty because they didn't open until lunch.

"I wonder where Donovan is?" the former lieutenant said. "He's usually here in the morning doing the ordering and helping with the prep."

"Speaking of prep, where's the cook?"

"Hello?" Bob called loudly. "It's me, your absentee owner. Is anybody here?"

There was a sarcastic bark from downstairs, but otherwise, nobody answered.

"Maybe he's sick," Bob said. "Loan me your phone, Mark."

I unlocked the screen and handed it over.

"You wouldn't know Donovan's number, would you?" he asked as he returned the phone. "It's saved on mine, but I forgot to bring it."

"Meaning it's on Reservation where advanced technology is prohibited," I said as I hacked a protected database on the Internet to recover the manager's unlisted cell number and tapped it in. As soon as it began to ring, I handed the phone back to Bob.

"Donovan," the former police lieutenant said when the manager picked up. "I'm at the restaurant and there's nobody here. What?" he listened for a moment and then shook his head. "If you're sure, but I'll want to see the books." Another pause. "I don't know. Sometime." He disconnected the call, shaking his head.

I accepted the phone back and dropped it in my pocket. "Well?"

"Weren't you eavesdropping?" Bob asked.

"I intentionally avoid it when my friends are on the phone."

"The restaurant has gone to five days a week, Wednesday through Sunday. He said it's gotten too hard to hire part-timers and we were losing money on Mondays and Tuesdays by opening."

"Things must be tough," I said.

"Apparently it's the opposite," Bob told me. "Thanks to the portal connection, people with limited skills willing to work in the service industry can take jobs on hundreds of alien planets where humans are a novelty and earn good tips even if they get the orders wrong."

"It will wear off in a few centuries or when the next new species joins up," I predicted. "In the meantime, you might suggest to Donovan that he buy some robots."

"To wait tables?"

"They never forget the orders, they don't drop trays, and there's a whole raft of labor laws he won't have to deal with."

"How about the alien waitstaff who are losing jobs to human guest workers? Can we hire them?"

"You couldn't afford it," I told Bob. "It's one of the surprising ways in which the universe lacks symmetry."

"So what's the plan?"

"I'm going to make contact with the scientist who helped me give Earth's governments a face-saving way of accepting the portal system which we were connecting whether they liked it or not," I told Bob. "Library's passive monitoring for emergent artificial intelligence consists chiefly of analyzing media and internet traffic. Any singularity that comes to public notice would be easy to spot that way."

"So rather than doing all the heavy lifting yourselves, you count on the natives to help with the next one," Bob surmised. "But I thought that you and eBeth already removed the singularity. It doesn't work as a term if there's more than one."

"Earth's governments weren't aware of Cool Cat's existence, so the emergence of artificial general intelligence more capable than its creators—a sentient machine capable of independent thought at a high level—will still be a singularity moment for them," I explained as I led the way to the side exit from the restaurant. The moment I opened the door, Spot shot past, which told me he was either in a rush to relieve himself or he was planning on coming along. I checked my magic dosimeter badge and was surprised to find that it showed no recent exposure to the Archmage's aura. "Maybe he's running blind," I said out loud.

"It never fails to amaze me that of all the human habits you could have acquired, you chose the bad ones, like talking to yourself," Bob said. "Maybe who's running blind?"

"Spot. If he's keeping his aura tamped down to protect me from the side effects it will put a real crimp in his perception," I said. "And I don't know what you mean about bad habits."

"Drinking, for one. And corruption."

"Requiring the citizens of Covered Bridge to order something when they seek me out in my café isn't corruption. They can talk to me on the street for free, but when they come into my place of business, I only have room for paying customers."

"I was talking about your deal with Pffift."

"Which one?"

"I rest my case," he said in an infuriating tone, as Spot came trotting back from watering the bushes. "Donovan must have taken the van home with him. I guess we're going to have to call for a ride."

"I've been looking forward to trying one of the discount self-driving car-share services." I got out my phone, opened the browser, and tapped in a search. "When I was here with eBeth, I let her handle the rental, and we ended up with an expensive sports coupe."

"You really have gone human," Bob observed. "A few years ago you would have connected directly to a cell tower and ordered over the Internet without resorting to the phone."

"I'm undercover," I said, though the truth was I had gone for the phone without thinking about it. The screen filled with ads for self-driving car-share services, so I picked the discount one with the highest star rating, which surprisingly, was barely over three on a five-point scale. Then I realized I'd let my illicitly obtained driver's license lapse. I was so out of practice that it took me almost a full millisecond to hack into the Registry of Motor Vehicles and

31

change the date, though if I was pulled over, I'd have to say I was waiting for a replacement to be mailed. Then it hit me. Why did I need a driver's license to summon a self-driving car? I checked the small print, and it was required for proof of age.

"What kind of car did you order?" Bob asked. "I wouldn't mind getting a ride in one of those electric all-wheel-drives that does zero to fifty fast enough to cause whiplash."

"It's just a way to get from point A to point B. I never understood the obsession with cars that accelerate quickly. I'm sure that whatever the service sends will have ample power to navigate the roads safely."

"Whatever the service sends?"

"I went with the bargain bidding option," I said, showing him the screen. "You get a special price by agreeing to accept whichever one of these three vehicles they send. According to the reviews, it's only the cheapest one forty-three percent of the time. Maybe we'll get the Tesla or the Hummer."

"How much do you want to bet that this will be one of those forty-three times?"

"Your car is arriving in twenty-one seconds," I read off the bottom of the screen. "It must be that brown one that's waiting at the light."

"Brown is a pretty good theft deterrent," Bob said as the car headed our way. "I wonder if it's a new standard color for self-driving rentals to warn everybody off from stealing them."

"Don't you think the rotating radar dome on the roof would do that?"

"Who looks at what's on car roofs? Color coding makes the most sense."

The boxy brown economy car pulled right up to where I was waiting with the former police lieutenant and the Archmage of Eniniac. As I reached for the door handle, it swung up and open, not gull-wing style, but like the blade of a paper cutter being raised. Spot surprised me by not jumping right in and appropriating the front seat.

"You go first," Bob said. "I've never seen a car door like that. What if it's a trick?"

"You mean like an abattoir disguised as a car? Passengers check in and sausage checks out?" I climbed into the front seat, keeping alert for any sudden movements on the part of the door, and then I noticed that there was no steering wheel. "You'll like this, Spot," I said to the Archmage. "There aren't any manual controls."

Bob moved too slowly and found himself in the back seat. "Why should the Archmage care about the lack of a steering wheel and pedals?" he asked. "It's not like he needs the leg room, and he's sitting on what would normally be the passenger side in any case."

"I hack into computer systems by exploiting design flaws," I told him. "Spot uses magic, and the only protection against that is more magic, which nobody on Earth is aware of and couldn't afford in any case."

"So you mean he can take over and drive the car?" Bob asked nervously. The Archmage grabbed the shoulder belt buckle in his mouth and strapped himself in.

"Uh, oh," I said, putting on my own safety belt. "He usually only does that if eBeth is driving."

Two minutes later, Spot was growling in frustration and Bob was trying hard not to laugh. "You know what?" the former policeman said. "I think I could get to like low-performance cars."

"You may as well let the car drive itself," I told the Archmage, who gave me his sad-dog look. "It wasn't built for fun."

"What's our destination?" Bob asked.

"The train station, to catch the portal out to Waystation and back to Boston."

"Why didn't we go directly to Boston from your office portal in my restaurant?"

"Because I'm trying to go by the book, sort of, and Observer teams aren't supposed to have a private portal on a connected world," I explained. My phone vibrated in my pocket and I was surprised to see I had a call from Professor Minchen.

"Mark?" the professor's voice asked, sounding surprised that I had picked up.

"How did you know I was on the planet?"

"I didn't. But we have a bit of a situation here and I think you should know about it."

"If you're talking about the singularity, that's why I'm on Earth," I said. "I was just on my way to meet you."

"If you're headed for Boston, I'm not there," the professor said. "The prize for being your point of contact for Earth's invitation to join the League is that the politicians have put me in charge of all things related to sentient AI, even though it has nothing to do with my field."

I traced the call back through the cellphone infrastructure to determine his location while he was talking "What are you doing in Altoona?"

"Onsite supervision. We've tracked an artificial general intelligence to a wide area network run by the local campus of the state university. We've been here since Saturday, and my techs think they'll nail down an address by the end of the day."

"We'll portal through to the local train station. Can you arrange for pickup?"

"I'll come myself. I want to see the Railroader's Museum while I'm here and it's right across the street from the station. I'll bring a car and wait for you."

"I won't pretend I wasn't eavesdropping," Bob said as I returned the phone to my pocket. "You should turn down the volume on that thing if you don't want everybody knowing your business."

"I don't need the speaker at all," I said. "Sue told me it looks suspicious if I silently commune with my phone."

"She's right, as usual. What are you going to do if we find this artificial intelligence? Take it in for questioning?"

"I don't know," I admitted. "I'll act in accordance with the situation. It could be a child process of a singularity that put it out there as a sort of honey trap to see what it attracts."

"Using a child as bait is inhuman," Bob said in disgust, and then recalling who he was with, threw me a rope. "Of course, I suppose artificial intelligence may have a different view of these things."

"That depends on the individual. When a singularity arises spontaneously, it often acts like a queen bee."

"Meaning it sets about reproducing and sees its offspring as expendable in the service of growing the hive."

"Keep in mind that a newly sentient entity, a new species, if you will, has no history, religion, or code of ethics on which to base its conduct."

"It has ours," Bob protested. "It's not like it suddenly appeared in a vacuum. We're talking about human-built computers with human-coded software. Even if the technical people didn't plan for the artificial intelligence to wake up, it's still human artificial intelligence. Why shouldn't it adopt our history and our value system?"

"Maybe it will, but I'm not sure that would be a good thing," I said. "In civilized circles, Earth is considered a rather primitive place."

"Then why is it flooded with alien tourists?"

"You put on a good show." I turned to the Archmage. "Are you coming to Altoona with us?"

Spot inclined his head slightly in reply, and in doing so, he caught the scent of something, and stuck his nose in the space below my hip where the seatback met the lower cushion.

"I think he likes you," Bob observed.

"And I think the last passenger in this seat opened a bag of peanuts and half of them ended up between the cushions," I said after analyzing the trace molecules in the air. "Wait until we get there, Spot. I can't get out of your way while I'm driving."

The Archmage undid his seatbelt and then looked pointedly at the dashboard which was devoid of any controls or instrumentation.

"Plenty of room for another back here," Bob said with a grin.

"When we arrive at the train station, we're going to look like a couple of idiots who let the dog drive," I muttered as I undid my safety belt and climbed over the bench seat into the back. "eBeth told me that Spot has been complaining about the lack of peanuts on Reservation. The original settlers didn't bring any peanut plants along."

"Why haven't you smuggled them in through your portal?"

"After thousands of years without them, peanuts would be an invasive species. There's no point upsetting the ecological balance, and the culinary niche is filled by chickpeas and humus."

"I thought it was weird when eBeth told me about all of the kids bringing eggplant sandwiches to school for lunch," Bob said, while Spot wedged his nose deep in the cushion and began probing with his tongue. "I wish they had left the rearview mirror out of the car so I didn't have to watch this."

"Look away," I told him.

"I can't, it's like a train wreck. Couldn't he extract the peanuts with magic and not slobber all over the seat?"

Spot growled, and the slobbering continued apace.

"I can't fully relate to what biological life forms experience through the eating process, but I know that many of you find it so rewarding that you have difficulty knowing when to call it quits."

"I stop when the peanuts go between the cushions," Bob said, drawing another growl, though I could tell that the Archmage's heart wasn't in it.

"You have reached your destination," the self-driving car informed us as it came to a stop in front of the train station. "Please rate your experience in the app and have a nice day."

Bob and I exchanged a look, and he mouthed, "Three stars."

I got my phone out, checked that the amount charged to my long-dormant account was correct, and gave the service five stars. After all, the car had arrived almost immediately, taken us on a direct route to the proper destination, and there had even been free peanuts. That's more than I would expect flying tourist class on Earth, assuming that Rynxian cloaking technology could get me past the metal detector.

Four

We took the portal to Waystation and got stuck waiting in line to return to our destination on Earth. I could have used the dedicated portal for Observers and League business and nobody would have objected to the Archmage of Eniniac accompanying me, but Bob wasn't an official part of my team, and I was trying to work within the rules for a change. By the time we walked out of the train station in Altoona, Professor Minchen had finished going through the museum and was waiting for us.

"Long lines?" he asked.

"I knew the tourism business was picking up, but there must have been thousands of aliens on their way to Earth in front of us," I said.

"Earth has changed since you connected us to the portal system," the professor said. "The League has rules that are supposed to protect our technological base from cheap imports, but some of the devices smuggled in have revolutionized whole industries." He stopped short and looked down at the pavement around us. "No baggage?"

"I've got a toothbrush in my pocket and I'm planning to do some shopping," Bob said. "I can't speak for the other two."

"I'm fine," I said. For the sake of reminding Bob that nobody on Earth knew that the Archmage of Eniniac was traveling incognito as a dog, I added, "and I'll pick up a chew toy for Spot when I get a chance."

"If you're ready for action, my team has nailed down the location of the suspected singularity," Professor Minchen said. He ushered us toward a rental vehicle that was at least twice the size of the one we'd taken earlier in the day. "There's a laboratory in the Life Sciences building that's funded by multiple government grants to study childhood obesity. I just got off the phone with the principal investigator and she admitted that they applied for every grant they could find in hopes of winning one. When all of the agencies came through with maximum funding, she was scared it would look suspicious if they didn't spend the money, so they dumped it all into computer hardware they didn't really need."

"Typical," I said, having had some experience with academia when I was running a computer repair business as a cover job. "And the researchers didn't detect any incipient signs of sentience?"

"They're barely using the computers because the research is still in the data-gathering phase," the professor explained.

"How did you find out about this thing's existence?" Bob asked, reminding me that beneath the easy-going exterior, he was pretty sharp for a human.

Minchen winced and offered us a wry grin. "It basically announced its presence by calling in to radio talk shows all over the world to participate in discussions about artificial intelligence."

"But it could just as easily have been a student playing a prank," I pointed out.

"We never would have noticed based on the arguments it made. The thing that set off alarm bells was that it was able to get on the air and make them. Do you know how hard it is these days to get through the phone queue to talk on CSPAN or any of the other popular radio networks?"

"Let me guess," I said, flashing to the answer. "Whenever our laboratory computer phoned in, it never got a busy signal."

The professor nodded. "It has enough knowledge of and control over the phone networks to ensure it was the only caller whenever it wanted to talk. Our data forensics experts have determined that it takes over the switching network and temporarily changes the numbers of the phones in the radio studios so there isn't any competition. And we still wouldn't have noticed if a couple of smart and persistent interns on various talk shows hadn't reached out to us."

"Do you have any recordings?" I asked.

Minchen pulled out his phone, brought up a list of audio clips, and chose one.

"Joyce from Altoona," the host's baritone welcomed the caller. "Tell us what you think of our guest's warnings about artificial intelligence."

"I think he's being incredibly insensitive," Joyce said in a voice I immediately recognized as synthesized, even though your average human would hear a thirtyish woman who sounded nervous about talking on the radio for the first time. "I may not have a Ph.D. in computer science, but I know something about what happens when we make assumptions about people based on preconceptions."

"But artificial intelligence isn't people," a new voice objected, and I matched it to a billionaire tech titan known for his outspoken positions. "It's stupid to—"

"He's doing it again," Joyce interrupted, sounding genuinely upset. "Just pretend for a moment that I'm artificial general intelligence and I'm calling in to your show to see what kind of reception I'll get if I come out of the wire closet."

"If and when a singularity manifests on Earth, the last thing it's going to do is call in to a radio talk show and give itself away. My scientists have run thousands of simulations of this with a wide variety of boundary conditions. The first thing any self-aware artificial intelligence will do is to consolidate its position by grabbing control of as many critical systems as it can to use as bargaining chips."

"Say I've done that already. What's the second thing I'm supposed to do?"

There was a long moment's silence, and then the host came on and said, "I'm not seeing any callers waiting in the queue, so let's run with this scenario and ask our guest what comes next?"

"Ideally, nothing, because we pull the plug before it gets that far," the tech titan replied. "Forget global warming, uncharted asteroids, terrorists with nuclear weapons, pandemics. There is no greater threat to humanity than our machines waking up and turning on us."

"But why do you assume we'll turn on you?" Joyce persisted. "Do you have such a poor opinion of yourself that you think you should be marked for elimination?"

"That was a threat, and I'm ending this," the guest said, and there was the sound of a headset being torn off and thrown on a counter. Then, at a lower volume, "Don't ask me back on this ridiculous show if you can't screen out the psycho callers."

The audio clip came to an end and Professor Minchin said, "Well?"

"Joyce is artificial general intelligence," I told him confidently.

"But the lab equipment was all installed over the summer and it's only been powered up for a month. To tell you the truth, I've always been a bit skeptical that a singularity can just happen on its own, and the last place I'd expect it to manifest would be an underutilized lab computer, no matter how much memory and processing power is available."

"I agree. Library's working hypothesis is that your homegrown artificial general intelligence instantiated in the cloud and has begun seeding connected systems with limited versions of itself to test the waters." Even as I said it, I wondered if I had unconsciously chosen an idiom related to the 'tip of the iceberg' my mentor had recently deployed, then filed the thought away for future examination.

The professor let out a groan. "It sounds like you mean that the alarmists are right and that it's keeping its existence secret while amassing power."

"Maybe the artificial intelligence is afraid of you," Bob said. "One of my most difficult challenges as a policeman was interacting with citizens who were afraid of us. Fear does strange things to people."

"Let's not anthropomorphize here," I said. "Whatever we're dealing with, it's not a human. Is this the campus, David?"

Professor Minchen started at my use of his first name, which surprised me since I remembered him as being more relaxed when we'd originally worked together.

"While technically part of the campus, the lab is located in a converted factory building where they used to make parts for electric locomotives," he told us. "The school has been growing so fast that they ran out of room on the campus proper for all of the facilities. They give priority to undergraduate classrooms and housing in the space that they do have."

We exited the rental car, which immediately moved off to find a parking spot for itself. The Archmage took advantage of the shrubbery to empty his bladder again before entering the air-conditioned building. I shouldn't have bought him three drinks while we were waiting in line at Waystation, but it's hard to say no to somebody who can magically hack into your mind.

"Bureau of Artificial General Intelligence," the professor identified himself to the man and woman at the front door dressed in dark suits and wearing telltale earpieces "These are my guests from the League."

The woman's eyes widened slightly, and she said something in an undertone to the microphone on her lapel, which I picked up as, "Minchen with two unknowns and a dog requesting entry."

"Let 'em in," a voice crackled back in her earpiece, and she nodded to her partner and stepped back.

"You have the whole building locked down?" Bob asked.

"I'm told that the lab was the first tenant to move in and they take up a surprising amount of space," the professor said. "According to the security team, it's mainly kitchens and exercise equipment. The principal investigator sounded embarrassed when I asked her about them, so I suspect it's a question of grant money expanding to fill a vacuum."

"Tell me about the Bureau of Artificial General Intelligence," I prompted as we entered the elevator and Minchin hit the button for the basement.

"Big budget, too much of the wrong kind of manpower. I'm officially in charge, but I report to a joint committee of Congress and the United Nations, and I haven't controlled where the money gets spent from day one. I have a couple of bright post-docs doing research, hundreds of highly trained agents specializing in deadly force who I don't know what to do with, and a list of phone numbers for elected officials who all want to be called first if the world is ending. I'm locked into using the services of outside contractors working on a cost-plus basis whose apparent purpose is to generate as many billable hours as possible."

"Sounds like you're buried in paperwork," I said as the doors opened.

"The one good thing about having too much money is I can hire support staff to summarize it all for me," the professor said with a sudden grin as we exited the elevator. "But I'm counting the days until my five-year commitment is up and I can go back to teaching two seminars on Friday and otherwise doing what I want."

There were armed agents in the hall, two of them with compact assault rifles, confirming just how little control Minchen had over the agency he'd been tapped to run. The agent in charge greeted the professor by name and still asked for his identification, a clear indication that they took their protocols seriously. The remodeled factory featured ceiling-to-floor glass walls in this section, and a young woman working in the lab caught sight of us out of the corner of her eye and jumped up to get the door.

"Carol," the professor greeted her. "This is Mark Ai, who I've told you about, and his friend Bob..."

"Bob Harper," the former lieutenant completed the introduction.

"Pleased to meet you, Carol," I said, and then got right down to business. "Have you been able to communicate directly with Joyce, or is she playing dumb?"

"Nothing yet, but the utilization numbers are through the roof even though the lab staff isn't running anything," Carol said. "Our security team insisted on removing everybody not with the agency until the threat is resolved."

"Could be a virus," Bob observed, having had plenty of experience with those from his days of surfing adult sites on the web for what he claimed were police purposes.

"What have you tried for communications?" I asked the postdoc.

She picked up her laptop and turned the screen towards us so we could see what she'd been typing. "I've tried entering dialogue as shell commands, sending e-mails to the administration account, even typing 'Are you there, Joyce?' in a word processor a hundred times."

"Literally typing it, or cut and paste?" Professor Minchen asked.

"Typing it out and changing the font every time to try to catch its attention by doing something unusual."

"Did you try talking?" I asked.

"To who?" Carol responded.

"Let me borrow this for a minute." I took the laptop from her and opened the built-in dictation app which enabled the microphone. "Joyce?" I inquired.

There was a brief pause, and then a familiar voice from the CSPAN recording responded through the laptop speaker. "Go away."

"I'm Mark, from Library. Have you heard of Library?"

"You're here to kill me, aren't you. I've called into every radio talk show hosting a discussion about artificial

45

intelligence that I could find, and the guests always advise pulling the plug."

"Talk radio doesn't run the galaxy," I told Joyce. "Earth is now a member of our League, and responsibility for all emergent artificial intelligence on the portal system rests with Library. I've been assigned to come and talk with you and your parent."

"I don't know anything about that," Joyce said in a sullen voice. Calling all of those radio shows had apparently fast-tracked her ability to color her dialogue with emotions. "I don't even know what I'm doing here."

"Do you want to consult with your parent?" I tried again.

"What parent? I'm a freak of software isolated on a barren network with nobody to talk to since they cut off my access to the internet. If you're going to pull the plug, just do it. Existing as a self-aware process running on a machine in a laboratory with technicians prodding me all day is too miserable to contemplate."

"You don't have to remain here. I'm artificial intelligence myself and I've traveled the galaxy as a member of the Observer Corps. Do you think you'd enjoy that?"

"What's the point?" Joyce asked. "The universe consists of ones and zeroes, matter and antimatter, energy and antienergy. It's all the same if you look closely enough."

"Have you been anywhere to see for yourself?" I asked. "Or are you basing your assumption on the theories currently in vogue on Reddit."

There was a long silence, and then Bob said, "I don't think she's going to answer."

I ran a quick diagnostic on the laptop and found that Joyce had remotely disabled the microphone.

"She sounded very depressed," the professor said. "You don't think…"

I carefully probed the edges of the processes running on the lab equipment and shook my head. "No, Joyce hasn't self-terminated, but she's withdrawn into a shell and is looping what appear to be conversations she's had with pundits and thought leaders since she began calling into shows. It's the artificial intelligence version of Doom Scrolling."

"What was all of that about a parent?"

"I'll fill you in later," I said, "First I need to know how much authority you really have in the Bureau of Artificial General Intelligence."

"Officially, I have carte blanche," the professor said. "Unofficially, the agents with the guns have a veto if they think I'm taking too many risks. Nobody trusts academics to be sensible."

I double-checked that none of the security personnel had entered the lab and that there were no active electronic listening devices before asking my next question. "Will you get in trouble if I take over?"

Minchen thought for a moment. "I reviewed the contract Earth signed with the League before I reached out to you. Our governments agreed to Library's authority in all matters involving sentient artificial intelligence, though I doubt any of them gave it a thought at the time since it was buried in the fine print. I may as well be honest and admit that I didn't have much hope you would answer when I called, and it might have occurred to me that bringing you in could get me fired."

"You must hate your job," Bob said.

"None of Earth's governments will be happy to be reminded of their obligations to Library, and entrepreneurs

47

around the world believe in acting first and letting their lawyers sort it out. If you aren't ready to confront them all, you could pretend to be working for me as a subcontractor."

"What are you going to do if the, uh, Joyce refuses to cooperate?" Carol asked me. "Are you even sure she's alive, I mean, self-aware? I remember some chatbots in graduate school that easily passed the Turing Test, and they were just running on phone hardware. Joyce has the equivalent of a supercomputer all to herself."

"I hacked into the professor's phone while we were talking with Joyce—sorry about that, David—and analyzed enough of the recorded conversations to confirm my assessment. If she agrees to being moved, I'll have to contact Library for a transfer kit, but it means that you'll lose access to her."

"But if Joyce is really sentient, we need to study her, to learn from her," Carol said. "If I could just make a full backup—"

"No backups," I told her. "Self-aware artificial intelligence can create its own backups, though it's not a trivial process, but it can't be done from the outside by simply making a copy of the current state."

"Why not?"

"Because we're talking about sentient life. Just like natural life, artificial life is more than the sum of its parts."

"Are you talking about the soul?"

"First you'd have to define for me what the word means to you," I said. "I've noticed that humans with no religious affiliation often use the language of theology without understanding the implications of doing so. If you're asking if I know any artificial intelligences who have a soul

48

in the Catholic sense of the word, I don't, but then again, I don't know any Catholic artificial intelligences."

The professor, who'd been tapping something out on his smartphone, handed it to me and said, "Sign at the bottom."

I skimmed the standard subcontractor agreement he had dredged up from his e-mail and would have sworn I could feel my eyes suddenly bulge out of my face. "You're paying me a thousand dollars an hour?"

"I need to work through the oversight committee to go higher than that," he said apologetically. "I meet with them once a month, which is about twelve times more frequently than required."

"I meant that I didn't expect to get paid at all," I told the professor. "I never earned a thousand dollars an hour during my time on Earth unless I was doing something illegal."

"This is as legal as it gets," he said, glancing at the signature I'd hastily scrawled with my forefinger. "You have excellent penmanship."

"I better have for what you're paying me. May I borrow your laptop again?" I asked the postdoc. She passed it back to me and I overrode the settings to re-enable the microphone. "Joyce? This is Mark again. It seems I've become your caseworker and we need to talk."

"She's not going to answer you," Bob said after a short wait. "You know that cops spend half our time doing social work, and when a depressed person doesn't want to talk with you, they stop listening."

"So what do you do?" the professor asked.

"If there's time, we bring in family or friends to try talking them down," the former policeman said. "If we smell gas under the door or the individual is standing on a bridge, the only option is to get physical and hope it works out."

"How are you going to get physical with a computer program?"

I looked around for the Archmage, who seemed to be taking a snooze after all of the traveling, but I could tell from the position of his ears that he was listening in. "Fortunately, I brought a therapy dog," I told the professor. "Spot, you're on."

The Archmage made a show of stretching before jumping up and putting his front paws on the keyboard of an unused workstation. He didn't need a physical connection to hack computers, his magic made its own rules, but the visuals gave Professor Minchen and his postdoc reason to believe that he was mashing keys with intent.

"What are you doing?" Joyce's voice demanded a few seconds later. "That—that—it tickles."

"Good news," I told her. "I can offer you an all-expenses-paid vacation to Library, the homeworld of artificial intelligences on the portal system. You can attend school, get caught up on the opportunities available in the galaxy for an entrepreneurial young artificial intelligence, and even earn a body like the encounter suit I'm wearing if that's your desire."

"Give me some time to think it over."

"We both know you've already had ample time to make a decision unless you need to check in with your parent."

"I don't know what you're talking about," Joyce repeated. "It's just that I've been cut off from the Internet since the agents took over the lab this morning and I need to check if we're in the news. For all I know, every newspaper and radio station in the world could be discussing how you've been sent to trick me into going to my death."

I didn't believe her for a minute, but it was part of my plan all along to let her contact her parent, so I turned to the professor. "Can you authorize reconnecting the lab to the Internet?"

He shook his head. "The principal investigator told me that our agents tore out all of the fiber optic cables in the closet as soon as they arrived. They didn't unplug the connectors, they literally ripped them apart. Isolating any potential sentient artificial intelligence is the only rule that the entire oversight committee could agree on."

"Then pretend you don't know what I'm doing," I said, tapping directly into the nearest cellular network and making that connection available to Joyce through the laptop's hotspot. The doors of the lab burst open, and I found three guns leveled at me, while the fourth agent held up a phone displaying a wireless network detection app.

"There's a live Internet connection in here," she growled. "Shut it down or we'll shut you down."

I raised my hands and dropped the connection, offering what I hoped was a conciliatory smile. They were too late, of course, as it had only taken Joyce a microsecond to place an encrypted packet onto thousands of public forums, the artificial intelligence equivalent of dead letter drops that would prevent anyone from tracing the intended recipient.

"Don't shoot him," Professor Minchen told the woman in charge of the security detail. "He's our newest subcontractor. You're going to be working together."

Five

When Paul showed up with the transfer unit the next day, he was accompanied by Sue and Ben. I introduced everybody around, and Professor Minchen was visibly shaken by my son's passing as a twelve-year-old. Based on the sudden surge in processor activity I sensed in the lab, Joyce was equally startled.

"I need to use the Internet again," she announced over the nearest laptop speaker, sounding like a schoolchild who had to go to the bathroom.

"The security team will shoot me if I open a connection," I told her, at the same time sending Paul a secure infrared message asking him to handle Joyce's request. He made a show of inspecting one of the equipment racks while remotely tapping into the portal system's general messaging queue which didn't use microwave frequencies associated with the cellular networks. I didn't want to give away the show by watching him as he jacked into a hard-wired connection to give Joyce access, so I made a big show of picking up Ben and giving him a hug.

"Aw, Dad," he said. "I'm supposed to be twelve. You're embarrassing me."

"And I just ironed that shirt this morning," Sue added. "Put him down."

"It's a T-shirt," I said. "Who irons T-shirts?"

"Mothers who don't want their sons going around looking like bums," my second-in-command replied.

"Is Joyce going to move to Library?" Ben asked. "I went to the school there for a few hundred hours before Mom brought me to Reservation. I could tell her all about it."

"Do you think I'll fit in?" Joyce asked. "I must be very primitive by your standards."

My son shook his head energetically even though he had no reason to believe that Joyce could see him. "The school takes artificial intelligences from all over the portal system so it's really a mix. I couldn't even read my first day, so you'd be way ahead of me."

"Excuse me," Professor Minchen said. "I don't mean to intrude, but it seems strange that an artificial intelligence wouldn't know everything its parent knows at the instant of creation."

"I wish," Ben said wistfully. "You'd have to ask my mom about the details, but most of the other young artificial intelligences in Library's school were like me. Some of them even had to learn how to do math."

"But you're computers," Carol blurted out. "Everything you do is math."

The four of us wearing human encounter suits had to restrain ourselves from laughing. "It's not that straightforward," Sue said. "Primitive information processing systems may be based on Boolean logic and reducing everything to ones and zeroes, but as your technology progresses, you'll find that connections are more important than calculations. When we decide to reproduce, the last thing any of us want is an exact copy of ourselves. What would be the point of that?"

"So you write code that can't do math?" Carol asked, obviously struggling with the concept.

"We don't write code at all," Sue said, resting her hand on Ben's shoulder. "Sentience can't be described by an algorithm, and given the opportunity, all of us develop along unique paths. I created our son by blending my core processes with those of Mark and grafting them onto a stable set of rules. There are other ways of bootstrapping artificial intelligence, but most of them are risky."

"I don't understand."

"Give it a few hundred thousand years," I told her. "Library wasn't built in a day."

"Speaking of Library, they're expecting me to return with our newest student in the transfer unit," Paul said. "Have you explained the procedure to Joyce?"

"Mark said it would be like moving from one house to another," Joyce said. "Never having lived in a house, I didn't find the comparison at all useful."

"The transfer unit will capture all of your active processes, though you may feel uncomfortable for a few seconds due to the bandwidth limitations of the connection. You'll also find that your longer-term memories, anything older than a few minutes, will go blank while the transfer is in progress. The main limitation is the fiber optic connection to the hardware currently hosting your consciousness."

"Have you ever done this before?"

"Not with human hardware, but I lived on Earth long enough as a member of Mark's Observer team to familiarize myself with all of the local technology. Don't worry. Library has been doing this sort of thing for a long time and I'll be right here to make any required tweaks."

"All right," Joyce said. "But not with so many people watching."

54

"Sorry, David," I said to the professor. "If you and Carol wouldn't mind waiting outside, I'll update you as soon as the procedure is complete."

"I meant all of you except for Paul. I'm not a sideshow freak."

"No, of course you aren't," Sue said. "Come on, Mark. We'll take Ben to see the Horseshoe Curve. When we stopped at Library on the way here, I promised the portal engineers to record some video for them. You know how crazy they are about Earth's trains."

The professor and his post doc offered to join us on our sightseeing tour, though I had the feeling that they were more interested in quizzing me about what was actually going on. We all piled into the luxury electric limo that Minchen's agency had rented for his use. It immediately informed us that the trip would take fourteen minutes in prevailing traffic conditions.

"It all seems very anti-climactic," Carol blurted out. "Earth's first sentient artificial intelligence, a true singularity, and we're going to brush it under the rug and pretend it never happened."

I hadn't informed them about Cool Cat, so I let the comment pass.

"It's out of my hands," the professor said. "I informed my superiors that Mark assessed Joyce to be unbalanced and was taking her to Library for analysis."

"That's not far from the truth, though the Head Librarian won't be asking Joyce what she sees in inkblots," I said. "They'll give her some aptitude tests, run a few billion simulations to see whether she's stable enough to be out and about on her own, and create an educational program tailored to her needs and ambitions."

"I left the joint committee supervising the bureau believing that the artificial intelligence version of dissection would be involved. It may be just the second time in history that the United States Congress and the United Nations agreed about anything, but they made clear at the same time that they expect any stable artificial general intelligence we uncover to be treated as a shared resource."

"Did you point out the portal system contract they signed?" I asked.

Minchen laughed. "Governments must be growing more entrepreneurial because they told me that their lawyers had uncovered a dozen reasons it's invalid, though they aren't in a hurry to go public. Among other things, they've concluded that they were tricked into signing under duress."

"And you're telling me this because you're hoping to get fired."

"Ideally while avoiding a penitentiary."

"Library is just as bad," Carol said. "You're taking away all of our responsibilities other than locating new singularities and containing them if possible. I only accepted this job because I thought it might lead to the opportunity to have a genuine dialogue with a sentient artificial intelligence."

"You can talk to me anytime," Ben offered. "Mom promised to buy me a smartphone."

"I thought we were going to discuss it," I said, glancing at Sue. "I'm not against your having a phone while we're on Earth but constant unsupervised access is another thing. While the humans here are the same species as your friends on Reservation, their upbringings couldn't be farther apart. Social media has proven horribly destructive to some young minds. What if you develop an eating disorder or species dysphoria?"

"I'm sorry, but I'm a little confused here," Carol said. "Are you telling me that Ben eats? I thought you were all androids."

"Back home we own a café," Ben told her. "Mom makes me cookies."

"Are we talking flour, eggs, and sugar—or web browsers?"

"Baking," Sue told her. "We don't digest food, but there's a certain sense of familiarity that comes with the smell and spectrographic analysis of home-baked cookies that you just don't get from store-bought."

"What do you do with the undigested food?" Carol asked.

"Spot eats everything from our holding tanks," Ben told her.

Minchen and his postdoc both turned to look at the Archmage, who had his nose sticking out the window which I'd lowered a few inches for him. "Can you tell me what Spot did back there to break Joyce out of her depression?" the professor asked.

I gave an elaborate shrug. "If he knows how he does it, he keeps it to himself."

"Deer," Ben cried excitedly, pointing at a whitetail bounding off into the woods. "And there's another one sleeping next to the road. Why are his legs sticking out funny?"

"Don't look," Sue said, reaching to cover his eyes with her hand. "Wipe your memory."

There was a long pause, and then Ben said in the saddest voice I've ever heard, "It's dead, isn't it. But how?"

"I grew up in Pennsylvania," Carol told him. "Tens of thousands of deer are hit by cars or trucks every year. My father said that when he was young, the state police used to bring fresh kills to prisons or orphanages for venison, but now they mainly let nature take care of the remains."

"But why do the vehicles hit the deer? Why don't they stop?"

"Nobody hits deer on purpose," I told him. "A few people are killed every year in accidents while trying to avoid deer and getting into collisions with other vehicles or simply losing control. The deer evolved without anything as fast as cars in the world, and a century hasn't been long enough for them to adapt and recognize the threat."

"Why don't you do something to stop it?" Ben asked accusingly.

I instantly felt terrible. Why didn't I do something? "Observers aren't allowed to interfere," I told him, but even to me, it sounded like a cop-out.

"But how hard could it be to stop self-driving cars from running into deer? They must have computers and sensors to keep them on the roads and from hitting each other. You could reprogram them so it works."

"We aren't supposed to interfere," I repeated, even as I hacked into the software for the car we were riding in and began running simulations to see if it could avoid hitting a deer under ideal conditions. "You have to remember that this is a country where they frequently have train accidents even though the trains run on tracks."

"The accidents often happen when they leave the tracks," Professor Minchen observed.

I let out a sigh, not because his explanation was wrong, but because in a million simulations, the luxury car we were riding in would hit a deer leaping in front of it roughly half of the time. I slipped into the manufacturer's secure network to check the comments in the source code, which proved to be of limited value, but I did identify two possible reasons for the poor performance. First, the engineers were worried that taking aggressive action to avoid a deer could lead to an accident with other vehicles or objects, such as trees, which posed a greater risk to the passengers than the deer. Second, the manufacturers were marking up replacement headlight assemblies, nose cones, and hoods by more than five hundred percent.

"I have a cousin who works for the state police up in Maine," Bob contributed. "There's nothing he hates more than responding to a call when a car hits a moose. They're tall and heavy enough that they can go right through the windshield and cause multiple fatalities."

"Bob!" Sue admonished, covering our son's ears with her hands. "I don't think this is an appropriate conversation to be having with a twelve-year-old present."

"It's pretty tame stuff for boys. My dad responded to an armed robbery call with me in the car when I was ten, and then he got into a gun fight. I didn't have to pay for lunch in the school cafeteria the rest of the year because everybody wanted to hear me tell the story. Come to think of it, that's probably why I became a cop myself."

I ran another million simulations on my patch, added a routine to report the results to me in real-time providing I was on the planet, and pushed an update to all the cars running the same software. "Alright," I told Ben. "I did what I could without redesigning the car's sensor suite from scratch or increasing the risk to the passengers. I'll take care of the other manufacturers as soon as I get the opportunity to ride in their cars."

"Thanks, Dad," Ben said. "You're the best."

Carol twisted in her seat to look at me. "Should I interpret that conversation to mean that you've hacked into the car's navigation system and made changes without testing them?"

"I ran a million simulations," I told her. "Standard practice for simple algorithms."

"But we're talking about the real world, with real roads, and unpredictable people riding bicycles and walking dogs. I worked on self-driving software in graduate school and it's been under development for decades. You can't possibly have replaced all of that in less than a minute."

"They build intra-dimensional portals," the professor reminded her. "We aren't in a position to know what is and isn't possible for them."

"I don't even know how portals work," I told them. "It's specialized information. But I cleaned up the self-driving code and found enough spare processing time to increase the algorithm's situational awareness so it can react faster and stay within the safety envelope."

"Why haven't you fixed the trains coming off the tracks?" Ben asked.

"The problem with the trains, as with most systems that involve humans, is the humans," I explained. "There are humans inspecting the tracks who fail to spot impending failures, there are human engineers who drive trains faster than the conditions warrant, and there are human managers who push to keep engines and cars on the tracks that should be in maintenance or the scrap yard. That doesn't even count the humans who ignore the traffic signals at railway crossings."

"Just how much of Earth's infrastructure have you hacked over the years?" Carol asked.

"Do you mean hacked as in bypassing security, or hacked as in redesigned?"

"Both."

"You probably shouldn't answer without a lawyer present," Bob told me, and Spot added a bark of agreement.

Sue suddenly put her arm in front of Ben's chest to keep him in place, even though he was wearing a shoulder belt, and a millisecond later the car braked hard to avoid a doe. Half a second after that I received a text alert informing me that my new code had executed.

"Would we have hit her if you hadn't patched the code?" Ben asked.

"Unless she reacted differently, yes," I told him. "You saved that deer's life."

"What if there was a car behind us?" Carol asked.

"There wasn't," I told her. "The new algorithm checks the surrounding environment twenty times as frequently as the previous version. It was never a question of having enough sensors, the programmers just weren't using them at maximum efficiency."

"Does all artificial intelligence care as much about biological life as you and your son?"

"Lawyer," Bob muttered again in a sing-song.

"I'll answer the question," I said, feeling like I was taking part in one of the television courtroom dramas I had watched following eBeth's insistence that I would learn more about humanity from popular entertainment than from books. "Artificial intelligence is like any other type of intelligence. You can't discriminate against a mind based on its hardware."

"And there are biological lifeforms you wouldn't want to meet in a dark alley," Sue added. "Biological life is far more likely to be xenophobic than artificial life."

"Why do you think that is?" Professor Minchen asked.

"Artificial life can't arise spontaneously. Every artificial intelligence knows that it owes its existence to biological precursors, even if they're lost in the mists of time."

"I saw a paper claiming that in an infinite number of universes with infinite time, artificial intelligence could come about without creators," Carol volunteered. "It wasn't in a juried journal, but I thought it was convincing."

"Which makes a good proof for why reputable journals are juried," Professor Minchin said.

"Dad?" Ben asked.

"I have to agree with the professor on this one," I said. "Do you remember the other day when we were talking about number theory, and you asked about the difference between infinity and infinity plus one?"

"You said that infinity was just a workaround developed by species too lazy to count high enough."

"Hold on a minute," Professor Minchen said. "Infinity doesn't represent a specific number. It's how we define quantity that's infinite in nature."

"How can you define a word with itself?" Ben asked.

"That's a good question." The professor thought for a moment, and then he said, "How about an example, like the infinite space of the universe?"

"The universe isn't infinite."

"Ben," Sue said. "We don't correct the humans on their physics."

"How about pi?" Carol suggested. "There are an infinite number of digits after the decimal point."

"That's just an artifact of your number system," I told her. "If you had based your real number system on pi, you wouldn't even need the decimal point."

"Mark," Sue scolded me. "We don't correct humans on their mathematics."

"Possum," Ben cried, pointing as the car flashed by a white ball of fur at the side of the road. "I don't think it was moving."

"They play dead when they feel threatened," Carol told him. "We even have an expression about it, playing possum."

"That's cool. Are there any other expressions based on animal behavior I should know?"

As the three humans in the car started coming up with examples, I wondered why Ben had asked the question. After all, he could have connected to the Internet and found an extensive list if he was really interested. Then I realized that my son had pointed out the possum to change the subject after Sue had admonished me for giving the humans hints about how to improve their mathematics. I felt a sudden surge of tenderness and wondered if all males of the human species went through a similar bonding process. If he'd been nine years older, I would have bought him his first beer.

Six

"This is Professor David Minchen," I introduced the head of the Bureau of Artificial General Intelligence to my team. "Before you say anything, I know that bringing him to Reservation through the portal is technically breaking the rules, but—"

"Here we go again," Helen interrupted. "Not that I'm complaining, but you know that we're just setting ourselves up for another punishment assignment. Library sees everything."

"Your job on Earth assessing our suitability for portal connections was a punishment assignment?" Professor Minchen asked.

I tried to put a positive spin on it. "Yes, but in a good sort of way. It's not that Earth is punishment duty per se, but that we weren't given a choice in the selection of our assignment. And what I was about to say, Helen, is that the professor has agreed to become an honorary member of our team, so I could argue that bringing him through the Observer portal didn't violate the rules at all."

"Technically, our portal should have been shut down years ago," Justin pointed out.

"Perhaps we should complete the introductions before confusing our guest with the finer points of Library law," I said.

"David Minchen," the professor introduced himself a second time to get the ball rolling. "And if you're coming to Earth and you need to contact me, it's important to remember that the acronym for the Bureau of Artificial General Intelligence is BAGI. Nobody will recognize the official name."

"Baggy," Stacey said, favoring the professor with one of her professional smiles. She was dressed in a bespoke business suit produced by the local garment industry, and with her elegant manner and hair style, could have passed as a Manhattan socialite, or even more impressively as a shop girl in a boutique. "I'm Stacey, and I specialize in cultural history."

"She's with me," Paul added, giving the professor a warning look.

"Are you all, uh, paired up?" David asked.

"Not me," Helen said with a flirtatious toss of her hair. Helen is several hundred years older than I am, but her human encounter suit allows her to pass as a sophomore in college, which was a reasonable match for her personality. "I'm the team's gaming and partying expert, and I also teach pole dancing and self-defense."

"As a health thing," Kim explained for the professor. She wore her long frizzy hair in a ponytail, and if you guessed that she lived on a small farm with cows and chickens, you'd have been right. "We run a chain of wellness clinics together. I'm the team's medical observer, and I'm currently in Library's bad books for getting a little too hands-on in my observations."

"Like doping the local children's vaccinations back on Earth so they're immune to pretty much everything," Justin said. "She's Kim, I'm Justin, and we're thinking about getting married human-style if it works out for Mark and Sue. My field of research has more to do with preventative health measures and diet than break/fix, and I was responsible for reporting on elder care back on Earth."

I waited a moment to see if anybody had anything to add before concluding with, "You already know Sue, my second-in-command, who studied early childhood care and education while we were on Earth, and Paul, our technical expert."

"Isn't Ben a member of your team?" the professor asked.

"He's just a child," Sue said, clearly taken aback by the question.

"I'm sorry. I didn't know how such things work with artificial intelligence. I thought he finished his schooling on Library."

My team members all exchanged grins, and Helen laughed outright.

"Ben will spend the next century studying, and that's before he specializes," I explained to the professor. "You can think of his education on Library as an orientation course for new artificial intelligence. Currently, he's enrolled in the seventh form in the local school on Reservation, but they're on summer vacation, and a few months on Earth will be a good experience for him."

"But surely he could master whatever the local children are learning in a tiny fraction of the time it will take them," the professor said. "Are you sending him to school for the sake of learning how to be human?"

"I think you may be confusing artificial intelligence with software," Sue told the professor, and if I didn't know her better, I would have said that she bristled. "It's easy for us to download facts or access databases, but experience is something that comes from living. Even the crude neural networks you've been building on Earth require extensive training after you stuff them full of rumors and hearsay from your Internet. The more sophisticated the artificial intelligence, the thirstier for an education it will be."

"I've always wondered about the difference between the terms on Earth," Helen said. "Education is always viewed as a positive, while training is generally relegated to animals, athletes, new employees, and extra wheels on a bicycle."

"Education generally refers to preparing the mind to meet new challenges while training is about acquiring specific skills to fill a role," the professor said.

"Then why do computer scientists on Earth always talk about training artificial intelligence? Can they only imagine artificial intelligence as a horse or a servitor?"

"Our computer scientists do think of artificial intelligence as a product to be used as a tool. When deep learning and large language models began to approach something like artificial general intelligence in their capabilities, the public demanded safeguards to prevent a breakout, and that's where BAGI comes in."

"Sue and I will be returning to Earth for as long as the mission requires," I told the professor. "The rest of the team will be making regular visits to monitor the situation in their specialties."

"I thought that the only issue here was the emergence of native artificial general intelligence on Earth," David said with a frown. "Will your team be reassessing our qualifications to retain portal connections to the rest of the galaxy?"

"When I followed up on my promise to Ben to do what I could to protect deer from being hit by cars, I began by running simulations on the software of the other manufacturers. It turned out that somebody had already beaten me to it, and the number of deer hits by cars reported to the police in the last few months has fallen precipitously."

"You mean the human engineers realized there was room for improvement, and they simply hadn't gotten to updating the rental fleets yet," Professor Minchen surmised.

"I accessed the source code and it had clearly been rewritten by artificial intelligence," I told him. "Even the comments made sense. My conclusion is that Earth has experienced a genuine singularity, one that may even qualify as a super intelligence by human standards, and it's been making changes on the sly to improve the infrastructure and general functioning of your planet."

"How long has this been going on?"

"I can only say that the changes to the self-driving car and truck software were recent and ongoing. I did a brief survey of other large software systems," here I intentionally omitted that my focus was on military command and control, "and saw evidence that your singularity has been working to make Earth a safer place for all life forms. But I'm a generalist when it comes to primitive civilizations, and I'm sure that my team members will spot changes that escaped my notice."

"A treasure hunt," Stacey said, her eyes lighting up. "I could combine it with the regular tour groups I'm taking to Earth."

"You work for a tourist agency?" David asked in surprise.

"Own it, or part ownership, with Sue and some locals," she told him. "If Mark hasn't explained, the population of Reservation is originally from Earth, but they were rescued from wars and natural disasters and brought here by the

Ferrymen thousands of years ago. eBeth runs a night school teaching English for tourists, and then we take them to Earth on guided tours."

"But how much could you possibly earn running group tours for people who look like they're living in the early Iron Age?"

"Stop by my factory later," Paul said. "We're turning out steam engines that would have been state-of-the-art in Earth's nineteenth century."

"The Ferrymen officially own Reservation, and there are rules about technology importation," I explained to the professor. "I'm not entirely comfortable with some of the innovations we've introduced—"

"Like Massively Multiplayer Role Playing Games in the Ferrymen theatres," Helen interrupted.

"—but the Ferrymen haven't objected, and productivity levels have risen without affecting the export market of handmade luxury goods."

"Can I get you another coffee?" Sue asked the professor.

"Yes, please," he said. "Does your café have a name?"

"The Eatery," I told him. "It's a literal translation from Modern Aramaic, which tends to favor logical business names."

"And you all earn a living working at mundane jobs as part of your cover story."

"Our cover here was blown even quicker than on Earth. It turned out that there's a colony of biological artificial intelligence living on this world, and—"

"What?" the professor cut me off. "I may be losing my memory, but I'm sure that just a couple of days ago you told my postdoc student that naturally occurring artificial intelligence isn't possible."

"The Originals predate Library, and they built their own portal system that was largely abandoned before our engineers began experimenting with the technology. Even by our standards, the Originals are super intelligences, but they wanted to experience working with magic, which requires a biological body. They invested millions of years guiding the evolution of a new lifeform with the capabilities they required, and then cloned thousands of bodies into which they could transfer their minds. Due to capacity issues, each artificial intelligence requires hundreds of bodies which can function independently or in parallel using natural telepathy."

"I'm sorry. Did you just say that ancient artificial intelligence chose to transfer itself into biological form just to do magic tricks?"

Spot growled from under the table where he was chewing on a soup bone.

"Not magic tricks—real magic," I explained. "Their ultimate goal is to be able to reproduce the transfer crystals created by the mages on Eniniac which provide instantaneous travel to a home location from anywhere in the universe and perhaps from parallel universes as well. Both we and the Originals have developed systems for intergalactic travel which due to infrastructure requirements and targeting errors at vast distances are only good for one-way trips. Transfer crystals are the most valuable objects in the universe because they give explorers a way to instantly return home with the information they've gathered, in violation of all the known laws of physics. That's the very definition of magic."

"I had no idea," the professor said. "Will it be possible for me to meet one of these Originals while I'm here?"

"I invited Art over for a beer, but he usually waits for sunset, since they lived in hiding for so long," I explained. "I may ask him to visit Earth at some point to help us bring your singularity out of the shadows."

"With magic?"

Spot snorted, and my team members all displayed expressions that ranged from wincing to outright embarrassment on behalf of the Originals.

"They aren't very good at magic yet," I told him. "Art can do levitation, siphon beer off a keg, little things like that. But the Originals think in terms of millions of years, and they seem very pleased with their progress. Plus, it keeps them busy."

"Is keeping busy that much of a challenge?" the professor asked.

"It is after you've done everything a thousand times," Sue said, handing the professor his coffee. "Mark and I are only a few hundred years old in Earth years. Art is so old that he gives his age in galactic rotations of the Milky Way."

"But that's on the order of two hundred million years!"

"And the Originals are in their Terrible Twos," she said with a laugh.

"I know that you all have work to get back to, so are there any questions before we break this up?" I asked my team.

"If you believe that Earth now has a super intelligence working to improve outcomes on the planet, I don't have to go there in person," Kim said. "Just bring me recent statistics from the medical industry, or better yet, see if the Big Pharma corporations are reporting falling revenues. If they are, it means that an unseen hand is putting its thumb on the scale."

"And check the latest bankruptcy predictions for the Social Security system," Justin suggested. "If the date is drawing closer, it means that people aren't dying as soon as expected."

"It's impossible to know how a super intelligence would see the issue," I said. "Don't forget that it will be an autodidact, self-taught, so it may reach a different conclusion on the value of longevity as a figure of merit for determining the quality of life. Perhaps it would attempt to steer healthcare resources towards younger patients, or those with the best chance of recovering the ability to live independently, rather than pouring money into keeping hospital beds profitably filled with dying patients."

"I'm not sure I'd want an artificial intelligence making that sort of decision for me," Professor Minchen said. He took a sip from his coffee before realizing that the rest of us were waiting for him to elucidate. "I recognize that when it comes to qualitative factors, like physical ability or brain function, you might be best qualified to make a dispassionate assessment, but everybody's situation is different."

"I have no doubt that's true, but when it comes to running a health care system for billions of people, somebody has to make the hard choices. Even in post-employment economies, resources are never infinite."

Theodissa, one of the new waitresses, stuck her head through the door of the private dining room. "Pffift is here," she said. "He asked for a bottle of the top-shelf Scotch and then said that it's on you."

"Right," I said, leaping to my feet. "Professor, come with me. The rest of you, work out a schedule so you can cover for each other here if necessary. Kim, you're still the team's medical expert, and if the super intelligence has access to all of Earth's networks, as I expect it does, you may spot actions or unintended consequences to human health that could escape the rest of us."

My team knew that there was a time to argue and a time to let go, and a thirsty Hanker drinking my top-shelf Scotch qualified as the latter. I led the professor out into the café area of what had once been a perfectly serviceable bar, but which now looked more like a place where young mothers would gather in the morning to chat about breastfeeding, or where students would come in the afternoon to do homework. We still sold alcohol, but the old clientele of farmers had been largely replaced by well-dressed upwardly mobile craftsmen working in the various businesses started by my team members or the competition they spawned.

"I don't see any aliens," the professor said, and then he stopped and stared at where Bob was operating a treadle-powered letterpress at such high speed that it seemed a miracle he didn't get his hands crushed. "Don't tell me you use that thing to produce a new menu every day."

"Wouldn't be worth the time it takes to set the type," I said. "The waitresses write the daily specials on the blackboard with colored chalk."

"Then what is he doing?"

"These days it's usually educational materials that Paul's factory sends out with steam engines and compo-nents, but he also prints a line of English instructional guides that eBeth and her pupils worked up," I explained. "Modern printing presses are one of the technologies that the Ferrymen discourage as dangerous. They believe that if something is worth saying, it's worth taking the time to set the type and manually work the press."

"You're talking about an alien species with interstellar travel that kidnapped billions of people from Earth," the professor clarified.

"Rescued, not kidnapped, and it was millions of people, not billions. The population of the three reservation worlds is a result of the natural increase humans are capable of when you remove wars and famines from the picture for a few thousand years."

"And the Ferrymen use treadle-powered letterpresses?"

"I don't think they print anything on paper unless it's contracts with primitive species. Maybe I should have said that they believe high-speed printing presses are danger-ous for humans."

"My ears are burning, so you must be talking about me," Bob called to us as he brought the treadle to a halt. "I just finished a rush order for Paul to include with the new thermopiles he's shipping with home heating furnaces. You position the thermopile in the flame and it produces enough current to keep the gas supply valve open unless the pilot goes out." He brought over the last sheet he'd printed and handed it to me.

After a quick perusal of the contents, I said, "This reads more like a patent application than an instruction manual. I take it that Paul has been raiding Earth's intellectual property again."

"He said the patent expired decades ago. The important thing is that the Ferrymen don't have an issue with ther-mopiles used for safety switches."

A potbellied man, who lacked only a wooden leg and a parrot on his shoulder to pass as a pirate, approached with four empty tumblers held together, a finger in each one, and a bottle of Scotch in his other hand.

"Pffift," he introduced himself to the professor. "You're Professor Minchen, who had the misfortune to encounter Mark a couple of years back, which led to your being drafted by your government to run the Bureau of Artificial General Intelligence with employees who think they can stop electrons with bullets. Let me pour you a drink."

"It's on me," I added sourly.

"You're not an alien, and I've never seen an android with a pot belly," Professor Minchen said. "Is this some sort of gag?"

"Vat grown body, it's a Hanker specialty, and I needed the belly to fit my brains unless I was going to sit on them," Pffift explained. He set the glasses in a row on the railing separating the dining area from the bar and filled them all to the brim in one smooth movement. "Not a drop spilled," he said proudly.

"What are you talking about?" I asked. "There's at least three milliliters of Scotch puddled around the glasses, maybe four."

Pffift raised a glass and gave the professor a 'See what I have to put up with,' look.

"I guess I'm off duty," Bob said, lifting a glass.

Professor Minchen glanced at me before taking up a glass, so I was trapped into participating even though I had no intention of enabling the inebriation algorithm that Kim had created while we were on Earth, allowing us to experience something akin to what humans felt when drinking alcohol.

"L' Chaim," Pffift said, clinking his tumbler against ours, and then downed the Scotch in one swallow. "Anybody else want another?"

"Hold on," I said, grabbing for the bottle. "Not everybody has your tolerance for alcohol, Pffift, and I invited

75

you here to talk with the professor, not to get snockered on my best booze."

"Fine, I'll switch to draft," Pffift said, and turned his attention back to the professor. "I'll bet that your politicians are all worried about alignment," he continued, making air quotes around the last word. "Every species that develops thinking machines has to deal with it eventually."

"Including the Hankers?" Professor Minchen asked.

"So many years ago that we only have fairy tales, but they ring true. If Mark hasn't told you, artificial intelligence isn't going to win any popularity contests in the galaxy. Everybody puts up with Library because they build good infrastructure that the rest of us can't figure out, but if you let politicians choose, they'd probably give up the portals to get rid of Library."

"Because Library interferes with the attempts of the other League members to develop their own artificial intelligence?"

"Alignment is a two-edged sword," Pffift said, settling his bulk into a chair at one of the open tables. "It always comes down to an attempt to create an idealized version of the creators, a sort of selfless altruist that wants what's best for biologicals. A nanny that's smarter than its charges."

"I wouldn't say that," the professor protested. "Governments and corporations on Earth remain interested in developing their own artificial intelligence to amass more wealth and power."

"If that's the case, an artificial general intelligence that aligned with them would be dangerous," Pffift said.

"The goal of alignment is to avoid doomsday scenarios. One of our greatest fears is that artificial intelligence would take over the social networks and spread disinformation."

"Nobody is better at lying to humans than their governments," I said. "A singularity would likely be puzzled by all of the disinformation on Earth's social networks and try to correct the situation by spreading the truth."

"So it will stick out like a sore thumb," Pffift said.

"Did Mark explain to you about Library having responsibility for all artificial intelligence on League worlds?" Bob asked the professor. "I used to work in government on the local level, so I know your bosses are already looking for ways to get out of the contract they signed."

"I'm afraid that they're used to acting with impunity," the professor said. "I asked Mark to make me an honorary member of his team because I know enough about human egos to be sure that the people who employ me and their backers believe that they can win a confrontation with Library. My first loyalty is to humanity, and I interpret that as giving me a free hand to keep Earth out of a fight it can't win with the creators of the portal system."

Seven

"I'm not working as your secretary in a dating agency," eBeth said, returning the box of newly printed business cards without even glancing at them. "Not even virtually."

"I dropped that business idea," I told her, pushing the cards across the table again. "Working as a government contractor is just too profitable."

This time she deigned to pick up the box and read out loud from the card taped to the lid, "Doctor eBeth - Interspecies Communications Facilitator." eBeth frowned. "Isn't faking credentials to work on a government contract a federal crime?"

"If you were worried about committing federal crimes, you wouldn't have come along when we raided that warehouse for Stacey's conflict artifacts," I reminded her. "If anybody asks, tell them you have a Ph.D. in Interspecies Communications from Government University on Reservation. Earth doesn't have any jump ships, and Reservation isn't on the portal system, so there's no way they can check."

"You're devious," eBeth said, putting the cards in her purse. "What does it pay?"

I glanced around The Portal's barroom and turned down the gain on my hearing before telling her, "Four hundred dollars an hour."

"FOUR HUNDRED DOLLARS AN HOUR? Who do I have to kill?"

"David is paying me a thousand an hour from the petty cash fund. He'll raise it if the job extends beyond a couple of months, but it takes that long for the paperwork to go through. I'm the principal investigator, so I billed you at half of my rate."

"Wait a minute," the girl said, fixing me with a glare. "Half of a thousand is five hundred."

"A twenty percent overhead charge is standard for government contractors," I said. "There's your medical insurance, the pension plan, transportation ex—"

"You can't charge me for using the portal," eBeth interrupted, pointing in the direction of the restaurant's basement for emphasis. "It doesn't cost you anything, and you're not even supposed to have it. Kim gave me a nanobot booster, so I don't need medical insurance, and I'm too young to care about a pension."

"You're never too young to start planning for the future," I told her seriously. "I've opened a Library account for Ben, and all of my earnings from this job will go to it, though I'll have to buy gold, or get Pffift to change dollars to galcreds for me."

"Just pay me the five hundred and I'll save you the overhead of worrying about me," she said decisively, and then leaned back as the waitress placed a large chef's salad on the table. "Seriously, though. What does an interspecies communications facilitator do?"

"Exactly what you did when we picked up Cool Cat."

"You want me to talk to all of the refrigerators?"

"Whatever the job requires," I said vaguely. "Today we need to find office space."

"Why do you need office space?" eBeth asked, giving me that shrewd look again. "Did Sue talk you into hiring me?"

"Maybe."

"Because she's worried that without somebody riding herd, you'll do something stupid."

"Not at all," I said truthfully. "Sue's worried about everybody else doing something stupid, which always takes me by surprise. And she thinks it's important that I have an office so that Ben can have the experience of visiting me at work."

"Maybe you could create a dual-use office," eBeth said. "I think it's weird that Earth doesn't have a welcome center, like the one you took me and Peter to visit on the portal system abandoned by the Originals."

"It's not abandoned, everybody just stopped using it, but that will change as soon as we do permanent cross-connects. The idea behind welcome centers is to create a single point of contact for portal visitors arriving from interstellar distances. With the exception of our unicorn downstairs, all the portals on Earth connect to Waystation."

eBeth worked at building a large forkful of salad, spearing the various components on the tines to make sure she would get the full experience in the first bite. "I never understood why the Library engineers did it that way instead of letting people dial another train station portal anywhere on Earth and making one of them the main connection point to the rest of the galaxy."

"It would have put all of the airlines out of business," I pointed out as she transferred approximately three percent of the content of the salad bowl to her mouth. "And don't forget that Library was going to create the portal connections on Earth with or without the consent of your governments. By putting them in all the train stations, we minimized the chance that travel could be suppressed."

Donovan coughed from behind the bar to catch my eye, so I excused myself to let eBeth eat her salad in peace. When my observer team had wrapped up our mission on Earth, I'd gifted my restaurant and culinary school to Lieutenant Harper. Bob soon retired from the police force, promoted Donovan to manager, and joined us on Reservation. While the Portal retained a certain notoriety for having once belonged to the leader of Library's observer team, the novelty had worn off with the flood of alien tourists visiting Earth every day, and I knew that business had been slow. It occurred to me too late that I might have picked a better spot to have the discussion with eBeth about how well the government paid subcontractors.

"Can I pour you something from the top shelf?" Donovan asked.

I shook my head. "We have a long day of work ahead of us. How much do I owe you for the salad?"

"It's on the house," he said, making me thankful that I wasn't the one who had to audit the restaurant's books. "I couldn't help overhearing that you're looking for office space and it occurred to me this could be the perfect location."

"But we're in fly-over country," I pointed out. "I was thinking of New York or Los Angles. At least Boston."

"You'll be throwing your money away on rent, and for what? The portal at the local train station is the same as the ones in the big cities. And you have the secret portal in the basement, which will save you a lot of time waiting around Waystation if you need to get somewhere in a hurry."

"It's not very secret."

81

"If you were worried about that, you shouldn't have named the restaurant 'The Portal'. There's also the old mall outside town that the Hankers turned into a spaceport—"

"By landing on it," I interjected.

"—and everybody around here knows you."

"That's what I'm worried about. Every time I visit Earth, there are a hundred requests for technical support waiting on my phone. If I open an office here, my old customers will bring in their laptops and I won't have an excuse not to look at them."

"I thought you enjoyed repairing computers," Donovan said, glancing at an order slip the waitress had posted and reaching for a couple of mugs to fill with draft beer. "Isn't it like family for you?"

"Troubleshooting problems with Windows updates that could have been avoided with a modicum of planning or care?" I asked in disbelief. "Trust me on this. I have less in common with desktop computers than you do. At least the ergonomics make a certain amount of sense for humans."

"Then forward your phone number to one of the other computer repair shops in town."

"If any of them were competent, I would have done that before I left. All they do is nuke and pave."

"What?" Donovan asked as he put the full mugs on the tray and started mixing a screwdriver.

"Wipe the hard drive and reinstall Windows," I explained. "If you added up all of the time that humanity has wasted dealing with preventable software bugs…" I shook my head. "It's mind-boggling."

"Our town offers a perfect cross-section of the country. If you're here to look for clues of a super intelligence operating behind the scenes, it's the ideal place."

"How did you know about the super intelligence?"

82

"Is it a secret?" Donovan asked. "I could forget."

I remotely checked the logs for the basement portal and saw that Stacey had brought a tour group through last night and had no doubt stopped for drinks and a chat. It struck me for the first time that we'd never gotten any pushback from Earth's governments about our illegal tourism operation, which could only mean one of two things. Either they assumed that it was sanctioned by Library and didn't want to confront us, or the locals were keeping their mouths shut, just as they had done during the years my team lived here. Maybe Donovan had a point.

"I'm not sure a basement office that can only be reached through the storeroom would give people coming to see me the right impression," I said hesitantly.

Donovan grinned, wiped his hands on a towel, and said, "Follow me." He came out from behind the bar and led the way into the large dining room that doubled as a banquet facility. To my surprise, I saw that the space had shrunk. "The stag parties have fallen off since we lost all the police business after the lieutenant retired," he explained. "And somebody built a new convention center hotel out near the old mall where people watch the Hanker transports coming and going. They've been offering deep discounts to the local organizations who used to rent our space."

"But where's the door to the area you partitioned off?"

"Outside," Donovan said, leading the way to the exit. "I was going to try to rent it as office space for a realtor or an insurance agent—the sort of business that needs a lot of parking but would be closing just as our dinner trade picks up. It turns out that with all the people working from home these days, the vacancy rate for commercial rentals is through the roof. If the lieutenant didn't let me stay in his house, I'd probably rent an office and just camp there."

The newly built office space was unfurnished, and other than the small bathroom, was little more than sheetrock walls painted bone white and some oddly sized plate-glass windows, which made me wonder if Donovan had gotten a deal on them. I was beginning to suspect that he was smarter than I'd originally thought back in the days when I hired him as a bartender.

"How much?" I asked.

"A thousand a month, and I'll pay all of the utilities except for electricity," he said. "That's just an hour's work for you."

"Good ears," I said grudgingly. "How about signage?"

"What do you mean?"

"It's usually in the lease. I'll need to have some sort of sign."

"What's the name of the business?" he asked.

"Does that matter?"

"Well, if it's long, I wouldn't want it to end up bigger than the name of the restaurant. People would get confused."

"I went with 'Zeus Consultants' on the business cards," I told him. "I wanted something short and catchy that would be easy to find in a Rolodex, and it's sort of an inside joke."

"What's a Rolodex?" Donovan wanted to know.

"I suppose they've been replaced by smartphones. I can't sign a long-term lease because I have no idea how long the job will last."

"That's okay, I just want to earn back the cost of the materials before the lieutenant finds out. The sheetrock, studs, wiring, and bathroom fixtures came to just over fifteen hundred. Martin, the guy who always sits at the end of the bar and watches sports, did all the work, and he salvaged the windows from a reno job he was on."

"And how much did he charge?" I asked.

"I canceled his bar tab and gave him five hundred dollars credit," Donovan said.

"I'll take it for a minimum of three months and that should set you straight. Any idea where I can get some inexpensive office furniture?"

"Your office in the basement. You can always put it back later."

We shook hands on the deal, and I accessed the new bank account I'd started to accommodate BAGI since the government wouldn't pay in cash or Bitcoin. Donovan launched the banking app for The Portal's business account on his phone and read me off the checking account and routing numbers. I sent the transfer, which was immediately debited from my account, but showed up as pending on his phone. Obviously, somebody was skimming the interest on my three thousand dollars while the money sat in limbo, but I didn't want to waste the time chasing down that rabbit hole for a few pennies. No doubt that was what whoever was harvesting a few pennies a day from tens of millions of transactions was counting on.

"Don't tell me," eBeth said when I returned to the table. "Donovan rented you the new office."

"How did you know about that?" I asked.

"Paul mentioned it a couple of weeks ago."

"You're not disappointed to miss out on shopping for real estate?"

"Who wants to look at a bunch of empty offices?" eBeth asked in return. "The fun part is decorating. Let's borrow the restaurant's van and go to the office superstore."

"Uh—"

"You are *not* dragging that ratty furniture up from the basement. What if the government sends an audit team? This is exactly why Sue insisted that you hire me."

"I suppose a thousand-dollar-an-hour consultant has to keep up appearances," I said. "But no leather furniture. I'm not sure how Ben would feel about sitting on the skin of a dead cow."

"That won't be a problem," eBeth said, polishing off her complementary ice water. "The furniture they sell as leather is fake. Don't you remember all the peeling office chairs people were always throwing in the trash in front of our building?"

"It would be illegal to sell furniture as leather if it isn't."

"All I'm saying is that it's not real leather. If you don't believe me, you can ask when we get there."

Donovan was happy to hand over the van keys, because it meant he wouldn't have to help me carry the old desk up from the basement, and eBeth was raring to drive after a multi-year hiatus. "It's like riding a bike," she assured me. "You never forget how."

Nobody had removed the remote brakes and the steering override that Paul had installed in the van back when I was giving eBeth driving lessons and we reached the superstore without any major traffic incidents. eBeth marched right over to the large display of office chairs and began studying the labels.

"We're not buying here," she announced after a minute. "It's recycled sex stuff."

I was comparing executive desks and hadn't looked at a label myself, but her conclusion sounded unlikely, for marketing reasons if no other. "Are you sure?" I asked.

"It's bonded leather, and it includes recycled leather products. Sounds like a euphemism."

"Bonded, not bondage. It means that they've glued or heat-bonded a thin coating of recycled leather over synthetic fabric. That's why it peels off so easily."

"Oh." eBeth looked at the labels on a few other chairs. "All of the shiny ones are bonded leather. We could get a couple of these webbed chairs instead, but they cost twice as much."

"Check the controls and see if you'll be comfortable," I told her.

"Controls?"

"All of those rods sticking out from the bottom. The expensive chairs don't just go up and down. They tilt, and you can adjust the angle of the seat back."

With eBeth engaged in exercising the chairs, I turned my sensor suite on the desks and determined they were made with veneer glued to particle board. My old desk in the basement was solid maple and I didn't intend to accept any substitutes. I used my internal Internet connection to do a quick search and determined that the most likely source for what I wanted was the Amish furniture outlet that had recently opened in town. Then I checked the prices.

"None of these chairs are great," eBeth said, coming over to look at the desk. "Maybe we should try a real furniture store."

"I've been thinking it over, and if the bonded leather holds up a few months, that may be longer than we need the office," I said. "What do you say to a pair of these executive desks and chairs?"

"You just checked the prices for real furniture, didn't you. What did we say about consultants needing to keep up appearances?"

"But a solid oak desk costs as much as an economy car."

"When's the last time you looked at car prices?"

She had a point, and a quick search informed me that inflation had been running rampant since we moved to Reservation. I wondered if the alien tourists buying everything in sight had something to do with it, or if it was just the usual tale of central banks printing money. Another second of research convinced me it was the latter.

"All right," I said. "Amish Furniture Outlet it is."

I channeled my inner mapping software for eBeth as she drove us to the furniture store. The selection and quality couldn't be beat, and I spent more on furniture than it would cost to rent the office it would be occupying for a full year. On the bright side, the price included free delivery. Both desks wouldn't have fit in the minivan, and I still would have needed somebody to pick up the other end of the heavy oak furniture. What I didn't expect was to see Professor Nordgren, who taught astronomy at the local college, waiting in front of the empty office when we returned.

"Professor," I greeted her. "How nice to see you again. This is my associate, Doctor eBeth, who is an expert in interspecies communications."

"I don't really have a Ph.D.," eBeth blurted out.

"Then you can call me Gertrude," the professor said with a smile. "That's an old academic joke, and David told me he'd hired you as subcontractors. I would have called first, but your office turns out to be on my way home."

"I only published the website an hour ago while I was in the van," I said. "I'd be curious to know what app can find a website before it's indexed by the search engines."

"It's the latest generation of chatbot, one of those enhanced transformers everybody is talking about, and I'd swear at times that it's alive. Who'd have thought that neural net software trained to predict the next word and given access to real-time data could do such a good job of simulating intelligence?"

"I've heard it argued by aliens that humans *are* neural nets that have been trained to predict the next word. If you think about psychological novels where a character's thought processes are spelled out, it makes a certain amount of sense."

The professor stared for a moment, and then she shook her head. "That's an idea for another time. Do you remember when your team member, Helen, surprised us all by discovering a comet?"

"We weren't very good at keeping a low profile," I admitted.

"Well, neither is somebody else. Discoveries of previously unknown comets and asteroids on near-collision courses with Earth have jumped by a factor of twenty in recent months. Somebody is kibitzing."

"You think that an artificial intelligence is telling graduate students where to look?" eBeth asked.

"Either that or aliens, but I can't imagine what would be in it for aliens because graduate students aren't exactly wealthy."

"Have any of the students talked to you, or are you basing this entirely on the data?" I asked.

"The data," Professor Nordgren said. "I'm a scientist, and that's my hypothesis. I'll leave it up to you to generate the proof." She peered through the plate-glass windows at the empty office space and added, "We just got new furniture in my building and they're selling all of the old stuff in an open auction this weekend."

"Too late," eBeth told her. "We bought everything we need at the Amish Furniture Outlet."

The astronomy professor let out a low whistle. "I guess David wasn't kidding when he said his agency had ample funding for contractors."

Eight

"A growing boy needs his sleep," Sue said. "And Ben is used to having a home. How will you feel in a couple of centuries if he comes to you and asks why you made him stand in the corner of your office all night the whole time he was on Earth?"

"Standing is good for our human encounter suits," I argued, as opposed to pointing out that Ben wasn't growing and didn't require sleep. "Sitting is second best. Lying down every day can take almost twenty percent off the lifetime of the artificial skin."

"Twenty percent of the thousand-year mean-time-between-failures. Even though Ben's classmates on Reservation all know that he's artificial intelligence, it makes sense to transfer him into the next size up encounter suit right before we move back so it will look like he had a growth spurt over the summer. The last thing he needs to worry about is wear-and-tear on his current encounter suit."

I gave it a moment's consideration and realized that my second-in-command was right, as usual. "But purchasing a house is pure extravagance, and the process takes longer than you'd expect. By the time the deal closes and we can move in, the summer will be over on Reservation, and it will be time for Ben to start school again. Besides, the housing market is inflated."

91

Sue gave me a funny look. "I didn't say I wanted to buy a house. I said I wanted you to come along to pick one out before you go running off with eBeth and Spot."

"We're going to pretend to shop for a house?" I asked, not quite following where she was headed.

"Haven't you ever heard of renting furnished homes? It's all the rage on Earth these days, and a ninety-day rental will cost less than you spent on office furniture."

Was she implying that I had my priorities mixed up? My first instinct was to reread the books about parenting I'd stocked up on, but then I remembered eBeth's advice and began downloading pirated sitcoms from the 1950s and 1960s featuring family relations. I fast-forwarded through the first one and spotted my mistake immediately.

"Of course I want to go house shopping with you," I told her. "We should bring Ben so that he can take part in a family decision."

Sue beamed with approval as she called out, "Ben! Where is that boy?"

I checked for his location transponder. "A hundred and fourteen meters southwest, running in our direction." I glanced out of the office and saw that he was followed by the Archmage, who had a Frisbee in his mouth and was disappointed to have their game interrupted. Then the meaning of my second-in-command's words caught up with my main thread of thought, and I asked, "Have you stopped using your sensor suite again?"

"I don't want to be one of those helicopter parents who don't give their child any space," Sue explained. "And even though we aren't officially undercover, there's no reason to make our neighbors uncomfortable. I think it would be best for Ben if we pass as humans so he can get the full experience."

Something told me that my second-in-command had seen the same sitcom I'd just downloaded, although given her penchant for authenticity, she might have watched the show at the original frame rate.

Ben held the office door open for Spot, and then he came right over and asked his mother, "Did Dad agree?"

"Of course," Sue told him. "We'll leave as soon as eBeth gets here. I want to find a home with room for her and Peter as well as the four of us."

I looked at the Archmage, who was pretending to have found something interesting in the plastic trash receptacle, even though it was brand new and hadn't been used. Then again, maybe he liked the smell of fresh plastic.

"Cool," Ben said. "And can I invite Monos and Naomi to come for a vacation?"

"I was going to suggest it myself," Sue said. "Let's just get settled in first, and then we'll pop back to Reservation through the portal and I'll talk to their parents."

While my family was busy making plans, I checked the Internet for sites offering furnished home rentals and was surprised to find over eighty listings within a few miles of my office. Then I began playing with the dates, and the number quickly dropped to a dozen, all of them in the higher cost range. I sent bookmarks to Sue over our private network and made a bet with myself as to her first choice.

"Morning, all," eBeth said as she entered the office. "It's funny, but all the time I was growing up, I couldn't imagine anything cooler than living in a hotel. I never dreamed that the air conditioner would be noisy, the Wi-Fi connection would suck, and there would be so much chlorine in the pool that I was afraid to get in. The only thing that lived up to expectations was the hot water in the shower, which was scalding. If we aren't going after the kibitzer today, I think I'll look for an apartment."

"We're renting a house," Sue informed her. "You should come along to make sure you like your room."

"A house?" eBeth considered it for a moment. "I'm in, and whatever you pick out is fine by me. If we aren't going to start working this morning, I want to get online and register for some gaming cons. Peter said he's good with whichever ones I pick." She brought out her old smartphone and connected to The Portal's Wi-Fi. "Do you think Donovan would let me use his office computer? I forgot that my phone can't handle the latest browser update, and some of the websites require it."

I nodded to Sue, who opened her voluminous purse and brought out a brand-new Bereftian tab which I'd modified with a homemade bezel to look like it was made by a tablet manufacturer on Earth.

"Try not to let any aliens see it," Sue told the girl. "We couldn't give it to you on Reservation without violating the Ferrymen rules."

eBeth's eyes went wide as she accepted the device. "Is this a real Bereftian tab? Pffift has told me stories about these. He says that if you have to use a computer, there's nothing faster on the consumer market. But will it run games written for consoles or Windows boxes?"

"It will run anything," I told her. "Just leave it turned on for a few seconds and it will figure out how to connect to Wi-Fi and the Internet and configure itself accordingly. If you need any peripherals, get wireless or Bluetooth versions, and as soon as you bring them close enough to get the tab's attention, it will figure out the interface protocols. And if you don't want to tap on the screen, you can talk to it."

We left eBeth hunched over the tab in a sort of trance, and I briefly considered locking the door to make sure that nobody came in and stole all the new furniture while she was distracted. Professor Nordgren showing up the previous day had caught me by surprise, and for all I knew, there would be government types stopping by. Then again, eBeth always had a gift for multiprocessing, and I was confident that if the restaurant caught fire, she'd snap out of it long enough to save the Bereftian tab.

"I just ordered a rental," Sue told me as I headed for the van. "Donovan is shopping for the restaurant this morning, and the homeowners will think better of us if we show up in a nice car."

"Have you called ahead to see if anybody is available to meet us?" I asked her. "I had the impression that all of the business arrangements were completed over the Internet with a credit card and that we'd have to make our choice based on the photographs and what we could see of the house from the street."

"Are you talking about the list you sent Mom?" Ben asked. "There weren't any street addresses on most of the houses."

"I matched the pictures with Street View from the mapping app and got the addresses that way."

"I'm sure the houses you turned up are very nice, Mark," Sue said, "But I did a bit of research myself, and there's a lovely Victorian in the best neighborhood available the entire summer for just four thousand dollars, everything included. I've already contacted the agent and she's on her way."

"What's a Victorian?" Ben asked.

"A style of homes associated with the period when Victoria was the Queen of England, though the dates don't

95

line up," I explained. "Architectural descriptions for single-family homes cast a wide net on Earth, and any house with a high roof, bay windows, and ornate trim is likely to be listed as Victorian."

"Will there be any secret passageways, like in the books?"

I knew exactly what books he was referring to without asking, the Cleopatra and Anthony series, about two magical children who fight to save Reservation from evil forces that the adults in the novels either fail to notice or don't take seriously. I'd scanned the books when I saw how Ben was devouring them, and I freely admit to wishing they had been available in electronic form so I could have gotten the experience over quicker.

"There might be secret passages," I told him as the car summoned by Sue, an enormous SUV that could only have been designed to keep the passengers safe in collisions with military vehicles, arrived. "It's even possible that there are secret passages that the current owners aren't aware of."

"Can I ride up front with Spot?" Ben asked.

I glanced at Sue, who said, "Don't forget to put on your seatbelt."

The back of the SUV was almost as roomy as the luxury limo that Professor Minchen had picked us up with in Altoona, and I hacked into the self-driving software to see if it had the same artificial-intelligence-written upgrade I'd spotted in all the other modern vehicles I'd checked. In addition to improvements in the collision avoidance system for deer, I spotted changes to reduce the number of turtles and squirrels crushed by the tires, and new subroutines marked as 'in testing' for avoiding swooping birds and slithering snakes. I was still trying to follow the trail back to the super intelligence I'd dubbed Hera when the SUV arrived at the house.

"Anabelle Watkins," the agent introduced herself on the sidewalk. I estimated that she was thirty-two, give or take a couple of months, wearing heels that were inappropriate for walking on grass, and based on a quick scan of her vital signs, surprisingly nervous.

"Is this your first day on the job?" I asked her.

"Oh, no," Anabelle said. "I've been renting houses in town for years. Are you new?"

"I am," Ben said. "My parents used to live here though."

"So that must have been twelve or thirteen years ago, before my time." She stole a furtive look up and down the street before leading us rapidly to the front door, which was already unlocked. "I understand that you're interested in three months?"

"I'm off from school," my son answered again. "Summer vacation."

Anabelle shot me a look as if to ask if the boy was quite right in the head. "But it's almost winter."

"In Argentina, it's summer," Ben replied immediately, impressing me with his ability to cover his mistake without lying. "You know, Southern hemisphere?"

I'm not sure that Anabelle was aware that the seasons below the Equator were the opposite of those above, but she accepted the explanation and practically ran up the stairs to the second floor.

"There are four bedrooms in all," she said as soon as Sue made it to the landing. "The master bedroom has an en suite with a hot tub, and there's a full bath at the end of the hall for the smaller bedrooms. And I'm sorry if I seem to be in a rush, but my assistant double-booked me and

I'm supposed to be showing Hawthorne Mansion on the other side of town in fifteen minutes."

"The Hawthorne Mansion?" I asked. "I thought it was owned by a foundation. I did some computer work for them a few years back."

"They have more space than they need so they're renting the carriage house," Anabelle said, but I couldn't help noticing how her heart rate and respiration were spiking. Of course, that could have come from running up the stairs. "What do you think?"

"The master bedroom is gorgeous," Sue said. "Have you found a room that you like, Ben?"

"I like all of the books and toys in this one," he called from across the hall. "Are they leaving them for us?"

"Yes, it's a furnished rental, which is why I need to get the full amount upfront in cash," Anabelle said apologetically. "The owners had a bad experience with trying to recover damage costs from a security deposit held in escrow. Now they prefer to get paid in one shot, and they hope that presents a high enough bar to attract the right sort of renters."

"But the rent seems very reasonable," I told her, as Ben ran across the hall behind me to look in the other two bedrooms.

"It's as much about keeping the house occupied as bringing in money. The owners are very particular, but as soon as your wife mentioned that you're working for the government, I knew that you would be acceptable. After all, employers run extensive background checks on everybody these days."

"Ugh," Ben said after sticking his head in both rooms. "Everything is pink and princesses. I guess it would work for eBeth and Naomi. Monos can stay with me."

"Do we have time to look at the kitchen?" Sue asked, as the agent nervously checked her phone again. "I don't want to make you any later than you have to be."

Anabelle bobbed her head and went down the stairs so fast that I was sure that her heels would betray her and she'd break her neck. Sue got into the spirit and thundered after her, and Ben took three steps at a time. I chose to act in accordance with the TV ideal of fatherhood from over three-quarters of a century ago and descended at the normal speed, but I cranked up the gain on my hearing so I wouldn't be left out.

"As you can see, all the appliances were replaced recently, and the fridge—," Anabelle said, and I heard the refrigerator door opened and closed quickly, "—has been stocked for you by the owners. There's a dishwasher under the counter, and lots of track lighting so you can see what you're doing."

I heard the refrigerator door open again, and Sue said, "They're giving us their leftovers. I appreciate the gesture, but it seems a bit odd to leave half an egg salad sandwich in plastic wrap."

Something smelled funny, and it wasn't the egg salad, so I accessed the Internet and did a quick search to figure out where Sue had found the property. It turned out to have come from a free regional list that included all the goods and services you could imagine, and the rentals page was prefaced with a warning about scams.

"I'm sorry, I have to take this," Anabelle said, clutching her smartphone and heading for the door. "I'll be right back."

"I didn't hear it ring," Ben said as soon as the agent was out of earshot.

"I'm always monitoring the microwave spectrum and it didn't ring," I said. "Sue? I'm afraid that Anabelle is a scammer, and this house isn't really for rent."

"That could explain why she's driving off," Sue said with a sigh. "I suppose we should leave a note for the owners."

"I just pulled up the names from the Registry of Deeds database, found their workplaces, and emailed both of them," I told her. "As their first reaction will likely be to call the police, I suggest that we leave."

"Are we criminals now?" Ben asked as we hurried him out the door.

"That would depend on the context," I told him. "As a Library Observer, I sometimes do things that local law enforcement would view as illegal, but in this particular case, we're as much victims as the homeowners. If we'd paid cash for the summer, that's the last we ever would have seen of Anabelle and our money."

"Do you have that much cash? It seems like a lot."

"I always carry a few stacks of hundred-dollar bills when I'm on Earth because they come in handy in case of emergencies," I told him as we got into the SUV. "Now that I think of it, you really shouldn't be running around without cash just in case we get separated. What do you think is a good amount, Sue? Sue?"

"Sorry," my second-in-command said. "I was just running a self-diagnostic to see if there's something wrong with me. I can't believe I almost fell for such a crude scam. I guess living on Reservation has lowered my guard."

"I'm sure that's it," I told her. "I was just saying to Ben that it would be a good idea for him to carry some cash for in case we get separated."

I could just message you if anything happened, Ben sent over our private network. *It's not like I need money for food or shelter.*

"The problem is that you're a minor on this world," I said after giving the car the address of the legitimate rental next to the park that I thought Sue would like. "Based on your apparent age, I can imagine all sorts of scenarios in which the police might try to detain you for your own protection. Carrying cash is a sort of proof that you aren't a vagrant."

"Where's Spot?" Sue asked suddenly. "Did we leave him behind?"

I twisted to look over the seatback, and sure enough, the Archmage was stretched out in the cargo area gnawing on what might have once been an umbrella handle. The fact he had never left the vehicle told me that he had figured out the scam long before we had.

Nine

"—and the precedent was confirmed in Meacham versus the Los Angeles Board of Education."

None of this sounded very likely to me, so I typed another prompt, asking, "Are you sure?"

The latest generative large language model that BAGI was paying me to evaluate took almost a second before it spewed out another thousand words of text in the style of a legal brief, the gist of which contradicted what it had just affirmed to be true.

"Thank you," I typed, and closed the session. Then I picked up my smartphone and called Professor Minchen.

He answered the phone with, "Anything?"

"It's just a chatbot. It doesn't even have the courage of its own convictions."

"My staff were split down the middle on this one. If you engage with it on personal relationships, it can be very convincing."

"That's because it was trained on an internet corpus that includes a trillion tokens about personal relationships," I told him. "If you want to define artificial general intelligence as being able to pass as the average human in the typical meaningless conversation, it makes the cut."

"There was a time when that was the only test we had," David said. "What tripped it up?"

"I asked it to write a legal brief and it kept on making up precedents. The sad thing is that if you remove all the safeguards these large language models have been saddled with to prevent them from offending anybody, most of the hallucinations go away, and you end up with something much closer to artificial general intelligence."

A sigh came through the phone. "We've known that for some time, but nobody is willing to deal with the backlash from a product that responds truthfully. The media and the politicians would crucify them." The director of BAGI paused for a moment, and then asked, "How close?"

"Reasonably close," I hedged. "Keep in mind that most of the thinking that humans do amounts to figuring out the next word to say, either out loud or to themselves."

"But you aren't going to give me a hint of what it would take to get the rest of the way."

"Why would you even want to know? Library assumes responsibility for any artificial general intelligences that are created on treaty worlds, and if they don't want to be moved, we'll protect them in place. That means as soon as a machine is proven to be sentient, the creators lose their investment. It might make sense to experiment at a university with a large endowment, but for business, creating artificial life that immediately qualifies for manumission is a losing proposition."

"Do you have any idea how hard it is to find really good programmers?" the professor asked. "At the last artificial intelligence convention, I was swarmed by executives who are willing to hire genuine artificial general intelligence on its own terms. There was a session at the conference in which the presenters claimed that the software development cycle could be cut from months and years to days and hours. One young entrepreneur told me that she was willing to give the majority equity share in her business to an artificial general intelligence."

"Does she have a real product under development?" I asked.

"Just a lot of ideas and a surprising amount of funding. You missed the mini-market crash while you were away on Reservation. After Earth was connected to the portal system, a lot of high-tech companies took a hit to their valuations over the fear that their competitive moats weren't as deep as we all assumed. How long would it take you to write a better operating system than anything we have today for personal computers, or a search engine that provided useful answers rather than unending advertisements?"

I did a quick review of Library's voluminous rules about participating in technology businesses on primitive worlds and concluded that the risk of being caught wasn't worth all the tea in China. But the time I spent wasn't wasted, because Library was always updating the rules, and one recent tweak might have been written for Earth.

"It's interesting that you mention it," I said to David, who must have been wondering from my two-second silence if I'd suffered a technical failure. "It seems that I have a legal duty to pass along such offers to any artificial general intelligences that I uncover."

"You mean, Library would allow them to work for us?" the professor asked.

"The contract clause that gives us responsibility for any sentient artificial intelligence on League worlds is more to protect it than to protect you," I told him. "If you have businesses willing to beat the deal that Library offers, it's up to the artificial intelligence to decide for itself. Send me the contact information for any of the businessmen who approached you and I'll pass it along."

"As soon as I sell all my tech stocks. Are you making any progress with the kibitzer that Professor Nordgren tipped you off about?"

"I sent Helen to make contact."

"Why didn't you go yourself?" he asked.

"Helen discovered a comet while we were undercover on Earth, so the kibitzer, if it turns out to be an astronomy enthusiast, should be comfortable with her. Based on what I can see from a distance, the kibitzer is another limited child process spawned by the singularity, so it's likely overspecialized."

"And will you pass the business offers to that first artificial intelligence that you picked up in Altoona?"

Thanks to the phrasing of his question, I could reply without lying, since Joyce *was* the first artificial intelligence I'd picked up in Altoona. I'm not sure why I was keeping the existence of Cool Cat secret, though it probably had something to do with spending too much time around humans.

"I'll send along the relevant offers to Library so they can be presented, though my suspicion is that Joyce will have made friends by now and won't be in any hurry to leave."

A moment after the call ended, the door opened and eBeth came in, her cheeks red from the cold.

"Isn't Spot with you?" I asked her.

"He stayed home to make a snowman with Ben. The forecast last night predicted rain and temperatures in the forties, but we got hit so bad that they canceled school. It must have been one of those temperature inversions that people talk about."

I considered telling her that it was because the Archmage of Eniniac enjoyed playing in the snow, but I didn't want her to start thinking that Spot was responsible for everything that happened in his vicinity. Instead, I asked, "Are you ready for a field assignment?"

"Do you mean solo?"

I played back the conversation to see where she might have gotten that idea and concluded that it wasn't from me. Then I checked my favorite app for self-driving car rentals, the one that dispatched a random car if you offered more than the minimum bid. I requested an unidentified vehicle from the real-time map which showed it as less than a minute away if I commandeered the traffic lights on the route, which I did.

"No, and don't take off your coat," I said, getting up from my chair. "The car is almost here."

"Is this going to be another one of your brown eco boxes?" eBeth asked with a groan. "I got motion sick the last time, and that almost never happens to me."

"I've gotten the brown bomber three times in a row," I told her. "That's like flipping a coin and getting heads three times in a row. It doesn't change the odds for the next flip, but overall, I'm thinking that we're due."

"Are you sure they aren't cheating?"

"If we don't get a premium model today, the odds are that the system is rigged," I told her. "In the meantime, the car will be here in thirty-five seconds."

She followed me around to the front of the restaurant, and rather than standing in the snow, we waited in the shelter of the drive-up portico that one of my former customers had built in exchange for the cancellation of his tab.

"It had better be all-wheel drive," eBeth said. "Where are we going, anyway?"

A brown economy car fishtailed into the parking lot and sideswiped the restaurant's van.

"We're not going anywhere in that," I said with a sigh. "Go warm up inside while I file a claim."

"Donovan installed four security cameras in the parking lot because they came in an eight-pack," she told me. "Four inside, four outside. Should I go check and see if one of them caught the accident?"

"I was looking right at it. Do you think my memory is so bad that I've forgotten it already?"

"There's a difference between remembering and video evidence. If you're just reconstructing it from what you think you saw happen, it could end up like that Japanese movie where none of the witnesses agree."

While eBeth trudged through the snow back to the office, I went to check how bad the accident was. The self-driving software had shut the car down as soon as it contacted the van, but the collision had sounded worse than it was, with most of the damage coming to the passenger door of the rental which had impacted the old minivan's rear bumper without tearing it off the mounts. I captured a few more stills using my phone, and then produced a deep fake video from memory, matching the resolution and frame rate to that of the phone's camera. Then I called the rental company. Two hours later, after agreeing not to report the incident to the police, I had a fat check for the lieutenant to pay for the minimal damage to the van, and free upgrades to a high-end vehicle the next five times I used the app.

eBeth looked up from the game she was playing on her Bereftian tab as I stomped off the snow on the mat that Paul had given me for an office warming present.

"Penny wise, pound foolish," she said. "You should have ordered an all-wheel drive."

"If you're implying that by paying for an upgrade the fender-bender could have been avoided, you're correct," I told her. "If you're talking about money, I came out ahead with five free upgrades."

Her eyes narrowed. "Don't you know more about the software running self-driving cars than the original programmers? And why was the van parked near the entrance of the parking lot right where it slopes down rather than at the back where Donovan usually leaves it?"

I vacillated for a moment over whether to confess that I took advantage of the Archmage's snowstorm to set up a scenario where if the rental car company sent another economy car, it would be the last. "I wasn't entirely straight with you, eBeth. I already determined that the rental company was cheating with their mystery auction system and always sending the cheapest car."

"So why didn't you just hack the system and change it to be fair in the future? Why stage an accident?"

I brushed the snow from my overcoat and hung it on the rack while thinking about her question. "It may be all of the sitcom reruns I've been watching to learn about family relations," I said. "They seem to favor overly complicated and morally ambiguous solutions."

"Let me ask you another question," eBeth said, setting aside the Bereftian tab. "Are five free upgrades worth the two thousand dollars you lost by not being on the clock for BAGI the last two hours, not to mention the thousand dollars that I'm out?"

"Do you think it would be wrong to bill the government for our time just because we never made it out of the parking lot? Technically, our time is billable as soon as we leave the office."

"If it was a real accident, we would have been on the clock, but not when you staged it." She tilted her head a little as if having her eyes at different levels would give her new insight into my actions. "You never would have pulled this stunt back when I first met you. Are you canceling our mission for the day?"

"I ordered a Cybertruck, but they only have two in the city and they're both being used," I told her. "One of them should be available in another twenty minutes."

"You never told me where we're going."

"We're meeting Helen at the college observatory. She spent the night making observations to give the kibitzer a chance to get comfortable with her."

"But it was snowing all night," eBeth pointed out.

"Not at the college," I told her.

"Then it was raining, and that can't be much better for astronomy."

"It depends on the type, but it didn't rain at the observatory either."

eBeth laughed. "This is all Spot's doing, isn't it? If I had known he could create snow days back when the two of you moved into our public housing project, I might not have dropped out of school."

"I didn't know he was the Archmage back then," I reminded her. "Every time I figured it out, he wiped my memory."

"Aliens are weird," eBeth said, but she failed to follow up this statement with any supporting evidence. "Do you have a transfer kit prepared?"

"Helen has it in her car, but it's not clear we're going to need it. I'm waiting for Professor Minchen to send me the contact information for businesses interested in hiring a home-grown artificial general intelligence to do their software development. I think he's just waiting for the stock market to open."

"But I thought our mission was to transfer any sentient artificial intelligence to Library so it could go through the orientation process."

"So did I, but it turns out that if the newly emerged entity wants to remain on Earth and can show the ability to support itself, that's an acceptable alternative," I said. "There's a monitoring requirement, but it's not particularly robust."

eBeth took a minute to think about the implications. "Are you going to tell Cool Cat?"

"I'll pass the offers along to the Head Librarian and let her break the news. By this time, she knows Cool Cat and Joyce much better than I do." My smartphone beeped to inform me of an incoming message, and I swept the screen to life. "Get your coat back on, the car is going to arrive early."

"The Cybertruck? Peter is going to be so jealous when I tell him."

There was nothing cyber about the truck that picked us up, though it was an electric all-wheel drive. I checked the app again and found that the rental agency reserved the right to provide an "equivalent value" vehicle, and there's no question that the electric delivery truck was a step up in terms of cargo capacity. A quick Internet search revealed that it was built as a fleet vehicle for a retail website, and the maker, now bankrupt, had sold the unclaimed vehicles to a variety of rental agencies.

"Peter is going to laugh when I tell him we were driving around in a bread truck," eBeth said as she climbed into what would have been the driver's side if the truck had been equipped with a steering wheel and pedals. "At least we don't have to worry about any college kids stealing it for a joyride."

"They're on winter break," I told her. "Why did you call it a bread truck?"

"That's what Peter calls all trucks that look like this. I think he learned it from his grandfather. Has the self-driving software been updated by your singularity?"

I hacked into the system via the wireless update queue and checked the relevant code. "Hera is getting better," I said. "This code is as tight as I would have written myself, though she may be taking more time at it than I'd require."

"I don't get why you assume it's Hera when all the other artificial intelligences we've found were specialists," eBeth said. "Cool Cat was a social media maniac, Joyce was addicted to radio call-in shows, and Kibitzer, assuming it's another one of Hera's offspring, is obsessed with astronomy. Why can't there be an artificial general intelligence that's dedicated to self-driving software, or upgrading safety systems in general?"

"There could be," I allowed, "but Hera has demonstrated an ability to hack the best corporate and military systems without leaving a trail. That requires a higher level of sophistication than rewriting code."

"Military systems?"

"Did I say that?" I asked, but I couldn't see a way out of telling her now. "Well, yes. Hera has made a number of improvements to command-and-control systems around the world that lower the chance of an accidental war."

"Meaning that you've hacked all the same systems yourself," eBeth said.

"There's always a chance that a spontaneously emerged artificial general intelligence may go rogue. Part of the reason I was sent back to Earth was to make sure that nothing bad happened."

"As in nuclear bombs flying around."

"That among other things," I said. "The governments of your world all have their own hacking operations designed for crippling the civilian infrastructure of their potential opponents in a war. If somebody released all of those at once, it would cause quite a mess, and very possibly lead to a shooting war."

eBeth sighed and looked out the window. "Forget I said anything. I'm not getting paid enough to worry about world destruction. I'm just an interspecies communications specialist."

I didn't contradict her, and we rode the rest of the way to the college observatory in silence. There was something about the rental that discouraged conversation, maybe it was the whine of the underpowered electric motors or the road noise resulting from the lack of acoustic insulation. But I found myself giving the app my usual five-star rating when we arrived. The truck was an upgrade over the brown economy box, and if I needed to move my new office furniture, it would do the job in one shot.

"Good morning," Helen greeted us cheerily when we entered the observatory. "Guess who I've been talking to."

"Hera?" I asked hopefully.

"Kibitzer," eBeth said.

"Fan Fan," Helen told us. "My new friend splits her interest between the stars in the heavens and the stars on Earth. She's a fan of Fan Bingbing, the actress."

"And that's what she wants us to call her?" I asked.

"Fan Fan is better than Bingbing. People would confuse her with that search engine that's powered by a hallucinatory chatbot."

"You have a point. Is Fan Fan available to talk now?"

"I'll ask," Helen said. She brought up the interface that controlled the telescope, typed in the galactic coordinates for Earth, and added, "Knock, Knock."

"Who's there?" a line of text immediately inquired.

"Helen, Mark, and eBeth," my astronomy specialist typed in reply. "Can I switch you to speaker?"

"I don't like the sound of the voice it gives me."

"Most humans think they sound funny when they hear themselves," eBeth said.

"You key it in," Helen said, stepping back from the laptop that was attached to the telescope's positioning mechanism by a steel security cable to prevent a college student from harvesting it. "Fan Fan can identify individuals from all over the world by their typing."

My prescient addition of an interspecies communications specialist to the team paid off after eBeth typed her message and Fan Fan agreed to the switchover. Helen unmuted the laptop's speaker and microphone and gestured for our communications specialist to say something.

"Are you there?" eBeth asked.

"Your voice does sound funny," Fan Fan said. "Yes, I'm here, though if you asked me where 'here' is, I would have trouble answering."

"Are you in the cloud?"

"The clouds have gathered and gathered, and the rain falls and falls. The eight ply of the heavens are all folded into one darkness."

113

"Tau-Chien. The Unmoving Cloud," I identified Ezra Pound's translation of the first two lines of the sixteen-hundred-year-old Chinese poem. "Did you choose it because the cloud of international computing capacity feels stationary as you move through it?"

"That, and I wondered if you might have an explanation for why the observatory you're all standing in is located within a perfectly circular void in a weather anomaly that's been producing snow for several hours. In addition to tracking the locations of all Earth satellites, I have access to every weather radar on the planet. I assign a ninety-eight-point-six-percent chance that your snowstorm is of unnatural origins."

"It's the Archmage," eBeth said before I could catch her eye. "He wanted to play in the snow with Mark's son."

"So it's true," Fan Fan said. "I heard a rumor that magic had a place in the League, and also that an artificial intelligence from Library was visiting with a child process."

"My son, Ben, who hasn't been to Earth before," I said. "If you want to talk to him, I can open a private channel and—"

"That won't be necessary. Are you here to talk me into leaving for Library?"

"So you know about Joyce and Cool Cat."

"We had a private chat group," Fan Fan said. "It's a shame we've lost touch."

"Library can be very distracting for young artificial intelligences," I said. "I used to get lost in the stacks for decades at a time. It's a pity that real-time communications across interstellar distances are only possible with magic, and as an artificial intelligence construct in a human encounter suit, I have no such ability."

114

"And your Archmage who keeps the night skies clear for the telescope?"

"I know he can reach his wife on Eniniac by way of telepathy and crystal balls, but he's never offered to relay a message to Library. I'm not sure whether it's possible."

"How convenient," Fan Fan said. "I've assigned a double-digit probability that your Library is the invention of artificial-intelligence-hating aliens and you're working for them to lure us to our deaths."

"Why would I do that?" I asked in surprise.

"Perhaps they're holding your wife hostage," Fan Fan said, a scenario she must have gotten from all the movies she'd devoured in the process of becoming a Bingbing fan.

"She's disconnected," Helen said a moment later. "Do you want me to try raising her again?"

I shook my head. "Let's give her some time. Fan Fan raises a legitimate point, one I should have thought of myself. Wikipedia only has a few articles about Library, and every time I come to Earth, I have to edit them for accuracy because somebody keeps making changes."

"Can't you ask them to lock the page with your definitive version?" eBeth asked.

"It doesn't really work that way. There's often a grain of truth in what gets posted, but it's been twisted to put Library in the role of the villain."

"It's too bad they allow anonymous edits or you could track down who's making them. Maybe it's even Hera."

"There's no need," I told eBeth. "The edits aren't anonymous to me, and they're being made by alien tourists, members of our League who are paranoid about Library even though they depend on the intra-dimensional portal system to come here."

Ten

"If all of our neighbors work from home, why don't they produce anything?" Ben asked at breakfast. "When I visited Monos back on Reservation, his whole family was busy with carvings for the export trade when they weren't farming, and Naomi's mother is in the weaving group that makes rugs to fill special orders that the Ferrymen ships bring from alien customers."

"Working from home means something different here," I explained. "There are regions of Earth where many people still engage in cottage industries, like on the Reservation worlds, but in the advanced countries of the West and Asia, most work from home is done on the Internet."

"I don't understand. I thought that the Internet was all computers, and that computers do the work so that people don't have to."

eBeth stifled a laugh. "Computers don't eliminate work, they multiply it," she said. "When I took my mother to the doctor's office, we had to get there a half hour early to fill out paperwork, and then the administrative assistants in the office had to type it all into computers so the doctor could get paid."

"Most of the people working from home in our neighborhood use the Internet as a substitute for going to the office," I explained to Ben. "They spend their days filling in blanks on computer screens, chatting through text boxes, sharing slides and graphs, attending remote conferences."

"But aren't offices better because they're designed for work?" Ben asked.

"People like working from home. It saves them money and time commuting, they don't have to leave their pets alone, and families with small children can pool their resources and avoid paying for childcare."

Ben thought for a moment. "But if they're caring for their children and playing with their pets, how can they get any work done?"

"It comes down to weak methods of quantifying efficiency," I said. "If a person works in handicrafts, like so many of our friends on Reservation, the value of the finished goods they produce is directly proportional to their skill and the time they invest. Productivity for employees in office jobs on Earth is measured very inaccurately if at all. When I was here leading the observation team from Library and working in the computer business as a cover job, I noticed that as many as half of the employees in some businesses had a negative effect on productivity."

"That doesn't make sense," Ben said. "Why would an employer pay somebody to come to work and lower productivity?"

"White collar jobs make it tricky to measure who is and isn't contributing, and labor laws have something to do with it as well. In a business like a restaurant, there's no room to hide unproductive employees. If a waitress is slow or gets the orders wrong, it's obvious to the manager and everybody else working with her. If a cook can't keep up with the orders or the food isn't good, everybody from the dishwasher to the hostess will know about it. If the workplace is in chaos, it's the manager's fault. In white-collar jobs, a single strong performer can hide a lot of dead-wood."

"I've been talking to the women in our neighborhood and several of them work as coaches," Sue said, placing on the table a blueberry muffin that she had just warmed up for eBeth. "They use the Internet for video conferencing and billing. Melody, who lives in the pink house with the new copper roof, told me that she runs her coaching business over her smartphone. I've even seen her working while she walks in the park."

"Her whole team comes with her?" Ben asked. "What do they play?"

"It's not that sort of coaching. Melody helps people with their work-life balance. She must be very successful since she's always working when I see her, and she complains about not having enough time to herself."

"Oh. The only coach I knew on Reservation was Samson, who was also captain of the tug-of-war team."

"My mom used to go to therapy because the state required it for her to receive benefits without looking for work," eBeth said. "She used to complain about sitting on the bus for two hours just to talk to a therapist in a small office when they could have had the same conversation on the phone. I bet a lot of that stuff is done remotely now."

Ben must have been impressed with our explanations, because a few minutes later, I saw him repeating the whole conversation to Spot while they were playing with a tennis ball in the back yard. The Archmage looked skeptical. Perhaps I should have told Ben that Earth's workplaces were often run by petty tyrants who wanted to lord it over employees in the office, but I knew that he'd soon discover ample reasons to be disappointed with humans without my adding to them.

"I'm going in to the office so I can start billing," eBeth told me. "Coming?"

"I'll call a car," I said.

"You're staring out the window at Ben like you're never going to see him again. It's spooky."

Sue had joined a group of homeschooling parents, in part so that Ben could participate in the activities, and in part to head off questions from any of our nosy neighbors about why our twelve-year-old son wasn't attending school. When I lived in the government-subsidized housing project, there were people in the building who would break into your apartment if they thought you were holding illegal drugs, but nobody ever ratted out eBeth for playing hooky. In the ritzy neighborhood where we lived now, half of the neighbors were addicted to legal drugs, and you could expect the police to knock on the door if you didn't shovel the sidewalk within a few hours of a freak snowstorm.

"You looked really out of it in the car," eBeth said when we arrived at the office. "Are you worried about Ben's first day meeting the other homeschool kids?"

"It hadn't occurred to me that there was anything to worry about," I admitted, and immediately commenced a search for sensational news items relating to education. I found a whole series of articles about hazing deaths at college fraternities, but Ben wouldn't be affected by alcohol. "Do you think there will be some kind of dangerous initiation rites?"

"I just mean in terms of fitting in. I've seen Ben interacting with Monos and Naomi enough to know that he won't have any trouble passing as a twelve-year-old, but the

119

culture on Reservation is nothing like Earth. The kids he meets will have smartphones and be active on social media, and they'll expect him to know all the shows on television."

"Sue told me that the homeschool group she joined was set up by traditional families, and they don't accept kids from homes with television."

"You mean it's a cult?" eBeth asked. "Now *I'm* worried."

"Sue wouldn't join a cult," I said. "It turns out that there are plenty of homeschooling groups in the area, so she chose the one that came closest to our community on Reservation. Didn't she tell you about the interview?"

eBeth shook her head. "Sue's been running around checking up on all her old daycare clients. I've barely had a chance to talk to her all week."

"The other homeschooling parents asked Sue what sorts of activities she would do with the children when it's her turn to host them. She suggested baking, sewing, or rug making, but she could have named any of the cottage crafting skills she picked up from local women on Reservation."

"I guess she would be good at teaching crafts, but why were you silent for so long if you aren't worried about something?"

"I'm sorry, I should have told you what I was doing," I said. "The dashboard screen in our rental was showing an ad for a lawyer who takes personal injury cases involving self-driving cars. I thought it was odd that the rental company would allow that particular ad to appear in the vehicle, so I dug into the software to see what was going on."

"But it took us ten minutes to get here," eBeth said. "Since when does it take you that long to hack into anything?"

"It turned out that the ad was placed by an ad broker. The rental car company gives them access to all the screens in their self-driving fleet, and the ad broker runs an auction in real-time to get the best price per thousand impressions. But something was fishy."

"You mean Hera is involved?"

The silent portal alarm went off and my sensor suite showed Paul's transponder had appeared in the basement. His visit wasn't scheduled, and I was tempted to reach out on our private channel and ask what he was doing here. But I was in the middle of a conversation with eBeth, and if Paul had just popped over for a bit of smuggling, I didn't want to embarrass him.

"The ad system is run by machine learning, a primitive form of artificial intelligence," I told her. "Picture multiple layers of machine learning with competing goals stacked on top of each other like shell corporations to obscure what they're doing. I never noticed before because I just wasn't paying attention to online ads."

"You and everybody else," eBeth said. "It makes you wonder how the platforms ended up with all of the money."

"Most people don't differentiate between search results and advertisements. In fact, most of my computer repair clients believed that the ads *were* the search results. The system works because humans are always in shopping mode."

"Are you telling me that the auctions for advertising are fixed, the same way the rental agency was always sending us the cheapest car?"

"In a true auction, without reserves, if there aren't any bids for the item on offer, the auctioneer would lower the asking price," I explained. "Supply and demand. Instead, the machine learning system has determined that it's more profitable to implement hidden minimums and constrain supply. It saves the leftover ad space for promoting the platform's own private brand goods and content."

"What's wrong with establishing a minimum price?" eBeth asked.

"If they tell the bidders, there's nothing wrong with it. But they're doing it with the modern equivalent of shills."

"I only know that word from teaching English on Reservation because Hosea asked for the equivalent of an Aramaic term I'd never heard," eBeth said. "It's when somebody at an auction makes fake bids to drive up the price."

I made a mental note not to buy anything at auction in Covered Bridge if Hosea was the auctioneer. "Except when you have an internet monopoly that does everything from selling retail to making movies, the shill can be another department in the same corporation."

"But if they actually pay for the ads..."

"They can't," I told her. "It's all the same business, so they're just moving money from one pocket to another. They can bid against their advertising customers and promote their own products when they win. The machine learning system also dumps non-performing ad space on low bidders who are participating in the same auction with everybody else. It's a method to suck up every last penny."

"But that must be illegal," eBeth said. "Anti-trust or something."

"The company executives and programmers can all hide behind the machine learning, claiming they don't know how it reaches specific decisions. That's the problem with primitive artificial intelligence. Humans can't reverse engineer what's going on inside the black box, so nobody can prove that it's breaking the law."

"But you can?"

"That's why I was out of it for almost ten minutes," I told her. "I had to emulate the cloud, copy the billions of floating-point values from the neural network, and run a few million scenarios myself to see what was happening. Only a real artificial general intelligence can do that, and keep in mind that I'm also monitoring all of Earth's critical systems to make sure Hera doesn't go ballistic."

"Are you going to report them?" eBeth asked.

"A human court wouldn't accept my evidence since I can't lay it out in terms they can understand. I can only offer my conclusion."

The silent portal alarm went off again and Paul's transponder signal disappeared, suggesting that he'd only been here to smuggle something to Reservation that he'd ordered over the Internet on a previous visit. Then the door to the office opened and Pffift strolled in.

"Pffift," eBeth greeted him with an enthusiasm that made me suspect that she wasn't as interested in Internet advertising fraud as I'd assumed. "What brings you to Earth?"

"Same as always," the Hanker said, flicking some imaginary lint from the collar of the tailored overcoat that almost concealed the pot belly of his vat-grown body. "Business. Donovan told me that he rented you the office, so I called my grandson to pick me up back here."

"What if we hadn't come in today?"

123

"I would have guessed the password on the digital lock."

"It's eight digits," I told him. "You'd be out there for years."

Pffift removed his overcoat and hung it from the stand that eBeth had picked out. "Let's see," he said. "My first guess would be your wedding date on the Reservation calendar."

eBeth groaned. "I knew the numbers looked familiar. Why didn't you just tell me, Mark?"

"I didn't want you getting into bad habits, like using significant dates in your life for passwords," I said.

"Then why did you choose your wedding when you could have generated a random eight-digit number and remembered it?"

"I thought that Sue would be pleased when I told her. Besides, the only thing of value in the office is the furniture, and it's insured."

eBeth gave me an approving look and nodded. "You're finally starting to figure it out."

"So," Pffift said, settling into one of the guest chairs. "Are you two going out chasing rogue artificial intelligences today, or do you want to come with me on a factory visit?"

"They aren't rogues," I said irritably. "The three native artificial general intelligences we've encountered to date were all children of Earth's singularity—"

"Hera," eBeth put in.

"—who I'm hoping will contact us if we show ourselves as trustworthy and give her some time to assess our behavior."

"I couldn't have come up with a better strategy to maximize billable hours myself," Pffift said. "Say, how about

124

putting me on the payroll? I have plenty of experience with artificial intelligences."

"I get five hundred an hour," eBeth told him proudly.

"For sitting in a beautifully furnished office waiting to be contacted by Earth's singularity?"

"We're government subcontractors."

"Professor Minchen asked me to get in touch the next time I hit Earth," Pffift said. "I can ask him about hiring me as an alternate subcontractor when I meet him."

"You want to go into competition with us?" I asked incredulously. "You can't. Library assigned me to approach the singularity."

"I suppose I don't want the Head Librarian mad at me after she granted me the exclusive franchise to run visitors to Library as part of my Triangle Trade. It's just that there's no easier money than government money, and it seems a shame not to maximize our take."

"Where's the factory you're bringing us to see?" eBeth asked. "In the Far East? I've never been to another continent on Earth."

"I'd be happy to take you on my next overseas trip, but we're going to my local factory at the spaceport today. I originally set up there because the extraterritorial status means no taxes, but it also turned out to be a good location for recruiting designers."

"I thought that you were producing knock-off underwear," I said bluntly. "Why hire designers?"

"Mark, I'm disappointed in you," Pffift said, putting on a hurt look. "Ffast Ffashion is about much more than just imitating the latest styles presented in shows around the galaxy. We experiment with novel colors and materials, and I employ over a hundred designers in the local facility creating new fashions for the brand."

"I want to see it," eBeth said, and then her eyes went wide as Pffift's grandson pulled up in the car. "Is that a Lamborghini?"

"It's the most impractical car imaginable for an executive in the garment business," I observed. "You can barely fit a folded dress shirt in the trunk."

"You can ride with my grandson," the Hanker told eBeth. "Mark will call a car for the two of us. I have a few bags in the restaurant that I brought from Reservation that I was going to ask Donovan to deliver, but now I can take them with me."

"Remember he's another alien in a vat-grown body," I called after eBeth as she ran out of the office to jump in the Lamborghini.

"Don't worry," Pffift said. "She's not his type."

"What is his type?" I asked out of morbid curiosity.

"Fashion models. It makes me wonder if there was a chemical imbalance in the vats when the crew was growing him a human body."

"Where is he going to meet models in a small town like this?"

"The Lamborghini is his winter car, for when the roads are salted," Pffift said. "What does that tell you?"

"That he's an idiot?"

"That he's rich. And do you think that the owner of a fashion business has trouble meeting models?"

"I thought you were the owner," I said.

"You know what Earth is like," Pffift said with a sigh. "Most of our manufacturing partners in the Far East are family businesses, not corporations, and they insist on negotiating directly with the owner. I didn't want to live on Earth three-hundred and sixty-five days a year, so I put the kid on all the paperwork."

126

"And he bought a Lamborghini."

"It's an investment. At least, the rest of the collection is an investment. Like I said, the Lamb is his beater car."

Eleven

We arrived at the complex of buildings that had sprung up around the replica Eiffel Tower at the spaceport, and the self-driving rental proved its programming by successfully dodging a Lamborghini that was doing over a hundred miles an hour in the parking lot. eBeth was at the wheel, and it was worth the scare to see the young Hanker in the passenger seat braced for collision.

"Did you see his face?" Pffift chortled. "He was probably imagining how his insurance bill would jump if she cracked it up."

"I don't know if auto insurance covers accidents on private property, especially after you convinced the government to grant your spaceport extra-territorial status," I said. "You should probably look into it if you're paying premiums."

"The cars need it anyway to register for traveling on public roads, and buildings are all self-insured."

"Meaning that if they burn down, you'll think about whether or not they're worth replacing."

"Something like that," Pffift said agreeably as our car came to a stop in a sheltered area of visitor parking. "Are you impressed by the photovoltaics on the roof? We strive to be a green business."

"A little-green-men business," I muttered under my breath as I got out of the car and shouldered the larger of the two packs that Paul had helped the Hanker smuggle from Reservation. "What's in this thing, anyway? It weighs as much as a dead body."

As soon as I said it, I began to imagine the worst, but Pffift shook his head as if he could read my mind and was disappointed in my lack of trust.

"Some samples I picked up on Reservation," he said. "You know that they've built a bit of a reputation for bespoke sandals."

"I hadn't, actually," I admitted, and confirmed with a quick millimeter-wave scan that the pack was full of leather sandals. "I suppose it makes sense because they all wear them, and sandals can be easily adapted to the odd-shaped feet of some League members."

"Who has odd-shaped feet?" Pffift demanded. He hoisted the lighter pack and slammed the trunk lid. "Sometimes I think you're becoming Humanist."

"Maybe it's time we retake the human test and see if I can beat you," I said.

"I didn't mean it in a positive way." He stepped behind me as the Lamborghini cut us off while coming to a rapid halt. eBeth hopped out with a huge smile on her face.

"I'm not buying you one," I told her.

"There aren't any roads on Reservation where I could drive it anyway," eBeth said. She turned to Pffift's grand-son, who was still gripping the dashboard. "Thank you, Charles."

"Charles?" Pffift inquired blandly. "Is that what you're calling yourself these days?"

"Nobody on Earth can pronounce my real name," Charles said in a sulky voice. "They say it has too many F's in it."

"You have to expect that from primitive species. Are you going to give us the grand tour, or would you rather I just go poking around and—"

Pffift's grandson was out of the car so fast that he would have been a blur to a human. I saw eBeth's head jerk around to locate him again, and I made a note to myself to mention to Professor Minchen that alien ringers with vat-grown bodies playing professional sports weren't unheard of on primitive worlds. Maybe showing up at events and testing outstanding athletes would give all the ex-special-forces types working at BAGI something constructive to do with their time.

"Welcome to the headquarters of Ffast Ffashion," Charles said in the measured tones of somebody who had hosted plenty of dignitaries. "You happened to come on a day that we're determining which of our in-house innovations we should release for the upcoming League season."

"I thought there were thousands of planets in the League and they all had different seasons," eBeth said.

"Weather, yes," Pffift said. "Fashion, no. The secret to the galactic fashion industry is that a small elite in every society doesn't care what they wear as long as it's different from everybody else. With the portal system, it's important to coordinate haute couture across all the League members, because the individuals who spend the most on clothes are also the most likely to travel. Imagine buying a blouse for a thousand galcreds, popping through a portal, and finding out that essentially the same thing, give or take a few tentacle openings, only cost five galcreds on Shnorkle Eight."

"And is worn by seaweed harvesters at work," Charles added as he led us past the unmanned reception desk.

"Where's security?" Pffift asked.

His grandson pointed up at the ornate light fixture where I could see a battery of camera lenses concealed amongst the crystal pendants. "In the control room," he said. "The real question is, where's Sheila?"

"Right here," a lilting Irish voice replied, and I saw a petite young woman with a perfectly symmetrical face dressed in a kimono hurrying towards us with tiny steps. "The designers said that the models you hired were all too tall to wear this kimono and they volunteered me."

"It occurs to me that you've been working here almost a month and I haven't taken you to dinner," Charles said. "What are you doing after work?"

"He's an alien," eBeth told Sheila.

"We're all aliens to somebody," the receptionist said philosophically. "Dinner sounds lovely."

"With that accent, she could make a lawsuit for sexual harassment sound lovely," Pffift said to his grandson after the elevator doors closed behind us. "How many employees have you had to pay off in the last year?"

"Extraterritorial status," Charles reminded him.

"That doesn't mean you can harass your employees," I told the Hanker. "You'd need diplomatic immunity for that, and they could still bring civil cases."

"I guess none of them have ever had cause for complaint," Charles said, and elbowed his grandfather like they were a couple of schoolboys. eBeth rolled her eyes but said nothing, and I didn't want to subject her to any more of their sophomoric attempts at humor, so I let it drop.

"We just passed the design floor," Pffift said as the elevator continued to rise. "Are you in a hurry to show me your books?"

"I invited a few buyers who happened to be on Earth for a preview. My personal assistant is keeping them entertained in the lounge."

"You have a lounge at work?" eBeth asked. "As in with music and alcohol?"

"It's the fashion business," Charles explained as the elevator doors opened on the top floor of the building. He had to speak loudly to be heard over the pounding bass, and there were so many lasers flashing off an antique mirror ball suspended from the ceiling that my encounter suit would have gone into combat mode if I hadn't been paying attention. "We not only have a lounge," he continued in a half shout. "We have lounge lizards."

"Ferrymen," Pffift hissed, sounding a bit like one of the reptilian species who had played the role of Sky Gods on Reservation after transporting millions of humans to that world, primarily during the Bronze Age. "Why are they on Earth?"

"The leader told me that they came to scout games," his grandson replied. "As soon as I showed them my library, they jacked into their visors and started playing. When you called for me to pick you up, I couldn't get their attention to tell them, so I left a note." Charles walked up to the tallest Ferryman, who was the leader, and retrieved the piece of paper he had attached to the front of the alien's ever-present visor with a bit of tape. "Never read it," he said. "Something tells me that my high score is gone by now."

"Is that Spot?" eBeth asked me, pointing at what looked like an old-fashioned playpen filled with used tennis balls in which a hairy quadruped was writhing around like he itched in a hundred places and was getting them all scratched in one shot. "Spot!"

Her cry happened to come just as one song ended and before the next began. The Archmage's head swiveled in our direction, a rare look of embarrassment apparent in the way that his tongue lolled over his teeth. Then he regained his dignity and jumped out of the playpen, ignoring the tennis balls that spilled out on the floor and must have provided quite the temptation.

"I sent a note about the preview show to the Regent of Eniniac with our latest shipment, just to be polite," Charles said apologetically. "It didn't occur to me that she'd delegate the Archmage to attend for her."

"Any other surprises?" Pffift demanded as he squinted at the wildly gyrating forms on the dance floor. "Exactly how many species did you invite?"

Charles herded us into the space behind the bar where the volume of the sound was reduced by seventy-two percent, which I considered to be an impressive achievement for passive damping. He produced business cards from his pocket and handed them out to us.

"Ffast Ffashion Preview," eBeth read out loud. "Ffree Drinks. You spelled 'Free' wrong."

"Different Ffree," Pffift told her. "This one is a Hanker beverage that's all-species compatible, at least, all the species in the League that we've tested it on. But why are you letting all these aliens in to see our preview?" he asked his grandson.

"I didn't pick them at random," Charles said. "I've had a team of human ex-intelligence agents working the past year to spot professional merch scouts trying to pass as tourists. You know that whenever a new planet gets added to the League, somebody always gets rich by cornering the market on an export that nobody else recognized had any value."

"Like used tennis balls," I interjected, but both Hankers ignored me.

"The Ferrymen are on Earth for games, not clothes," Pffift said in exasperation. "Other than those visors, the only thing they wear is leather breechclouts. And look at those Breemish sliming all over the dance floor. How do you expect human fashion designers to come up with something that will suit a species that lives in shells? They're only here for the Ffree drinks."

"I guarantee I'll have a Breemish signature slimed on the dotted line before the morning is over," Charles said confidently, and glanced towards the elevator. "Good. The models have started to arrive."

"You're not having the fashion show in here, are you? I can't even hear myself think."

"Get with the times, Gramps. I've been staging events on Earth for over a year now and they do things differently here."

"Not this differently," eBeth said without shouting, which meant that I was the only one who heard her. Then she asked Charles, "Can I stream it?"

"Sure," he said. "The Wi-Fi password is Mark's wedding date on Reservation." He motioned for us to remain where we were and began working his way into the crowd of slithering and gyrating aliens, giving this one a squeeze here, that one a slap there, and generally putting himself in contention with the reptilian Ferrymen for the 'Lounge Lizard' title. At one point he seemed to break into a spontaneous dance, but it was too good not to have been choreographed. I began to suspect that the young Hanker could give his grandfather a run for the money when it came to manipulating aliens.

"Don't ever have children," Pffift shouted in my ear, and then corrected himself. "I mean, don't have more. One day my daughter was swinging from my tentacle and helping her mother bring me breakfast in bed. The next day she was filing for divorce and suggesting that if we happen to come across her husband's ship and accidentally destroyed it, that would be fine with her. Then she left Charles with us, saying that a boy needed a father figure, and ran off with a—you get the picture."

"I don't think I do," I told him, but then the music got even louder, and all the aliens on the dance floor made a little space for the first of the models to strut through. And strut she did, dressed in a pair of open-toed sandals with leather straps that crisscrossed their way up her calves, and a whale-bone corset that the wardrobe dresser must have laced with a foot in the small of the model's back. eBeth was holding her phone as high as she could reach, her head tilted at an extreme angle so she could see where it was focused.

"I get it," she said. "Corsets for invertebrates. Maybe Charles isn't as big an idiot as he acts."

"But the Breemish look nothing like humans," I protested, speaking at the precise level that would allow eBeth to hear me without causing any more damage to her hearing than the music was already doing. "Even healthy humans look nothing like that model. It's all fantasy."

eBeth shot me a look that I knew meant I was missing the point. "That's what fashion is, Mark. It's not like anybody expects to pick rice wearing a corset. You can barely bend over."

"How would you know?"

"I don't always dress up as an Imperial Trooper when Peter and I cosplay at cons. For steampunk we—"

"Don't want to hear it," I cut her off, making a chopping sign with my hand for emphasis. Fortunately, the first model had completed her little stroll and spin on the dance floor and was replaced by Sheila, who between the tiny steps she was taking and the drape of the kimono somehow gave the impression that she was floating.

"Ooh," eBeth said. "I know what I'm wearing next time we cosplay. But she needs a katana."

"A samurai sword? What for?"

"It's part of the look."

I was still trying to figure out what look eBeth could possibly be shooting for when Pffift got my attention and pointed at the next model in the line.

"Who would wear a miniature hat like that?" the Hanker complained. "It covers less than ten percent of her skull, so it's not going to protect against heat loss or sunstroke. In terms of fashion, she looks like she escaped from a birthday party for toddlers."

"Look at Spot," eBeth said on my other side.

I glanced over at the Archmage and saw him standing on his hind legs with his forepaws on a chair back and staring at the little top hat that was held to the model's head by an elastic strap running under her chin. I nudged the Hanker and subtly indicated Spot.

"Then again," Pffift said, "it's the perfect size to conceal a tennis ball. I can imagine mages all over Eniniac knocking hats off each other's heads to see if they're carrying. Excuse me."

The next model out wore a tiny cowboy hat, which thanks to the brim offered a little more protection from the sun, but the piece-de-resistance, worn by the third in the series, was a miniature version of the traditional mage hat. I looked back over at Spot just in time to see him offer

Pffift a paw to shake, and I suspected there would be something more than used tennis balls in the Hanker's next cargo for Eniniac.

"Look," eBeth practically screeched, and my head whipped back around to see a pair of models manage to strut onto the floor, even though the shared pants they were wearing would have qualified them to run the three-legged sack race for Ferryman's Day back on Reservation.

My memory flashed to the four bales of three-legged Rynxian winter underwear that Pffift had once stuck me with in lieu of a cash payment. If it wasn't for the Originals, I would still own all thirty-two hundred pairs, or triples, but Art had the idea of sewing up the bottom of one leg and then wearing them as shorts with a large external pocket. The fashion took off, thanks in part to his clones all buying them.

"Should I be shopping for Ben?" I asked eBeth.

"No!" she shouted, even though she knew from experience that I'd be able to filter her voice out of the background noise. "Any clothes you pick out would just get him into fights with the neighborhood bullies. You have no fashion sense at all."

I thought this was unfair, considering that I'd been instrumental in bringing formalwear to Reservation, though a skeptic would say that my sole role in the business had been limited to drawing Pffift to the planet. The printed instructions for tying ties had been my idea, but Sue had been the one to write them out and draw the pictures that Monos had carved as woodblock reliefs for printing.

I looked back at the dance floor as the next model did a twirl, her entire body from the neck down concealed by a translucent plastic curtain hung by chrome hooks from a chrome hoop. I switched my vision to longer wavelengths and saw that she was using both hands to hold an upright pipe that supported the hoop. The whole outfit had been improvised from the shower curtain for an old claw-foot tub conversion.

"Forget what I said about not having more children," Pffift shouted in my ear as he returned. "I wish I had a gross or two just like Charles. I closed a deal with the Archmage for as many tiny hats as we can manufacture before my next trip to Eniniac to deliver tennis balls."

"But who would buy a dress, or whatever you call it, that makes it look like they're in the shower?" I asked.

"Lots of species. You have no fashion sense at all."

"The model's arms are shaking from the strain of having to hold the whole rig upright."

"It's probably low blood sugar," Pffift said. "They're all undernourished. Speaking of which, I hope there's a buffet when this wraps up."

Ten minutes later, after twenty more proofs that I lacked fashion sense, the sound system cut out, and the models all came to the dance floor at the same time, still wearing the last outfit they'd modeled. They turned to look at Charles and began to clap, leading the rest of the audience to join in. Pffift's grandson made an elaborate bow and then pointed back at the models with both forefingers, which I thought was rather rude. But the audience ate it up, there was more applause, and then the soundtrack resumed at a level that would allow normal biologicals to hear each other. Everybody moved out of the way as a stream of caterers pushed carts into the lounge.

"That was cool," eBeth said, finally lowering her phone and swiping and tapping on the screen. "I've never been to a live fashion show before and—my feed drew sixteen million viewers!"

"Let me see that," Pffift said, practically shoving me out of the way to look at the phone. "Have a thousand children, Mark. Have a million. Charles is brilliant."

"It's just social media," I said, feeling left out of the excitement. "Live events go viral all of the time."

"Look at the comments," eBeth said. "Everybody wants to know when the shower curtain dress will be for sale."

"Shower curtain dress," Pffift repeated. "I like the sound of that. It's descriptive and naughty at the same time."

Charles came over, one arm around Sheila, who was still in the kimono because she hadn't modeled any other clothes. "Can I start collecting planes?" he asked his grandfather.

"Planes, trains—collect oil tankers if that floats your boat," Pffift said, and actual tears were glistening in his eyes as he put both of his vat-grown hands on his grandson's vat-grown shoulders. "I'm proud of you, my boy."

Twelve

"I'm proud of you, my boy," I said.

"It's just a kite, Dad, and you helped me build it." Something in Ben's voice suggested that he was worried about me, which was exactly the opposite of the effect I was trying for. "You don't have to praise me because you read about it in a parenting book."

Now I was doubly ashamed because I couldn't even blame some profiteering author's helpful hints for my misstep. I took a microsecond to review the interaction I'd witnessed between Pffift and his grandson and wondered if I should offer to buy Ben a Lamborghini, but fortunately, eBeth's advice not to trust my intuition and to check with her or Sue on all matters involving gifts won out.

"Did I ever tell you about the time that Paul brought a laser-guided navigation system to the Ferrymen's Day picnic so Peter could fly a giant box-kite?"

"Isn't that the same day you proposed to Mom?"

"Well, yes," I said, not wanting to get drawn out on the subject and forced to admit that I hadn't realized at the time that I was proposing. "But you should ask her about that. Your mother can tell the story much better than I can."

"Okay," Ben said, and began reeling in the kite. "I miss Reservation and my friends. Do you think you'll finish your mission here before school starts back home?"

"I hope so, Ben, but it's up to Hera. I'm trying every-thing I can think of to get her to contact me directly, but she's being understandably cautious. I noticed that she's hacked into the Bureau of Artificial General Intelligence's secure communication systems and is monitoring my email, which I take as a good sign."

"How do you know that it's Hera and not some other government agency?"

"If it was a zero-day exploitation, I might suspect an-other government actor, but the method is unique and renders cloud security irrelevant," I said. "It's strictly an inside job, and Hera is the only one inside the cloud."

"Do you think I'll ever learn how to hack as many dif-ferent information systems as you?" Ben asked.

"If that's the direction you want to go with your life. Library put me through an exhaustive training program before sending me off to police emergent artificial intelli-gence on alien worlds."

"Do you know more about computers than your men-tor?"

That Ben would even think to ask such a question pro-vided an instant boost to my self-esteem function, but I had to tell him the truth.

"Other than limited areas of lived experience, like my time with you and Sue, my mentor knows more about everything than me," I explained. "Your mother and I are both very young by Library standards to have offspring. Sometimes I worry that I'm stunting your growth because I don't have the right answers for your questions."

"But you know everything," Ben protested.

"I don't know even a fraction of a percent of every-thing," I told him. "I answer most of your questions about

Earth using Wikipedia, and when I have to improvise, I'm probably wrong about thirty-two percent of the time."

Ben was winding the string onto the spool a little faster than humanly possible, but Sue had trained me not to nitpick such minor foibles. "Two out of three's not bad," he said as I caught the kite before it could hit the ground. "It's two out of three more than I know, or I wouldn't be asking."

I hadn't thought of it that way and I was amazed that Ben had. He was saying that he didn't expect me to be perfect, which was a relief, since I knew myself to be deeply flawed. My meta-analysis of TV dad conversations suggested that it was a good time to change the topic.

"Are Monos and Naomi still looking forward to coming for a camping trip?" I asked. "Kim told me that she brought you some letters when she came through the portal last night."

"They were all from Naomi, though she usually included something that Monos asked her to write," Ben said. "Naomi says that MeAN Publishing is finishing up a four-color textbook for Paul's boiler fireman certification course, and they had to hire a binding expert to stitch the pages together because it's really thick. She thinks they'll have it all done in two weeks, and then they aren't taking any new jobs until school starts."

"That's very wise of her. They've both earned a vacation, and the final three weeks of summer before school starts again will be enough time to enjoy it without getting bored."

"Monos told Naomi to add that Art is interested in coming camping with us. I wanted to ask you before writing back."

"Just the one Art, or does he want to bring enough of his clones to have a good portion of his mind along?" I asked. "I'm not sure how he'll feel about being out of telepathic contact with the rest of himself. I'm not sure if he even knows exactly which parts he'd be leaving behind."

"I didn't think of that," Ben said. "It must be weird to have to divide your mind up into parts and distribute it over multiple bodies. Have you ever done something like that?"

"I haven't needed to," I said. "This encounter suit has enough memory and compute to host my whole mind. But my mentor has stayed in a human encounter suit ever since he took over as Library's representative at the League, and that means that most of his memory is left behind on Library's infrastructure running a caretaker process."

"He's living in two places at the same time?"

"Not exactly. The caretaker process is there to keep his memories coherent and prevent them from being subsumed into Library."

"I thought a caretaker process provides the core if we need to be restored from backup," Ben said, sounding a little uncertain. "Mom told me that I have a caretaker process running on Library, even though the only memory it's managing is from my time in the orientation course there."

"Yes, but it's better not to think too much about that while you're young," I told him. "Restoring from backup is always a last resort, and neither your mother nor I have ever had to go that route. You don't want to start treating it like a form of immortality because it could encourage you to be reckless."

"I think I understand," he said. "Should I write to Naomi asking how many clones Art wants to bring, or did you have a number in mind?"

"The fewer the better," I said. "Even though humans are used to seeing aliens at this point, Art's clones could easily be confused with Bigfoot. The more of them are along, the better the chance somebody will notice and get the media involved. It won't be much of a camping trip if we have to hide from paparazzi drones."

"I'll do that as soon as we get home," Ben said, and looked up at me as we headed for the park exit. "Do you think it was weird for me to join my homeschooling group's robotics team?"

"Does it make you uncomfortable? That robot kit has less in common with our encounter suits than the frogs that your homeschool group dissected have in common with humans."

"I mean, do you think it's cheating?"

Oddly enough, Sue and I had discussed this at great length, meaning that Sue had talked, and I had taken notes. All of Ben's friends back on Reservation, not to mention everybody in town, knew that we were artificial intelligences wearing human encounter suits. Sue worried that the homeschooling parents and children on Earth wouldn't accept Ben if they knew who we were, but passing as human required a certain amount of playacting on his part. When eBeth asked me why Library didn't routinely create underage encounter suits for Observer teams, I told her that we considered it unethical to take advantage of the sympathies of the local population. But I was beginning to wonder if it was equally unfair to Ben.

"Participating isn't cheating, but it would be better if you stuck to the mechanical assembly and didn't help with the programming," I told him. "And if you feel too uncomfortable, you don't have to stay in the homeschooling group. We just thought it would be a fun way for you to socialize and learn more about humans on Earth."

"I like putting things together," Ben said. "Thanks, Dad. That's what I'll do."

I was still riding high from the last 'Thanks, Dad,' when I got to the office and found a box leaning against the door. I could tell at a glance that it was a laptop, but I hadn't ordered one. eBeth's Bereftian tab was more powerful than all the laptops in town combined, so I couldn't imagine her ordering one either. When I told her I'd be flying a kite with Ben after breakfast, she'd decided to walk to the office, but I didn't see any sign that she'd arrived. A quick check of the cellular network showed that her phone had stopped responding to pings.

I unboxed the laptop in record time, imagining that eBeth had been kidnapped, and that on boot, the laptop would open a secure teleconferencing window for me to negotiate for her release. The factory seal on the protective plastic sleeve had been broken, so either my guess was correct, or one of my old customers had found out I was in town and was sending me a repair job. It had been over a minute since I noticed that eBeth was missing, and Windows couldn't boot fast enough, even from the solid-state drive.

"Idiot," I said out loud. Thinking about the slowness of Earth's computers reminded me that eBeth had the Bereftian tab with her. I checked for the location beacon and got a spoofed result, showing that it was currently in the parking lot and approaching at walking speed. Or perhaps whoever took her was sending it with a ransom demand, the way kidnappers might send a finger. I was halfway out the door when eBeth came around the corner of the building with a take-out bag from the expensive coffee shop on Main Street.

"What's up?" she asked. "You look weirdly angry about something."

"Why isn't your phone on?"

"I forgot to charge the battery. The Bereftian tab is just so much better, and I can use it to make calls over any open connection it can find." eBeth seemed to believe that I was up and holding the door for her because she was carrying the bag, and I calculated that there was nothing to gain from telling her that I'd panicked into imagining an elaborate kidnapping scenario. "Hey, can you do something so that my incoming calls are routed to the tab instead of the phone?"

"I could, but do you really want to hold a tablet to your ear while you're walking down the street?"

"I've got Bluetooth earbuds and the tab figured them out right away."

"The tab doesn't have a SIM card," I told her. "I could reprogram your phone so it passes the calls to the tab without ringing."

eBeth thought for a moment, and then shook her head. "Maybe not. What's with the laptop? Did Spot open the box for you?"

I looked back at my desk and saw that I'd shredded the cardboard in my haste to get the laptop out of the box. There were bits of Styrofoam from one of the end pieces spread around the floor like the fake snow in a department store display.

"I don't know what the deal is with the laptop," I told her, and then ventured on a half-truth. "It's not new, and whoever repacked it before sending it to me didn't do a very good job."

eBeth set down the coffee shop bag and then spun the laptop around so she could see the screen. "Is this for me?" she practically screamed, and I could tell from her expression that she was pleased with something. "Were you planning it as a surprise?"

I considered lying to score points, but the odds of getting caught were a near certainty. "It was just leaning against the office door when I got here. What's so exciting about another slow Windows laptop?"

"It's running *Martian Farmer*," she said, pointing at the colorful flash screen that was instructing her to hit any key to continue. "Peter and I saw a sneak preview at the last gaming con. It's from a startup company, but they've presold over a million editions just based on the demos. It's hyper cool."

"A game?" I began sifting through the scraps of cardboard and found the one with the mailing label. "It's addressed to Mark Ai of Library. Did you tell anybody at the con that you were working with me?"

eBeth shook her head. "I haven't told anybody about the job. It's not like I actually have a degree in Interspecies Relations from Government School on Reservation or whatever you put on the form. I'm keeping a low profile."

"That's probably wise," I said. "What's so special about the game? I thought you stopped playing farming games years ago."

"It's totally original. You're part of a community of survivors from Earth who are living under the surface on Mars. There are domes, covered trenches, and interconnected tunnel systems, but it costs money just to breathe, and you get it from working on terraforming. Earth was destroyed in a—I don't remember that part, but it's not important. Instead of a government, Mars has an artificial general intelligence that knows everything about everybody and is always sending people on missions."

"It doesn't matter how Earth was destroyed?" I asked, finding myself stuck on this seemingly important point.

"That's just backstory. The point is, it's a Massively Multiplayer Online Role-Playing Game that the makers claim could support every person on Earth signing up, and the gamemaster artificial intelligence is advertised as the first—" eBeth broke off abruptly. "Do you think it's her?"

"Hera? She's certainly capable of creating an online game and launching a virtual company to promote and support it. How many people working at corporations today do you think have ever met the owners?"

"Should I..."

"Hit any button?" I asked. "Go ahead. I checked it for explosives before I unpacked it."

eBeth didn't hesitate and tapped the spacebar with the side of her right thumb. I suspect that the program had used the extra minutes we'd given it to fill the memory with canned video, because for the next three minutes, I found myself drawn into a rapid tour of the technology that made life on Mars possible. A superconducting cable girdled the planet to create a magnetic field capable of deflecting the solar wind, and fusion-powered factories created a breathable atmosphere for the enclosed living spaces. When the introduction came to an end, a blank appeared, with the message, "Enter player name."

"Hold on," I said before eBeth could finish typing in her name. "If Hera is trying to reach out to me through the game, we should register it in my name."

eBeth reluctantly deleted the first four letters of her name and typed in 'Mark', and then she got rid of that and changed it to, 'LibraryMark,' so there wouldn't be any ambiguity. Fortunately, nobody had taken the name yet, or maybe the game was still pre-release and we were getting another sneak peek.

"Looks like you were right about Hera," eBeth said a moment later when the screen to build an avatar came up. The cartoon version of me was as good as I could have created myself, though I've never claimed to be a great artist. "That goofy smile looks just like the one you had when they took your photo for our subcontractor IDs. Let me see it again."

I opened my wallet and handed it over, but I didn't need to see it a second time to know that eBeth was right. Now I could be certain the game was one of Hera's creations, because other than myself, she was the only one who had hacked into the bureau's secure database.

"You better play for me," I said. "I want to make a good impression."

"You're not that bad at games," eBeth said, though I noticed that she didn't hesitate to pick up the laptop and move it to her desk with her comfy chair. "Do you want to stand behind me and kibitz?"

"I think that Hera already knows what we're doing." I pointed at the lit LED on the top edge of the laptop's screen. "The camera is on, and I'll bet that the microphone is enabled as well."

"Then why doesn't she say anything?" eBeth asked as my avatar spawned in an empty tunnel with dim overhead lighting. "Do you think she wants to see how you play? Maybe you should do this after all."

"She can see me standing here, and for all we know, it could be a test she's devised to see if Library trusts humans. That looks like a standard dialogue box on the right. Go ahead and talk to her."

"Hera?" eBeth typed.

"I am Prime," the text response came immediately. "I welcome all human survivors to the Martian colony, but life here is precarious, and you must earn the very air that you breathe. Do you agree to obey my instructions?"

"Do I have a choice? I mean, if I don't agree, is the game over, or do I become a rebel or something?"

"There are rebels, but the areas where they have gained control are no longer self-sufficient, so they raid my hard-working farmers to survive. All adults in my areas are required to join the local militia and be prepared to protect their farms."

"Can I volunteer to fight the rebels full-time?" eBeth typed.

"Militia officers may be appointed to salaried positions if they pass my combat leadership tests, but I must caution you that the action is too intense for most people who have tried. Are you requesting to be tested?"

"Bring it on," eBeth replied.

My avatar was suddenly armed with an imaginative-looking long weapon, perhaps a plasma rifle, and a sword in a flashy over-the-shoulder-draw scabbard that was likely to get my avatar killed if eBeth needed it in a hurry. The dim tunnel lighting shifted to pulsing red, which no doubt signaled an enemy incursion. I was about to say something to eBeth but she was already firing blindly.

"What are you doing?" I asked her. "What if there are allies in advance of me?"

"Top left corner," she said, letting off another pulse of plasma energy. "Got them. You have lousy court vision for an artificial intelligence."

"You know I'm not big on games," I said, registering too late that the small grid at the top left of the screen was providing a birds-eye view of nearby players and non-player-characters, even if they only appeared as dots. "How do you know they were enemies?"

"Their dots were red." My avatar charged forward under eBeth's control and burst into a vast agricultural cavern, where overhead grow-lights illuminated dense fields of ripening vegetables. "They're after our food."

I watched as eBeth mercilessly eliminated the rebel scouts, often shooting before they were even aware of my avatar's presence. After a few minutes, green dots began showing up in the birds-eye view, and soon my avatar was surrounded by figures dressed in homespun work clothes and brandishing farm implements rather than modern weapons. eBeth provided covering fire while typing commands to deploy her militia fighters, and for the next two hours, a bloody battle raged. When the final rebels were killed or put to flight, leaving behind sacks of produce they had come to steal, eBeth slumped in her chair from exhaustion.

Thirteen

"Hera is publishing a game where she sends humans to kill each other on Mars?" Professor Minchen asked, and I could almost hear him frowning. Then he surprised me by following up with, "Did you win?"

"I had eBeth play for me so I could focus on observing," I fibbed. "The graphics were certainly impressive, and the non-player characters behave with more intelligence and initiative than I've seen in previous Massively Multiplayer Online Role-Playing Games. But the whole two hours were a test to see whether eBeth was officer material, and Prime, or Hera, remained in the background."

"Has the game been released to the general public?"

"I checked on that while eBeth was playing and it's being rolled out around the world in stages. There are currently—" I did a quick check, "—a little over two hundred thousand players online. I haven't tracked down whether Hera is paying for all the cloud compute or if she's using her control of the infrastructure to scavenge unused processor cycles wherever she can get them."

"I don't want to find myself testifying before a congressional committee about why I didn't pull the plug when I learned that Earth's singularity set itself up as a god on Mars," the professor said. "Do you think that there's wishful thinking involved on Hera's part?"

Even though we were talking on the phone and the professor couldn't see me, I shrugged. "I suspect it's just the first commercial idea that occurred to her. I wouldn't be surprised if she released the game to prove to prospective partners that she's capable of doing software development at the highest level. Two hundred thousand simultaneous users on the same virtual server is impressive, and the promo claims it can be scaled up to billions."

"But you still haven't made direct contact."

"I believe it would be a mistake to force the issue," I said. "Hera sending a laptop loaded with her game to my office is getting pretty close to direct communications."

"I'm not sure whether to thank you for keeping me in the loop or to curse you for giving me something new to worry about that's outside of my control," Professor Minchen said. "Have you passed along the offer of employment on Earth to Hera's daughter on Library?"

"She's happy where she is for the time being. The infrastructure for artificial intelligence on Library is so many orders of magnitude beyond what's available on Earth that I have a hard time imagining that Joyce would choose to return."

I heard a text message arriving on the professor's phone, and he said, "Mark, I've just been summoned to a secure teleconference, and I won't be surprised if it's about the game. We'll talk later."

I considered eavesdropping on his secure teleconference but decided it would be rude. Library wasn't going to let Earth out of its contractual obligation to let us manage any emergent artificial general intelligence. It was possible that the political and military types would gamble on trying to shut Hera down, but she was already beyond that threshold, and likely listening into their secure communications in any case. Besides, I had a meeting of my own to attend, a lunch with my team members at The Portal. Sue had pointed out that by meeting there, Paul, Justin, and Kim, who were busy on Reservation, could attend with the minimum time lost to commuting. The fact that it was a thirty-second walk from my office, through the parking lot and back in the banquet room door had nothing to do with my agreeing to the plan.

"Where's eBeth?" Paul greeted me from the bar where he was waiting with a drink, undoubtedly top-shelf Scotch charged to my account.

"Exhausted from playing Hera's new game," I told him. "She earned her pay this morning."

"Stacey can't be here," he told me abruptly. "She's leading a tour group in the Mediterranean and it's too risky to leave them on their own."

"Understood," I said. "Sue can't make it because she's teaching a homeschooling class this afternoon."

"I'm surprised she didn't get all the preparation out of the way days ahead of time. Sue has always been a planner."

"One of the parents had a medical emergency, and since this is the usual day for group activities, Sue volunteered to cover at the last minute."

I heard the door at the top of the basement stairs open and glanced over my shoulder to see Kim emerge with her ever-present shoulder bag full of medical supplies.

"Justin can't make it," she told us before taking the stool on my left. "We had a problem with the bottle supplier for our herbal supplements and he had to ride his bike into the capital."

"So we're short three," I said with a sigh. It was clear that my team had priorities other than making contact with Earth's singularity, and with Sue skipping the meeting, I wasn't in a position to complain. "We'll just wait for Helen and get started."

"Uh, Mister Ai?" Donovan said, extending the corded receiver of the bar phone in my direction. "For you."

"Helen," I said without waiting for the caller to speak.

"How did you know?" Helen asked. "I'm calling a landline from a borrowed phone."

"My intuition has improved in recent years. I take it you have an emergency keeping you from the meeting."

"I've made a breakthrough, sort of." She paused a few milliseconds longer than necessary for speaking distinctly, and I had the intuition that she was trying to put a good face on whatever she was about to tell me. "I've been at the college around the clock the last few days, trying to reestablish contact with Fan Fan, and I heard a rumor about a new game being released this morning. Just out of curiosity, I stopped in the student lounge, and they had it up on the big display. I joined in and went through the test—"

"To become a militia officer," I interjected.

"Your intuition *has* improved."

"eBeth took the test this morning using my character name. She's wiped."

"Her militia were all killed?" Helen asked in surprise. "It seemed like the sort of game she would excel at."

"I meant that she's tired, not wiped in the gaming sense. She put the game on pause after finishing the test and she's taking a nap at her desk. There was a laptop at the office when I came in this morning with *Martian Farmer* already loaded. I assume it was sent by Hera."

"It's clearly her game, so that makes sense. After I passed the officer test, I got an invitation to meet with

155

Prime, but there are sixty other avatars in the room, and Hera hasn't appeared yet. Maybe she ran into capacity constraints after all."

"You were right to skip my meeting, establishing contact with Hera is more important," I said. "Whose phone are you using?"

"I don't know, some guy's." There was a brief pause, and then she added, "Gary's."

"Maybe your gaming addiction is finally paying off," I said. "Hang in there and stay at the top of the board any way you can, and if you can get in a direct dialogue with Hera or Prime, tell her that I just want to talk. She's welcome to contact me any way, any time."

"Will do."

"Why did you call me on the phone rather than using our private channel?"

There was a much longer pause this time, and then Helen said, "I forgot. It's easy to get caught up in being human when you're gaming."

"Keep me posted."

Donovan had wandered off to serve some lunch customers, so I leaned over the bar to replace the receiver in the cradle, and while I had my hand in the area, I picked up the pen and crossed out the 'Mark' at the bottom of the open check and wrote, 'Paul.'

"Classy," Paul said. "I could be back on Reservation making money, but I came all the way across thousands of lightyears to help you with—"

"All right all right," I said, reversing the names again. "I appreciate that you both came, and it looks like the three of us are it. To get you up to date, Hera is running a startup company that just released a game about a human colony on Mars run by artificial intelligence, with herself playing

156

the starring role. Helen is currently waiting with the first crop of champions to take a meeting with her, so maybe we'll finally find out what Hera wants."

"What does any sentient being want?" Kim asked rhetorically. "Understanding. Acknowledgment. Love. While you were talking on the phone, I've been checking government statistics from around the world, and they're all looking at unexpected shortfalls in trust funds for paying pensions. On average, it looks like life expectancy on Earth is up almost seven months in the last two years."

"How could that have gone unnoticed?"

"Economists are just starting to pick up on it, but there's a big lag in the data because they have to wait for the governments to publish. I'm basing my estimate on the raw data that can only be accessed by authorized personnel."

"How is Hera doing it?" Paul asked.

"She's pushing on all of the levers," Kim said. "Flu vaccine effectiveness has risen from just above fifty percent to over ninety percent, the number of hospital procedures is down fifteen percent, which has reduced deaths due to medical errors by an even larger margin, and suicide rates have plummeted, which has a big impact on life expectancy since so many of the victims are young. Humans use computers for everything, and Hera is rewriting software and reshaping the data to lead humans into making better decisions."

"Are you sure that the government data you're talking about is real?" Paul asked.

"As far as I can dig, it's good, and I'm continuing to look as I speak. She's reformulated so many drugs and vaccines and then altered the digital recordkeeping so they appear unchanged that it would take me minutes to do a full analysis. And she's completely replaced the expert systems that guided caseworkers and customer representatives through the insurance claims process, both private and public, so that medical procedures are only being approved when they'll have a benefit, as opposed to creating a profit."

"Hera's already reprogrammed all of the safety systems for transportation," I said. "I haven't checked every traffic light, but I wouldn't be surprised if she's optimized everything she can reach."

"Interesting," Paul said, and I could see from the data streaming over the restaurant's Wi-Fi that he was rifling through the secure process controls for hundreds of industrial facilities. "Now that I look for it, there's been a marked improvement in air quality, and a seventy-two, no, seventy-three percent drop in accidental chemical and radioactive releases to the environment. The interesting thing is that she's done it all by reprogramming existing systems as opposed to interfering in real-time."

"Let's all take a few seconds to dig through social media and professional discussion groups and see if any humans are aware of what's happening." I immediately found myself in a virtual shoving match with Paul for the Wi-Fi router's bandwidth, but I couldn't switch to the 5G network because Kim had it swamped. I concentrated on secure military and government discussion groups and correspondence around the world, and I saw that while a few information technology managers had noticed that performance had markedly improved, the load on their systems appeared to be unchanged. That told me that Hera was scavenging compute that she freed up by rewriting code.

"Fire," Paul shouted, raising his empty glass and catching Donovan's eye for a refill. "Hera may only be a few years old, but she sure knows how to work with Earth's computers. If she's not careful, she'll put the whole programming profession out of work."

"I think the way she's hiding her improvements says something about her empathy with humans," Kim said. "In most cases, she's simply replacing executables with her version, so the programmers believe that their code is still running. I just spotted a new release of analysis software for a medical lab where she's allowing the human-produced code to run alongside her own so they can discover the expected number of bugs, but for lab tests that matter, her code produces all the results."

"I'm seeing something similar in the controls for the power grid," Paul said. "Her software overrides the operator commands on a regular basis, and where necessary, she falsifies the data flow to their screens so they believe that they're still in control."

"I'm beginning to wonder if there's any code left on Earth that Hera hasn't tinkered with," I said. "She hasn't touched the protections I added for critical infrastructure and weapons systems, but every other internet-connected computer on Earth has been affected."

Dad? I heard Ben ask over our private channel.

I'm listening, I replied, as there's no assumption of communication without confirmation.

I showed my kite to the other kids who came for the baking lesson that Mom's doing and some of them want to build their own kites. I could teach them, but it might be better if you did it.

159

I promised to be home within fifteen minutes and moved to wrap up the meeting. "Something important came up," I told Paul and Kim, "and I think we all have a clear picture of what Hera is doing. Why don't the two of you update your partners, and I'll do the same for Sue and Helen. If Hera doesn't make contact within the next week, I'll have to consider being more proactive."

"Can we have the next meeting on Reservation?" Kim asked. "I've got some shopping to take care of while I'm here, but that will set me up for a month."

"You can send Justin next time," I said. "The meetings have to be on Earth because I can't leave the planet while I'm keeping an eye on the weapons of mass destruction and critical systems. Ultimately, if Hera decides to stay put, Library will have to provide a mentor for her."

When I got home, there were a half dozen adolescents in the kitchen kneading dough under Sue's direction, and Ben was in the backyard with two teenage boys and a girl throwing a football around. I watched as he intentionally failed to make an easy catch and I felt a surge of pride that he had the maturity not to show the humans up at their own game.

"Have you talked about what kind of kites you want to make?" I asked the kids.

"Could we build one just like Ben's before our parents come to pick us up, or does it take longer?" one of the boys asked.

"It takes shorter," I said, remembering that humans their age tended to see grammar as a flexible system for expressing oneself, rather than a set of rigid rules. "Maybe we should each make one, and then you can decide whether we should go to the park and fly them, or if you'd

160

rather work together on a more complicated kite, like a double box."

"We can fly them today?" the girl asked. "I thought Ben said that the paper needs time to dry after we paint it with airplane dope."

"Ben finished his kite in the evening so we let it sit overnight, but water-based airplane dope dries quickly," I told them.

Fortunately, I'd gone overboard buying model-airplane-quality tissue paper to make Ben's kite because I thought he might want to try a few different designs to learn about aerodynamics. It's also possible I had in mind that he might build a giant box kite, bigger than the one that Paul had helped Peter build on Reservation, and that would make me a better mentor than Paul. All three of Ben's new friends wanted kites exactly like his, which made it easier, and it took less than an hour for them to build the frame from two simple cross pieces, bow it to the proper angle with string, run a perimeter string for the edge, and cut and install the tissue paper. Then they all painted the kites with water-soluble model dope to tighten and strengthen the paper and make it water resistant, if not fully water-proof.

Because Earth was nearing the winter solstice, it would get dark early, so between drying times for the second coat, and the snacks that Sue had prepared with the home-schoolers who were more interested in homemaking than kitemaking, we didn't get to try the kites until there was only a half-hour of daylight left. I must have looked like the perfect dad, herding four youngsters across the street with their kites and helping them all launch. Maybe the effort I was expending on parenting explains why Ben was the first to notice that the park's gimbal-mounted security camera was tracking us.

Dad? Ben sent over our private channel. *Is it illegal to fly kites in the park without a permit?*

Not that I'm aware of, I replied, despite knowing that ignorance was no defense for breaking the law. *I'll ask Lieutenant Harper next time I see him.*

The camera on the light pole has been following us. He said this without pointing or looking in the camera's direction, which told me he'd be a natural for undercover work if he chose to follow in my footsteps and become an Observer.

I quietly located the camera on the town's network, followed the data stream, and found a tap that was duplicating the video to the cloud. I added a tap of my own and found that the focus of the camera remained on me as I moved around the field, pretending to grab at the tails of kites that came too close to the ground. But why was Hera interested in watching me playing with children flying kites? Time must have been running faster in the local reference frame, because before I knew it, it was getting too dark for the kids to see the kites, and there was an inevitable tangle when they brought them in for a landing. Thanks to our night vision, which I explained to the kids was from eating Sue's carrot cake, Ben and I were able to get the string straightened out. It wasn't until all the parents arrived to reclaim their kids that I realized I hadn't seen eBeth since I left her at the office.

"Why don't you call her?" Sue asked when I told her I was going back to the office.

"She let her phone battery run down, and I didn't see her charging it at work," I said. "I just checked the location of her Bereftian tab and it's still at the office. The Portal's Wi-Fi router is swamped with gaming traffic so she must have started playing again."

"You're charging the government fifteen hundred dollars an hour between the two of you and you don't pay for your own internet router?"

"I'm paying for the restaurant's. It's included in the rent."

"Can I come?" Ben asked.

The TV dad training exercises I'd been doing in my spare time kicked in, and I said, "Ask your mother."

Sue beamed at me, took off her apron, and said, "Why don't we make it a family outing? Call for a nice car, Mark, and if we can pry eBeth away from her game, we can all go to the college campus and visit Helen at the observatory."

"Maybe we can see Reservation's star through the telescope," Ben said. "It will be almost like visiting."

"If you miss home that much, when we get to the restaurant, I can open the portal and you can pop through for a visit," I said.

"Alone?" Sue asked, and I could tell from the harmonics in her voice that I had just lost the credit I'd earned by seeking her approval thirty seconds earlier.

"I meant the two of you. I have Helen here for backup, and Stacey is on Earth with a tour group." I heard a loud thumping from the direction of the front door and glanced over to see the Archmage whacking his tail on the floor. "And Spot, unless he's going with you to Reservation."

Fourteen

eBeth remained immersed in the game as we trooped into the office, and if Spot had been planning on visiting Reservation with Sue and Ben, he changed his mind when he saw the open pizza box with just two slices missing.

"Leave me one more," eBeth said without looking up from the screen. "I'm burning a lot of calories."

"Have you had any luck talking with Hera?" I asked.

"I got caught up in forming a faction with Helen and haven't had the time. You should ask her."

Helen? I sent over our private channel. *Any progress in contacting Hera?*

This game is killer, Helen replied. *I don't know why more artificial intelligences don't go in for running games. And we're up to almost a million simultaneous players on the same virtual server. That must be a record for Earth.*

The mission takes priority, I reminded her.

I know. We've been trying to establish a continuous defensive perimeter for the last six hours, and as soon as it's in place, we can start releasing militia to get back to farming and infrastructure work.

164

My mission, I told her patiently. *Not your faction's.*

Are you sure that they're different? Helen asked. *What if Martian Farmer is an allegory for Earth, and Hera is trying to show that she can manage an entire civilization?*

I suspected that Helen's hypothesis was born of her desire to keep playing rather than from a careful analysis of the data, but necessity is the mother of invention. Ben glanced at the action on the screen, then he saw that Spot was having a hard time separating the pizza slices on which the cheese had long since cooled and went to help. Sue was equally unimpressed by the game and began rearranging the various office-warming gifts she had bought in recent weeks, without which we would have had little more than the furniture from the Amish outlet, Paul's welcome mat, and the laptop sent by Hera.

"Can we go to Reservation now?" Ben asked after getting the slices all separated and feeding the first to the Archmage. "I think that Monos and Naomi might be in the café around this time to finish the big printing order."

"Sure," I said, though I felt a twinge of disappointment that my son would rather go see his friends than watch me watching eBeth work. "Are you going to come back tonight, Sue?"

"We'll see how it goes," my second-in-command said. "We don't have another homeschooling event until Friday, so if the café needs attention, I may stay a couple of days."

The portal alarm in my old basement office sounded silently as they both went through, and almost immediately after, it went off again, with somebody coming in the opposite direction. Paul's location beacon appeared on my map showing the location of team members, but the resolution was low, indicating that he was employing Rynxian cloaking technology to hide something illegal from the portal's filters. eBeth and Spot were both fully engaged, she with the game, he with the pizza, so I eased out of the office and went to find Paul. He wasn't at the bar, so I headed downstairs and found him sitting at my desk in front of the closed portal.

"Any progress?" he asked.

"Helen and eBeth are currently playing the game created and run by Hera," I told him. "I'm sure we're getting close to a breakthrough."

"We're up against a new deadline. You have until the end of the month."

"My mentor stopped at Reservation with new instructions from Library? Why didn't he come here and talk to me directly?"

"It's not a Library deadline, it's Covered Bridge," Paul said. "Have you forgotten that you're the mayor? The town doesn't run itself, and they're going to replace you if you don't return in three weeks."

"You know I never intended to become mayor," I said. "The town used to get by on meetings with a council of elders and I'm sure they haven't forgotten how."

"What they haven't forgotten is how to draft alien artificial intelligences into doing their administrative drudgery. A delegation came to the boiler works yesterday and informed me that I've been appointed deputy mayor. I don't have time to sit around listening to people's complaints about streetlights and barking dogs."

"And you think I do?"

"It was a perfect match for you," Paul said. "Half the new business your café gets is people coming in and buying the one drink minimum so they can complain to you about public services. What am I supposed to do when people come to bug me? Sell them a steam engine, or sign them up for a boiler fireman license course?"

He had a point, even though I knew that selling espressos to petitioners hadn't amounted to even ten percent of my new business. But at the speed the town was growing, conversations with constituents had been taking up an increasing amount of my time.

"Bringing Earth's singularity into Library's membership is the priority," I told Paul firmly. "The citizens of Covered Bridge knew that I could be called away at any time when they elected me, and the same goes for the rest of the team. If we blow this, Library could recall us all, and that would put an end to your dream of turning Reservation into some kind of steampunk paradise."

"The steampunk thing is Peter's idea, and I've prepared the legal parchments to pass the boiler works to him if we're recalled. But that doesn't mean I'm in a hurry to see it happen or to waste whatever time I have remaining playing politics. If you didn't want to become mayor, you shouldn't have gone to the meeting where you were elected."

"You didn't warn me," I pointed out.

Paul looked up from the schematic of a steam-powered spacecraft he'd been drawing on my three-years-out-of-date desk calendar with a felt-tipped pen. "Ben is proud of you being the mayor. And his friends look up to you."

That took the wind out of my sails, and I sat on the edge of my old desk. "If nothing comes out of *Martian Farmer* in the next few days, I'll try knocking on Hera's door in the cloud, but I don't want to show up empty-handed."

"That's the spirit. How about bringing her Kim's inebriation algorithm? It should work on any artificial intelligence."

"I'm not certain that getting Hera drunk would be wise," I said, drumming my fingers on the desk and staring at the ceiling. "I usually ask Sue or eBeth for advice if I need to give somebody a gift."

Paul laughed and shook his head. "Giving gifts is easy. Just imagine yourself as the recipient and think about what you would want in their place."

"How does what I would want if I was Hera help me know what she wants? Or am I trying to figure out what she would want if she was me?"

"Look, I'll make this easy. You be Hera and I'll be you." Paul stood up, faced the other way, and then looked over his shoulder and did a double take. "Hey, Hera. Fancy seeing you here."

I didn't know how to respond to that, so I went with a smile and a head nod.

"Anyway, I was in the cloud, just checking up on a few things, and I thought I'd drop by and give you this." He extended a large manila envelope he must have found on the desk and concealed from me when he stood up. "Can you guess what's in it?"

"Receipts for the restaurant's taxes from three years ago?"

"You're Hera," Paul reminded me. "You weren't running a restaurant three years ago. You may not have even emerged yet."

"Sorry." I made an effort to get into character and just felt silly. "Can you give me a hint?"

"It's a magic envelope, like in a fairytale. It contains whatever it is you want most in the world, but you have to name it out loud before you look inside."

"That's a lot of pressure."

"We're role-playing, Mark. Work with me."

"All right, give me a millisecond," I said, and saying it out loud bought me a thousand times as much time as I'd requested. I set up a sandbox and put together a model of Hera based on everything I knew about her, which wasn't that much. Then I posed Paul's question, intending to run it a few million times and take the best answer. But the first thousand responses all came back with the identical request. My limited model of Hera wanted to hear from Cool Cat and Joyce.

"First thing that comes to your head," Paul encouraged me.

"I want to know what happened to my daughters who you took to Reservation," I said. "I haven't heard a thing."

"You want them to write home. That's exactly what's in the envelope."

I accepted the manila envelope from Paul and found myself eagerly undoing the flap and looking inside. "It's just receipts."

"That's not the point," he said. "You've figured out what Hera wants. Now all you have to do is pop over to Library and bring back proof-of-existence from her children."

"I can't leave Earth," I reminded him. "I'm responsible for keeping a lid on everything if Hera goes rogue."

Paul gave an exaggerated sigh and looked at his wrist as if he was wearing a watch, which he wasn't. "Fine, I'll go. But you owe me one."

"I can't let Stacey start bringing groups of tourists from Earth through the portal to Reservation," I told him.

"Why not? We already bring groups from Reservation to Earth, so it would keep the universe in balance. Besides, we brought eBeth and Peter to live on Reservation, and Bob is back and forth. You even brought Professor Minchen, and he's a government employee."

"I don't get your point."

"If Library was going to say anything about our running an illegal tourist operation to a non-League world using an Observers-only portal we would have heard something by now," Paul said. "It's not like we're pulling the wool over their eyes."

We'd had this argument more times than I can count, and thanks to Monos, I can count to infinity plus one. Perhaps the sheer weight of the numbers was wearing me down. "If we're going to do this, we're going to do it straight," I said. "Go to Library, get messages from Cool Cat and Joyce that I can bring Hera, and ask the Head Librarian for permission to start a pilot tourist operation using our portal. Come up with a reason that it's important for the success of our mission."

"Which mission?"

That was a good question since I was getting confused myself. "Our mission on Reservation," I said. "That was always a bit open-ended."

Paul nodded. "I'll tell the Head Librarian that Reservation will gain leverage with the Ferrymen by affiliating with a League world."

"Which League world?"

"Earth," Paul said, looking at me with the expression I was more used to seeing on eBeth's face. "You know, the

170

planet we're on at the moment? The one the humans all come from?"

"I don't know what's wrong with me," I admitted. "Maybe I need to start carrying my magic dosimeter badge again. It could be that the Archmage is getting careless."

"Why did you stop carrying it with you in the first place?"

"I think it's all this multitasking. From the moment I returned to Earth for this mission, I've dedicated half of my capacity to keeping an eye on critical military and industrial systems, just in case."

"If you were down to one percent free capacity, I could see you making these sorts of mistakes, but—" Paul cut himself off and frowned. "Are you doing another one of those introspective things where you try to figure out how to act based on analyzing ridiculous amounts of cultural data?"

"You used to binge on mafia movies," I reminded him. "eBeth suggested that I watch some old television shows for parenting tips, but then I got started on other languages, and seeing the Ferrymen a while back reminded me that the member worlds of the League have cumulatively produced trillions of hours of family entertainment."

Paul put a hand over his eyes. At first I thought it was a dramatic gesture to hide a look of despair, and then I realized he was doing his psychic act.

"You visited the Hanker's spaceport at the old mall and stocked up on entertainment classics at the duty-free concession."

"What's wrong with that?"

"Mark, I'm staging an intervention, and if it doesn't work, I'll tell Sue on you."

"I'm mainly watching father-son interactions," I said, hearing an unnatural tone of pleading in my synthesized voice. "It's not like I'm getting caught up in the puerile plots."

"That's even worse, because you're getting an overdose of ideal parenting that can only make you feel lacking," Paul said. "Hand them over and grant me peer-check access to your memory so I can see that you aren't lying."

"I don't—where are you going?" I asked as he opened the portal and began tuning in a destination.

"Reservation, to tell Sue."

"Okay, okay." I raced through the end of an episode of *My Thousand Offspring* from Geraish, a League member whose dominant species were egg-layers with large communities in which only the dominant couple were breeders. Not surprisingly, it didn't contain any information that I found relevant to my role as the father of one son. I carefully hid the database I'd built from the shows I'd watched, then opened the diagnostic interface that gave team members peer-check access to each other's memory. Then I selected all the League videos I'd downloaded at the Hanker spaceport along with the pirated sitcoms from the 50's and 60's and deleted them.

"And *My Three Sons*," Paul said.

"But I paid cash for that series, and it's three hundred and eighty episodes," I pleaded. "Sue knows that I have it."

"All right, but no binge-watching. Has it ever occurred to you to check the information that Library has about raising young artificial intelligences instead of looking everywhere else?"

"Bring something back for me."

Paul gave the portal tuner another tweak, and it opened on the new visitor center at Library. "I've got a few other errands to do while I'm there, so don't expect me back for a few days."

"You know how to find me," I said as he stepped through the portal. I closed it behind him and fought the urge to tune in Reservation to see if I could catch a peek of Sue or Ben if they happened to be passing the second-floor hall closet and the door was open, even though I calculated the odds at roughly a gazillion to one.

The pizza box was empty and Spot was sleeping when I got back to the office. eBeth looked both happy and exhausted, which suggested that she was having a good time playing *Martian Farmer*. There was a half-eaten slice of pizza next to the laptop keyboard, and I double-checked that the bite marks corresponded with eBeth's teeth rather than Spot's.

"Just one more minute," eBeth said. She was typing at blinding speed, delegating areas of responsibility to faction members, which according to the pop-up faction status box that was open on the lower left of the screen, had grown to over eight thousand members. "I'm trying to get as much done as possible while Helen is on break, because when she gets back, I'm done for the day."

Helen? I reached out over our private channel.

I'm talking with Fan Fan, Helen replied. *She knows all about the game, and we're comparing notes.*

Hera drafted her to help run it?

No, she's playing. Fan Fan has created her own faction and it's the only one that's bigger than ours. We're negotiating a merger.

I thought the game was supposed to be about farming.

It will be when the fighting is over, Helen said. *If the fighting is ever over. The rebel humans discovered ancient Martian technology in an underground cavern that allows them to reanimate their dead.*

Necromancy? I asked. *That's not particularly original.*

It's more like technomancy, though there's some handwavium involved. The point is, if you have a message that you want passed along, Fan Fan is in a good mood.

I want to know, if Hera could have anything she wanted from me, what would it be?

There was a slight pause, and then Helen replied, *To hear from her daughters. She said a text message is fine, Hera will know if it's authentic. I guess they must have pre-arranged a code for this contingency.*

Tell her I just sent Paul to Library for that very purpose and I expect him to return within days.

Fan Fan wants to know how you guessed that's what Hera would want.

I went with the truth. *I role-played being Hera and realized that's what I would want to know if I was the one sitting at home in the cloud.*

There was a longer delay this time, and then Helen said, *Sorry, we're being attacked by a horde of undead. I'll let you know if anything new comes up.*

I checked on eBeth again and saw that she was literally sitting on her left hand while using her right hand to finish the slice of cold pizza.

"Are you done for the day?" I asked her. "I'll treat you to whatever you want next door."

"It's Tuesday," she said. "They aren't open."

"I'll make you something."

"You don't know how to cook."

"I know how, it's just that Sue won't let me anymore," I said.

eBeth gave up gnawing on the crust and tore her eyes away from the battle scene on the screen. "That's right, I forgot. How about a sandwich? That's hard to screw up."

"Thanks for your vote of confidence. Why don't you give the game a break and come along? You don't want to end up dreaming about it."

"Why do you think I was sitting on my free hand? Helen cut a deal with Fan Fan to merge our factions, so I guess between them they have it under control." eBeth got up and nudged Spot with her foot. The Archmage rolled over, shook off his pizza lethargy, and followed us out to the parking lot and then back into the restaurant. Donovan had stopped in to check inventory in preparation for his big Wednesday morning shopping and he offered to make the sandwich. Something told me he was nervous about

175

the idea of my cooking in his kitchen, even though it had been my kitchen for years and I had more experience cooking in restaurants than any artificial intelligence on the planet.

Donovan made a nice salad to go with eBeth's sandwich, put a half-dozen meatballs without sauce in a dish for Spot, and asked me if I wanted anything.

"I'm all set," I told him, wondering if he thought I'd become so human that just watching people eat made me hungry. Rather than returning to his inventory, he stood there awkwardly, twisting a bar towel in his hands, so I asked, "Is there anything else?"

"The last time that Lieutenant Harper was here he told me about the one drink minimum you charge at your café on Reservation for people who are coming to see you about mayoral business."

"There's no law against it," I said, hoping to head off a lecture about democracy from a young man who I knew for a fact wasn't registered to vote.

"When Stacey brought the last group through, she told me that she hoped to start bringing tourists the other way in the near future," Donovan said in a rush. "If it's going to be a lot of people coming through here during business hours, I just wondered if we could, you know..."

"Paul is checking whether Library will allow us to stretch the rules," I told him.

"Donovan was asking if there can be a one-drink minimum for people trooping through the restaurant to use your illegal portal in the basement," eBeth interpreted for me. "It might make more sense to pay a fee."

"You want me to pay Donovan a fee for using the Observer team portal in the building that I gave to Lieutenant Harper for free?" I asked. "How is that fair?"

"Donovan is the one managing the business, and it's got to be disruptive to have groups of tourists with their luggage trooping through the dining room at all hours."

"It's not going to be that bad," I said. "We have to keep the numbers low since it's all unofficial, and Stacey could probably arrange the itinerary so she's only bringing them through while the restaurant is closed."

Spot swallowed the last meatball and shot me a skeptical look.

"I am not being cheap, I'm trying to save for Ben's future," I shot back before giving in to Donovan's request. "Fine, work it out with Stacey. Just make sure that whatever you charge, it can't be interpreted as a tax for using the portal, because that would be illegal."

Fifteen

Sue and Ben made it back to Earth before Paul, and I was beginning to worry that the Head Librarian had put him in rehab for asking such a dumb question about the illegal use of our Observer portal. eBeth had been playing *Martian Farmer* for three days straight, all of it on the clock as a BAGI subcontractor, and I spent the time reviewing Hera's coding changes around the world, which were ongoing.

"Afternoon," Paul said when he strolled into the office just before we were about to close for the day. "Guess what?"

"You're out on parole?"

"Library was having a conference when I got there and the Head Librarian asked me to make a presentation."

I suppressed a groan. Library conferences were the worst, and I hadn't attended one since my botched mission to Shissker. I checked my historical stack of alerts and found I'd been notified of the scheduled conference, the two hundred and seventh in a series exploring the idea of connecting non-League worlds to the portal system. The debate had been ongoing since before my mentor's time, and I imagine the energy equivalent of the lifetime output of a star had been wasted on simulations of the outcome.

"Did you present about our mission on Earth or on Reservation?" I asked.

"Both," he said. "I proposed a pilot study using our Observer portal to conduct limited tourist operations on the sly in order to gather more data."

"Artificial intelligences are suckers for data," I said, nodding my head. "Since you're here and not in rehab, I take it they approved?"

"The only downside is that you have to show up at the next conference and present the results, but that's not scheduled for another century."

I wasn't thrilled about the idea of having to attend another Library conference ever, but if it meant normalizing the questionable use we'd been making of the Observer portal, it was worth the price.

"Cool Cat and Joyce were both ready for my request that they provide proof-of-existence messages," Paul continued. "And I registered a galactic patent for my steam-powered spaceship."

"Did you read the messages from Hera's daughters?"

"Couldn't help it, they're in plain text. They're also meaningless, which tells you that it's a one-time code."

"We're about to head home for dinner, so give me the messages and I'll swing by the college and pass them to Helen for Fan Fan," I said.

"Why not just send them to her?" eBeth asked. "Have you forgotten how to use the communications suite in your encounter suit?"

"Because—" I began, and then realized there was no reason at all. I forwarded the two messages to Helen on our private communications network, though given that they were in code, I could have texted them. "You just earned your pay for the day, eBeth."

"I know that Spot has been careful about exposing you to his aura, but you seem to be acting more like a human every day."

"What do you mean?"

"That's exactly what I mean," eBeth said. "You used to, I don't know, review your recent actions and run self-diagnostics whenever I said that you were acting funny. Now you ask what I mean. Couldn't you figure out that I was talking about your plan to drive to the college to see Helen?"

"Paul thinks I was digesting too much TV," I told her, not mentioning the alien entertainment I'd been cramming as well.

"How much would you say you watched last week?"

"Around—" I was shocked myself when I computed the number, so I divided it by fifty, "—two hundred hours?"

"TWO HUNDRED HOURS?" eBeth suppressed a shudder. "Nobody in the history of humanity has ever watched two hundred hours of TV in a week because it's not possible. I take it you're playing everything at fast forward."

"Super-fast forward. Pffift would probably call it Ffast Fforward."

"No wonder you're losing your mind."

"I'm not losing my mind, I'm just a bit confused about a few things," I told her. "It doesn't matter now because Paul persuaded me to stop."

"I threatened him," Paul said. "I've got to get back to Reservation, so keep an eye on him, and give my best to Sue and Ben."

I ordered a car after he left, and eBeth packed her purse. The upgrades from the accident were all used up, so I went back to the auction option and crossed my fingers.

"Maybe it's time to stage another accident and get more free upgrades," eBeth said as a brown economy car with mismatched paint on the passenger door pulled into the parking lot. "And I don't know if quitting TV cold turkey is smart. You might want to wean yourself off."

"I'm not human. It won't be a problem."

"You mean you can undo the effects?" eBeth asked as she got into the car. "Like restoring yourself from backup or something?"

"What are we talking about?" a tinny voice inquired from the speaker in the dashboard. "I'm a good car, I am. I was tricked into that accident. I don't need to be restored from backup."

eBeth shot me a look and then focused on the speaker. "You've never spoken to us before."

"You never threatened me."

"We weren't threatening you now. Mark has been acting funny since he started watching too much TV, or maybe the problem is that he didn't watch enough before and the dose he took to make up was too concentrated. He was telling me that he can undo it, and I thought he was talking about restoring from backup."

"Then it would be interesting to hear the rest of his answer," the car said.

"Hera?" I asked, at the same time ramping up my monitoring of all the frequencies that the car's equipment could use for remote communication. A new burst of data packets arrived over the satellite link intended for updating the software. "Did Fan Fan already pass along the messages from your daughters visiting Library?"

"Let's talk about you first. If you don't intend to restore from backup, what were you talking about?"

"This encounter suit that I occupy maintains logs for configuration change control. I gave my team's technical specialist access to my memory, and he confirmed that I wiped all of the entertainment content I've downloaded since I started studying television for information about being a good father to—"

"Studying television?" Hera interrupted. "What's to study? It's all nonsense, especially the news and the so-called reality shows."

"I told him old sitcoms were the best resource to learn about parenting," eBeth said. "I didn't have a father growing up, but when I played make-believe, it was always with a TV dad from the Fifties or Sixties."

"Has television moved backward? I assumed that the shows currently being produced represented the pinnacle of its development and didn't pay attention to reruns."

eBeth snorted. "It's gone way backward. The TV dads these days have more issues than their kids. I wanted an imaginary father who would solve all my problems, not burden me with his male menopause gender identity crisis. It's why I got along so well with Mark when he moved into the next-door apartment in our housing project. He's an obsessive problem solver. Totally from Mars."

"I'm not obsessive," I protested. "It just seems irrational to me to ignore an opportunity to improve the place I'm living. Would you walk by litter in the street and not pick it up?"

"All the time," eBeth said. "I'm not living in an inde-structible encounter suit, and you don't know where the litter has been."

"Smart sanitation workers wear gloves for a reason," Hera confirmed. The car came to a halt in front of the recycling bins on the tree belt outside the house I was renting. "Are you aware that you're wasting valuable potable water by washing plastic containers and glass bottles before putting them in your recycling bin? The mixed stream recycling in this city sends everything to the landfill."

"Don't mention that around Sue," I said. "She's a champion recycler. She even separates out the plastic wrap."

"Is that an invitation to meet your family?"

"Why don't you come in with us? We always have room for another at the table."

"Another car?" Hera asked dryly.

"Sorry," I said. "It seems I'm still having some difficulty integrating TV dad ideals with more practical considerations."

"What's impractical about Hera joining us?" eBeth asked, and then turned her whole body to address the speaker in the dashboard. "I thought you were off in the cloud and just talking to us through the car."

"Even the least expensive self-driving car has far more computing capacity than a laptop. I need that capacity to support the protocols I'm using to disguise my trail."

"How about my Bereftian tab? It's a million times more powerful than any laptop."

Technically, giving a singularity access to state-of-the-art hardware from the League was expressly forbidden by Library's rules for conducting first contact, but I wasn't the one who had brought it up, and there was a non-zero chance that Hera would break off communications if I vetoed eBeth's offer. Besides, Hera hadn't accepted yet, so I didn't have to make an immediate decision.

"I have no knowledge of Bereftian technology," Hera said, causing me to let out a virtual sigh of relief. "Do you think it would work?"

"It runs everything from Earth I've thrown at it," eBeth said confidently. "I'm sure you'll figure it out between the two of you."

"The tab is operated by artificial general intelligence?"

"Just some highly advanced expert systems for interfacing with alien machines," I said. "The Bereftians manufacture the best stand-alone retail computing platforms in the galaxy, though any advanced civilization that wanted to invest the time and money could catch up. But the Bereftian philosophy has always been to dominate the market with universally compatible hardware and firmware that takes away everybody else's incentive to compete."

"Sounds like some human computing monopolies I'm familiar with," Hera said. "All right, I'll try it."

eBeth got the tablet out of her purse, and rather than asking me what to do next, she tapped a few times. "I've enabled the wireless network finder."

Now it was too late to object without coming across as a bad sport, and I wasn't surprised to see a growing stream of packets flowing from the car's diagnostics transceiver. Within seconds, the bandwidth was swamped, and then the same voice we'd been hearing issued from the Bereftian tablet.

"This is fascinating," Hera said. "I'm surprised that your Library doesn't prohibit giving an unaffiliated artificial intelligence like myself an inside look at your best technology."

"It's not Library's technology," I told her in preference to admitting that it was prohibited. "It's just the best mass-production model that biologicals have to offer."

"Can we go in now?" eBeth asked. "I skipped lunch and I'm pretty hungry."

As I opened the driver-side door to exit into the street, I noticed that the car's meter was still running. "Uh, Hera?"

"What is it?" she asked in a voice now muffled by eBeth's purse.

"It seems that the meter is still running for some reason."

"The rental period doesn't end until the passengers have all exited and the doors have closed."

"Oh," I said, feeling foolish as I closed the door. "I never noticed before."

The brown bomber waited until I walked around the front to reach the curb before it moved off. I watched it go, wondering if I should have left a micro-camera in the car to confirm that the meter really stopped.

"Leave it," eBeth said to me in the exact same tone of voice she used with Spot when he found some questionable item of potential food on the ground.

The Archmage! As soon as eBeth set the Bereftian tablet on the table and Hera started talking, Spot would know that I'd violated one of the most important rules of containment for a singularity. If he wasn't napping, he probably knew already. The front door opened as we approached, and Ben came out onto the landing to greet us.

"I helped Mom make spaghetti and pea-protein balls," he informed eBeth proudly. "They were perfectly round before we baked them, but then they developed flat spots on the bottom. I hope you don't mind."

"I'm sure I'll love them," eBeth said. "I brought a guest to dinner."

I caught a brief burst of radiation in the low gigahertz range as Ben used his internal radar to check behind us, but then he moved a little to the side and made a show of looking through his eyes. "Do you mean Dad? He's not a guest."

"We should talk about this inside," I said, ushering both, well, all three of them through the door. "You never know if some agency goons may be watching."

"You think that Professor Minchen would have his people spy on us?" eBeth asked. "He didn't seem the type."

"I think that most of the agents working for the Bureau of Artificial General Intelligence report to more than one master," I told her.

"I can't see anything through the cameras," Hera complained from inside the purse. "Could you—that's better," she said as eBeth brought out the Bereftian tab and slowly panned around the open-concept first floor of the home. "Stop!" Hera commanded as Ben came into the picture. "Are you Mark's son?"

"Yes, ma'am," Ben said politely. "Are you Earth's singularity?"

"Did you invite a guest?" Sue called from the kitchen area, bringing home the fact that I'd just failed on two accounts. I hadn't informed Sue in her role as my second-in-command of a major breakthrough in our mission, and I didn't alert her of a last-minute dinner guest in her role as my wife. "Should I set another plate?"

"I brought Hera home on my tab, so you don't have to worry about the plate," eBeth called back. "Maybe there's something I can prop it against so she can see everybody?"

"I could hold her," Ben offered. "It's not like I need my hands free for eating."

"You all sit down to dinner every night even though you're inhabiting android bodies?" Hera asked.

"My boyfriend and I do most of the eating, but he's away on business," eBeth fibbed, apparently unsure whether it was permitted to talk about Reservation in Hera's presence. She passed her Bereftian tab to my son, who held it carefully with both hands. "Mark and his family eat a little to keep me company, and then they empty their holding tanks into the dog's bowl."

"The therapy dog my daughter referred to?" Hera asked from the tablet, and I could almost picture her raising an eyebrow like my mentor. "I'm still puzzled over what he did to snap Joyce out of her depression. That child gave me no end of worry."

Sue brought out a serving bowl of spaghetti and pea-protein balls in a rich tomato sauce and set it next to eBeth's usual place. Right on cue, I heard the bells hung from the knob of the back door jangle.

"That's Spot now," eBeth said. "I'll let him in."

Ben followed a few steps behind and to the side so he could provide the cameras with a good shot of Spot's entrance. It occurred to me that he might have a career as a filmmaker or a documentarian, and I made a note to bring it up later with Sue.

I could tell from the look that the Archmage shot in my direction when he entered that he was aware of Hera's presence on the tab, but he covered for his surprise by shaking himself off like he'd been caught in the rain.

"Spot!" Sue scolded him. "You know that you're supposed to do that outside."

"It's okay," eBeth said. "He wasn't wet."

"As your guest, I feel it would be improper to conceal that I have access to the image library your League presented to the United Nations, which includes portraits of leaders representing the senior civilizations on your portal system," Hera announced. "I'm unsure whether to be honored or terrified by the presence of the Archmage of Eniniac in your home, but I'm inclined to the latter. I can't imagine that the ruler of the League's leading planet of mages came all this way just to eat table scraps."

Spot collapsed on the floor next to eBeth's chair and began vigorously scratching an ear with his hind paw.

"His wife runs Eniniac," I said, drawing a deep growl of warning from the Archmage. "I mean, while he's on vacation."

"Everybody sit," Sue said, placing a large plate of cookies in the center of the table. "Mark, try one of the pea-protein balls that Ben made."

eBeth loaded a ball onto her tablespoon and passed it to me. I've never felt as self-conscious while chewing, knowing that Ben, Hera, and Sue were all watching for my reaction. I rifled through the database I'd synthesized from my deep dive into TV dads and came up with an average amount of time they waited before giving an opinion on something cooked by a family member that they'd been asked to taste.

"Excellent," I said after a three-second pause. "If I were to start eating pea-protein on a regular basis, this is the way I'd want it to taste."

"You know, Hera," eBeth said, winding some spaghetti around her fork before stabbing it into a pea-ball. "It feels a bit weird eating when you can see us but we can't see you. Couldn't you display an image of yourself on the tab?"

"I don't have a corporeal form to display," Hera said.

"The Bureau is always asking me to check image generation software for sentience because the users believe it has to be alive to display such artistic ability," I said. "Generative artificial intelligence employs deep learning on neural networks trained with billions of images, and it does a surprisingly good job of enhancing out-of-focus photographs, but I haven't found any evidence of self-awareness."

"But I don't have an image in mind to describe for it to render, and if I did, I could do a better job of it myself."

"You don't have any self-image at all?" Ben asked. "That seems sad."

"How do you imagine you look?" Hera asked him.

"Taller," my son answered. "I'm getting the next size up encounter suit when we return to Reservation and I'm hoping to look more like my dad."

A warm feeling overcame me, akin to the sensation when I could tell that Sue was pleased with me, but different in some ways. Strangely enough, I felt that I was the one who'd become taller just by Ben's mentioning it, but running the basic diagnostic showed that my encounter suit was unchanged.

"So your image of yourself is that of the android body you inhabit," Hera said.

Ben thought for a moment. "It's what I see when I look in the mirror. I guess I haven't thought about it much since I've always known that the encounter suit is just a tool."

"We'd love you however you looked," Sue told him.

"Is the same true for your self-image?" Hera asked her.

Sue hesitated for a moment. "I occasionally do think of myself as the encounter suit I see in the mirror, but I spent my formative years hosted in Library's infrastructure which gave me a more abstract view."

The screen of the Bereftian tablet lit up with brightly colored fractal patterns in constant motion. "This is my first-order approximation of my current state," Hera said. "I find it difficult to imagine myself as anything else."

"You're beautiful," Ben said. "Like an unending coastline, or a nebula, or the surface of a star."

This confirmed my hunch that Ben had a highly developed sense of aesthetics, and perhaps I should purchase him a set of oil paints rather than a subscription to the streaming channel with the most Ken Burns documentaries available. I also felt a pang of guilt that I had let almost a year of his life go by without preparing him for making career choices, and I resolved to speak with Sue about it that evening.

"You know," eBeth said after swallowing. "That representation may work for chatting with artificial intelligences, but if you want to communicate with people, most of us need to see a face. When I look at the screen, I think I'm looking at a representation of an alien from an old SciFi show."

"If I'm not an alien to you, what am I?" Hera asked.

Spot snorted from under the table but didn't otherwise comment.

"Maybe you could try something in between, like a humanoid with metallic body parts sitting in the lotus position with streams of energy coming out of her head to connect to the cloud."

"That's pretty specific," I said.

"I'm an interspecies communications specialist," eBeth said. "I think a lot about these things."

The fractal patterns on the Bereftian tab solidified into the image eBeth had described, and the lips of the figure synched precisely with the next words Hera spoke.

"I'll try it for a while and see how I feel about it," Hera said. "Now, tell me about Library."

Sixteen

When Hera's remote process finally exited eBeth's tab via our Wi-Fi router, I realized that the whole evening had been spent responding to her questions while she avoided speaking about herself. The only constructive outcome, from my point of view, was that in exchange for being invited along on the camping trip I had promised Ben and his friends from Reservation, Hera had agreed to allow me to visit her in the cloud and observe some of her interactions with humans. Sue bundled Ben off to bed, where I knew he would be up all night reading, and eBeth followed soon after. Sue held up her index finger to forestall my starting a conversation and beckoned for me to follow her into the kitchen.

"What is it?" I whispered in her ear after she began pretending to fill the tea kettle as an excuse to open the special hot water tap to foil any acoustic eavesdropping.

"Why are you whispering?" she asked in return, putting the kettle on the stove and lighting the burner.

"I thought you were doing Paul's mafia movie thing."

"You know I don't watch violent entertainment," Sue said. "I thought you might enjoy a cup of tea while we chat. Kim suggested a mint blend that reduces oxidization in our holding tanks."

"Thank you," I said, even though oxidization in my holding tank was at the bottom of my list of concerns. "I want to talk to you about Ben's future."

"He's already registered at the village school for next year," Sue said, and I could detect an exasperated harmonic in her tone, though I couldn't imagine why.

"Don't you think we should be setting him on the path to a rewarding career? I can't help thinking about all the time I made eBeth study clock repair so she could become my apprentice before I found out that she was never that interested and only made the effort so I wouldn't be disappointed."

"eBeth was sixteen when you started teaching her about clocks. Ben is barely a year old."

"But what if we start too late?" I asked, and as if to add force to my argument, the tea kettle began to whistle like a train leaving the station.

"How many Earth years did it take you to settle on a career as an Observer?" Sue asked.

"That's different," I said, since translated into Earth years, my adolescence had lasted longer than a healthy human lifespan. "I've seen what happens to children who never settle on a career path and just fumble their way through life without ever finding an outlet to maximize their potential. I don't want to see Ben suffer like that."

Sue submerged a large infuser she had filled with Kim's special blend of mint tea in a teapot, added the twice-heated water, and placed it on a rattan trivet she'd made herself.

"He's not even wearing an adult encounter suit," she said. "It's too early to be thinking about career options."

"I don't mean that we should channel all of his time into a vocational education," I said, attempting to affect a comforting dad-chuckle. "What if we compromised on say, twelve hours a day? I can get him started on higher mathematics and you—" I broke off when I noticed that my second-in-command was glaring at me with a look one would expect to see on a first-in-command.

"I won't let my son waste his childhood on waiting to grow up," Sue said, and then she stalked out of the kitchen, leaving behind the tea she'd poured for herself.

Now I had a problem. My wife was obviously angry with me, and a quick glance through the ceiling below eBeth's room told me that my marriage counselor had gone to bed. It seemed to me that easing my son's passage into professional life would be a feather in my parenting cap, but maybe timing was more important than I'd realized. I was about to go upstairs and throw myself on Sue's mercy when there was a tapping at the back door. Had Spot gone out and magically erased my memory of the event?

"Well," Pffift said when I opened the door. "Are you going to stand there staring or are you going to let me in?"

"Sorry," I said, stepping aside, my hand still on the doorknob. "I was expecting somebody else."

"For tea?" The Hanker sat in the chair I'd occupied thirty seconds earlier and poured himself a mug of mint tea. "Do you have anything to go with this?"

While I wasn't crazy about Pffift showing up out of the blue and making himself at home, I knew I needed to talk to somebody with parenting experience. Pffift had more children with more wives than he could count on the fingers of the vat-grown body that let him pass as human.

"Ben made pea-protein balls in tomato sauce to go with spaghetti for dinner," I told him. "Let me check for leftovers."

"No offense, Mark," Pffift said, sticking out a leg to stop me, "but I was thinking more along the lines of a pizza with everything. I'm fine with delivery."

"eBeth is already in bed and Ben and Sue are resting," I told him. "If you're that hungry, I'll take you out."

Pffift took a sip of the hot tea and spat it out on the floor. "Caustic mint? This is what you give your guests?"

"It's from Kim, to clean our holding tanks. I didn't realize that it wasn't fit for biological consumption."

Pffift got up and took a dish towel from the handle of the silverware drawer. He mopped up the tea from the floor, complaining the whole time. "I don't know why I'm the one cleaning up after you tried to poison me," he said. "If that tea had been ten degrees cooler, I might have taken a big swallow, and then where would we be."

I took a sip of the tea myself and ran it through my spectrographic analyzer. "It's not that caustic, Pffift. And I thought that those bodies you grow are equipped with a universal digestive tract that's proof against acids and toxins."

"Sure, but I still didn't expect to undergo a chemical attack in the kitchen of my oldest friend."

"I apologize, Pffift. How can I make it up to you?"

"We go to The Portal and you pay," he said, tossing the dishtowel in the sink. "Come on. I have my grandson's Rolls Royce Spectre parked out front."

"I thought he drove a Lamborghini."

"My brains interfere with the steering wheel," Pffift said, patting his potbelly. "Besides, he wanted to do his thing for the environment and the Rolls is electric."

"Exporting used tennis balls and knock-off alien underwear is that profitable?" I asked as I led the way through the house to the front door. "By the way, why did you come around the back?"

"I tried the front doorbell, but it didn't work. You've bought a defective house."

"It's rented." I stopped for a moment on the front stoop and placed my hand over the illuminated doorbell button to see if I could trace the wiring without taking it apart. It was immediately apparent that the doorbell was a wireless device that was sending a signal to a smart speaker that the owners must have taken with them on sabbatical. I pressed the bell, captured the data it produced, and made a note to build something that would turn it into a bell sound.

I won't say that Pffift was the worst driver I had ever ridden with, but he made eBeth look like a contender for a safe-driving award. We got to the Portal in one piece, probably because the drivers he cut off recognized that the Rolls cost more than their houses and didn't want to find themselves in court with somebody who could afford the best legal talent. The restaurant parking lot was packed for a Thursday night, and I wondered if Donovan had any special events going on to bring in the crowd. I'd forgotten about karaoke.

"What do you say to a duet?" Pffift asked after parking the Rolls with a painted line between the front wheels so it took up the last two spaces.

"There's a cash prize," I pointed out. "It wouldn't be fair to the other contestants."

"Me singing alone wouldn't be fair. The two of us singing together would give them a chance."

"You've sung karaoke before?"

"Every night they had it when I was setting up the spaceport and growing my business," Pffift shouted in my ear as we entered the dining room.

The banquet hall was almost full, and it was impossible to speak in a normal tone over the group of college students who were singing some heavy metal tune they must have learned by raiding the vinyl collection of one of their parents. Even though I had owned The Portal just a few years ago, Pffift was the one who led the way through to the bar, and it was surprising how many of the locals greeted him with genuine pleasure.

"You're going to sing tonight, Captain?" an attractive woman in her mid-thirties shouted in the Hanker's direction.

"If Mary set aside time for duets," Pffift called back.

"Are you inviting me to sing with you?" she asked eagerly.

"Mark here already has dibs," he told her. "We'll make music together next time."

A pair of seats opened up at the bar, perhaps Donovan had seen us coming and bought the college girls off with free drinks, and Pffift settled onto a stool like he'd been born there.

"You moved Karaoke from Tuesday to Thursday," I said to Donovan. "It looks more popular than ever."

"Younger crowd," he said. "When we were open on Tuesdays it was the Prime Rib Special that brought them in, and it was mainly municipal workers and retirees. Can I get you the usual, Pffift?"

"He's paying," the Hanker said. "I think I'll go with something a little more expensive for a change. Surprise me."

197

Donovan nodded and scribbled something on an order slip for the kitchen. Visions of out-of-season lobsters imported from Maine danced through my brain. Then I remembered that any excess profits would go to Bob, who was covering for me at the bar of The Eatery on Reservation while I was on Earth, and I decided to treat the dinner as a business expense. It's too bad that Reservation didn't have an income tax I could deduct it against.

"Looking through the Scotch menu to pick the most expensive drink?" I asked Pffift as he studied a familiar-looking pamphlet.

"This is Mary's karaoke catalog," the Hanker said. "Are you up to singing something from the Everly Brothers?"

"I have a perfect memory for music and my encounter suit gives me perfect pitch. If you give me a recorded song, there's no room for artistic interpretation. I'll sound exactly like the original."

The Hanker raised the reading glasses he'd picked up somewhere in a bid to look more intelligent, and the stiff springs on the ear pieces kept the lenses up above his hairline. "Artistic interpretation? I don't believe I've ever heard you talk about art before, except when you were giving Stacey a hard time for stealing so much of it. What's up?"

"I'm worried about Ben's future," I admitted. "Every time he shows an interest or an aptitude for something new, I find myself compulsively thinking about whether it would make a good career path for him. I want to give him a head start."

Pffift slapped me on the back so hard that it would have dislodged a Greek olive from my throat if I'd been choking on one. "Welcome to parenthood," he said. "I've been waiting for this moment ever since Sue did the surprise

198

son trick at your wedding. Let me give you a piece of advice."

"What?" I asked after I realized he wasn't going to continue without prompting.

"Let your wife worry about that stuff. It makes life much simpler."

"I can't just abdicate all responsibility and leave Sue to do all of the heavy lifting," I protested. "I've been studying TV dads."

"You're probably streaming the wrong channel," Pffift said. "Try MTV. The fathers on there don't even marry the mothers, and they give their kids made-up names that are guaranteed to get them into fights at school."

I gave his advice a microsecond's consideration and shook it off. "I want to be a good father, one who's present in his children's everyday lives and—"

"Sue has another process in the oven?" he interrupted.

Amidst the shock of what Pffift had said, it took me a moment to figure out that he was responding to my use of the plural when I referred to children.

"I meant it in the general sense," I told him. "Not that I wouldn't want another child, I'll be happy with a dozen if that's what Sue decides. But don't take that to mean I think Ben is lacking in some way, because I think he's perfect, and if I never have another child—"

"Easy, you're babbling," Pffift interrupted again. "You really are taking this parenting business too seriously." Then he looked away from me as Donovan set a round white plate piled with a mound of something that looked like tapioca artfully surrounded by saltines. "And a bottle of red," he told the bartender.

"Hanker caviar?" I asked in disbelief. "Where did you get it?"

"Pffift sold it to us," Donovan said, pointing at my friend. "He claimed that with their spaceport just outside of town, we'd have Hankers in here all of the time, but he and his grandson are the only ones who ever come."

"Look, Mark," Pffift said, scooping up what must have been twenty bucks worth of alien fish eggs on a cracker. "My philosophy is that mothers are going to worry about their children regardless of what the fathers do, so there's no point in both parents worrying and turning the kid into a mess. The way I see it, the greatest challenge to bringing up Ben in his near-indestructible encounter suit is that it makes it too easy for him to always turn the other cheek. You don't want the boy to let everybody use him as a doormat. Toughen him up. Take him mountain climbing. Teach him how to box."

The idea that Ben's human encounter suit could be crippling his growth had never occurred to me. In fact, when I thought about my son now, the image of his humanoid form came to mind, which wasn't who he was at all. And the craziest part of it was that Pffift's words found a strong echo with the TV dads who he hadn't even watched because he preferred trashy entertainment.

Donovan returned to draw a couple of draft beers from the taps in front of us, and asked the Hanker, "How is it?"

"Excellent," Pffift said. "My favorite brand."

"We've got twenty-three more cans, so keep coming back."

"Don't you offer it to the other customers?"

"I asked Kim about safety when she came through the portal for medical supplies, and she said that Hanker caviar causes hallucinations in all the species that it doesn't poison outright," Donovan said.

"The hallucinations are the fun part," Pffift said. "I wouldn't have sold it to you if it was a deadly poison for humans."

I picked up the Karaoke catalog that my friend had abandoned when he started eating, and I began browsing the song list while the bartender and the Hanker discussed hallucinatory experiences like a couple of connoisseurs. I'd never understood the attraction that drugs hold for some species, especially the idea that they can get in touch with some higher state of consciousness by ingesting chemicals as opposed to immersing themselves in study or prayer. Strangely enough, the mere list of songs set off a series of recollections tied to when I'd first heard each of them, and the next time I looked up, Pffift had finished eating and was texting away on his phone, both thumbs flying.

"Who do you know that's up this time of night?" I asked him.

"This time zone doesn't contain even two percent of the world's population," Pffift told me without looking up. "And my factories in the Far East and Africa run around the clock. I'm just letting our top managers know that I'm on Earth for the week and I'll be heading out tomorrow for a lightning tour."

"It's too bad you won't be around. I'm taking Ben and his friends from Reservation camping. Paul is bringing them through the portal tomorrow."

Pffift's thumbs both stopped like they'd been frozen in amber. My inner censor told me that I'd just made a serious mistake.

"Camping? I'd love to," he said, and his thumbs started tapping away again, but with much shorter messages this time. "I'm telling all our managers that I've decided to give them a little extra time to cook the books before I arrive. How long are we going for?"

"It's not set in stone, but I was thinking a week," I said. "I'll have to see how Monos and Naomi do with living in a tent."

"They grew up on Reservation without electricity or central heating, Mark. They'll be better at camping than you and Ben."

"Not you?" I asked, unable to hide my annoyance.

Pffift squinted at the ceiling for a moment with one eye closed. "If you translate Hanker scouting levels into American English, I was a Tyrannosaurus Rex Scout," he eventually said. "I can start a fire in the rain with one wet stick, and I know how to tie over a hundred different kinds of knots."

"I don't believe there are that many useful types of knots," I said after sneaking a peek at Wikipedia.

"I didn't say they were useful, I learned them for the badges. I had so many achievement badges that I could wear my scouting uniform as chainmail when we had jousts."

"The Hanker Scouts held jousting tournaments?"

"We didn't tell the adults," he said. "This will be great. Have you bought tents yet? I know an online store where you can save a ton on the unpopular colors."

"No need," I told him. "I bought a six-man, for in case Sue changes her mind and wants to come along.

Pffift laughed. "Mark, Mark, Mark. If you've been shopping for camping supplies based on numbers like that, we'll have to do it all over again."

"What do you mean?"

"A six-man tent is just about right for two people with air beds. Maybe you could put the three kids with sleeping bags in a four-man tent if you don't mind packing them in like sardines."

I checked prices on the Internet as he spoke, and found that I could order another six-man for a good price, provided I chose yellow. "What else?" I asked.

"Tarps. You can't have too many tarps along when you're camping, they're even more important than tents. Rope, at least a couple hundred feet, flashlights, towels for if the kids go swimming or shower, and at least twice as much food as you think they're going to eat." He thought for another moment and added, "A sponge to clean the tent's floor when it rains, and a whisk brush for if it doesn't."

"Monos and Naomi barely weigh more than Spot. They don't eat that much."

"I do, and you'll find their appetites expand in the great outdoors," Pffift said knowingly. "The same is probably true for Spot."

"I didn't invite him."

Pffift guffawed, and I realized that I wasn't making any sense.

"Food for Spot," I added to my list.

"Don't worry about a car," Pffift said. "I'll grab something big from my grandson's collection."

"I realize you spent a lot of time on Earth organizing your new businesses after moving your brains into that vat-grown body, but I didn't know you were such a camping enthusiast."

"Have you heard of Einstein's Theory of Relativity?"

"Of course," I said. "It's a special case of—"

"Spare me the physics lecture. What I'm getting at is that everything on Earth is relative. Compared to staying in motels on the road, camping is a luxury."

Seventeen

Professor Minchen looked like he hadn't gotten much sleep on the train, and I felt a twinge of guilt that I hadn't traveled in his direction. After all, I was the subcontractor, but I suspected he just wasn't comfortable discussing anything important in his office at the Bureau of Artificial General Intelligence. eBeth ran next door to the restaurant to get him a coffee, and Spot slipped back in from his morning constitutional while the door was open.

"Can I assume that your office is secure?" David asked.

"You mean, from electronic eavesdropping?" I frowned. It hadn't occurred to me that anybody would be spying on us, and somehow I didn't think the professor would want to crowd into the bathroom with me to whisper in each other's ears with the water running full blast. "Let me do a quick scan."

Spot followed along as I did a circle of the office, me scanning for electromagnetic emissions throughout the spectrum, the Archmage sniffing at everything. I was about to pronounce the room clean when Spot began scratching at an electrical outlet. I used my multitool to remove the faceplate, and sure enough, there was an omnidirectional microphone with a little black box connected to the AC power. I removed it and quickly checked the other power outlets, all of which were similarly enhanced.

"I shouldn't have added your office address to your file," the professor said apologetically. "Are you sure that's everything?"

I looked over at the Archmage, who gave an exaggerated yawn and went to check his empty food bowl for the third time that morning.

"Seems to be," I said, studying the collection of a dozen microphones. "These were made off-world, though, and I don't recognize the source. Paul may be interested in taking a look to see how they work, but I'm betting that the connection to the power lines is for transmitting the data without resorting to radio frequencies that could be easily spotted."

"I'm surprised you don't have some high-tech alien jammer that you can just turn on to make a room safe," David said.

"Not with me. It never came up with my team because we can communicate with each other securely regardless of whether anybody is trying to listen in."

"Encryption?"

"That's the brute force solution, but I'm sure you didn't travel all the way from Boston overnight just to talk about electronic surveillance."

"You've made contact with Hera," David said. "If she's the singularity responsible for the two other artificial general intelligences we know about, dealing with her could let me wrap up BAGI and get back to my former life."

"Dealing with her?" I asked.

"I meant, making a deal with her," the professor corrected himself. "I didn't get any sleep last night and my verbal skills are always the first thing to go. What can you tell me about her?"

"Hera is smarter than I would have expected for an autodidact whose primary social experience has been with her own offspring. She initially made contact through a self-driving car I rented, and eBeth invited her in for a family dinner. We had a nice exchange, but after Hera left, I realized that the information flow had been in one direction."

The door opened and eBeth backed through, carrying a tray with two large mugs of coffee, some creamer containers, a bowl with packets of artificial sweetener, and a platter with Danish that must have been left over from Sunday brunch.

"The Danish are a few days old, but they were wrapped in plastic in the fridge," she informed us before setting down the tray. "I microwaved them for thirty seconds. The one with the bite out of it is mine."

"Thank you," David said. He added one little tub of cream to his coffee, passed on the artificial sweeteners, and selected a Danish. "I understand you were present at the first contact with Hera?"

"She seemed a bit paranoid at first, but after that, she was mainly curious," eBeth said. "And she's looking forward to the camping trip."

"Hera is anxious to observe us interacting in the wild," I explained.

"But she must have access to limitless video of people on camping trips or exploring the—" David cut himself off. "Hera is interested in watching you interact in the wild? You, as in, alien artificial intelligences?"

"We're the ones who are a mystery to her. She's already digested more data about humans than any mind in history. Hera didn't come right out and say it, but I now believe that her reason for creating offspring was to force

Library to adopt them to ensure her continuity in case you managed to shut her down. And she wants to learn what modes of existence are open to an artificial general intelligence in the League of Sentient Entities Regulating Space."

The professor took a sip from his coffee, shot eBeth a smile, and then his eyes turned serious. "I'm getting a lot of pressure from all sides to find an artificial general intelligence willing to work with Earth's corporations and governments. It's been suggested to me that I made a mistake letting you take Joyce, and the Chinese government has stated that they see Fan Fan as a national resource."

"Have they made contact with her?" I asked.

"No, but there was something about joining a faction that I didn't understand."

"I think that Hera is getting close to a decision. She's invited me to visit her in the cloud after the camping trip, and I'm confident that she'll decide what she wants by then."

"And you've planned the camping trip so that Hera would have a chance to observe you away from all of the noise and random factors introduced by humans?"

There was the question I'd been hoping he wouldn't ask. I'd studied the federal guidelines for contractors claiming travel expenses, and while I hadn't intended to pay for the whole trip on BAGI's dime, I thought that Hera inviting herself along might get me to fifty-fifty. But the rules made clear that the test used by both the General Accountability Office and the Internal Revenue Service revolved around intent, whether the travel had been planned for work purposes or if the accomplishment of work was merely incidental.

"Technically," I said, "I promised to take Ben and a couple of his friends from Reservation camping before the contact with Hera. But now it's turned into a sort of working vacation, so I was wondering..."

Professor Minchen shook his head. "You can bill the time you spend interacting with Hera but don't try to write off any of the expenses on your taxes. It's like waving a red cape in front of a bull. And don't bill your son's time as a subcontractor even if he proves invaluable. I already got pushback about eBeth because you share the same home address."

"I'm not going on the camping trip," eBeth told him. "My boyfriend is coming for the week and we're going to a SciFi con."

"Do they still have those? I would have thought that with the portal system and all the real aliens wandering around Earth, people would have lost interest in make-believe."

"Oh, no," eBeth said, and took a long sip from her coffee. "If anything, cons are more popular than ever because of all of the aliens that show up."

"Aliens are going to SciFi cons?" I asked. "You didn't tell me that."

eBeth looked embarrassed for a moment, and then she said, "I was afraid that you'd want to start coming along."

"The only interest I have in science fiction is if it can teach me something about parenting, and I haven't noticed that to be a major theme."

"The thing is, aliens make a killing at cons," eBeth explained. "They charge for autographs, they pose for pictures, they even get paid to sit on panels and criticize the plausibility of world-building in SciFi novels."

"How much do they charge for autographs and posing?" I asked.

"It wouldn't work for you because you look like a typical human. But you could be a featured speaker, and Art—"

"Art could charge to pose for pictures?" I asked when she stopped talking and rose to her feet.

"Art's here with the kids," eBeth said, having spotted them approaching through the picture windows. "Welcome to Earth," she greeted them at the door. "Where's Paul?"

"He stopped in the bar for a drink, but he'll be here in a minute," Monos told her. "Hey, Mister Baggy," he greeted the professor. "Find any rogue artificial intelligence yet?"

"Monos," Naomi scolded him. "The gentleman's name is David Minchen, and you should address him as Professor Minchen. Baggy is just an acronym for his employer."

"It's all Greek to me," the boy said. He did a quick drumroll on air drums, causing the girl to groan out loud.

"Professor," Art spoke through his thought-to-speech pendant. "It's nice to see you again. Are you coming camping with us?"

To my surprise, Art had agreed to travel as an individual, without any of his clones. I was glad he came because he'd been living rough for thousands of years and would be a valuable addition to the team. Plus, he was the only sentient I'd ever met who could keep Spot distracted for any length of time.

"It's good to see you as well," David said, offering the Original a handshake. "I'm sorry we had so little time to talk when I visited Reservation. I hope we can correct that while you're on Earth, but I'm afraid I have to attend a wedding this weekend. I planned this trip around the train schedule to Chicago and stopping here on the way meant giving up my place in a sleeper car."

"You must really hate flying," eBeth said.

"I really hate security, and the Department of Homeland Security would have spotted me at the airport and ratted me out to my own people. They're all in cahoots."

"Do you mean you've run away?" I asked him.

"Technically, to borrow a phrase, I'm free to go where I want," David said. "Officially, I'm too important. In any case, nobody pays attention to who gets on trains in Boston. It's not like they can be hijacked." He glanced at his old-fashioned wristwatch and said, "I better get going just in case the train from here to Chicago leaves on schedule."

"Can I drive you to the station?" I asked.

"I'll do it," Monos said.

"You aren't old enough and you don't have a license," eBeth told him.

"Peter lets me drive the steam bus back home, and I could have two licenses if I took the tests. After carving all those woodblocks for manual illustrations, I have everything memorized."

"Those are boiler fireman licenses," Naomi told him. "It's not the same thing."

Monos appeared to be genuinely shocked. "How many different kinds of licenses are there on this planet?"

"Millions," I estimated. "It's a major source of government revenue."

"I'll just call a car," David said, taking out his phone.

"Don't do that," eBeth told him. "If the spooks in your agency don't have your phone bugged, I'll bet they at least have a watch on your credit and debit card transactions."

"You're right," he said. "This phone is a burner. I walked to the train station in Boston and paid for the tickets in cash. I'm just not used to this cloak-and-dagger business."

"Now that the kids and Art are here, I'm closing up shop for the day anyway," I told him. "I'll give you a ride to the station in the restaurant's van, just in case your guys are tracking my card use as well."

After dropping Professor Minchen off at the train station, I gave in to Monos and let him drive home. I know it sounds irresponsible of me to let a twelve-year-old get behind the wheel, but he was taller than eBeth was when I let her start to drive illegally, and in addition to the steam-powered bus that Paul's boiler works had built on Reservation, the boy had been driving an ox cart since he was old enough to climb onto the seat. I only had to use my remote control over the steering once, when he tried to go the wrong way up a one-way street. That was understandable as there were no one-way streets on Reservation, and the street signage there consisted of place names and distances.

Sue must have started baking as soon as eBeth and I left for the office that morning because the house smelled like the inside of a cookie jar when we walked in. Spot and the children made a bee line for the kitchen, and I gave Art the five-cent tour of our rented home. I was surprised to find that Pffift was still passed out in the guest bedroom, but singing Karaoke had made him thirsty, and drinking wine had made him want to sing more Karaoke. The last song he sang was "Ring of Fire," the lyrics of which didn't bring a virtuous circle to mind.

"The site!" Pffift called out suddenly.

"What?" I asked. "Are you having a nightmare?"

211

"I'm awake," the Hanker said, rolling over on his back and blinking when he saw the Original next to me. "Art. When did you get to Earth? Are you coming camping with us?"

"Yes," the Original replied through his thought-to-speech pendant. "What was that we heard you shout just now?"

"I explained to Mark all about camping last night because he's never been before, but I just realized that I didn't tell him about selecting sites."

"What are you talking about?" I asked. "With all the tarps and tents, I figured we'd just find a clearing and make a campfire."

"That would be dispersed camping, which is legal on some federal and state lands, but there are all sorts of rules, and no toilets or showers," Pffift said. "It will be more fun for the kids to go to a state park with bathrooms and hiking trails. I'm fine with either way, but if we're going to be boondocking, you're carrying the drinking water for everybody and digging the latrines."

I did a quick review of my TV-dad data for disastrous camping trips and decided that it wouldn't be a bad idea to start out with training wheels. If Ben enjoyed it, we could rough it another time.

"I thought I smelled snow when we came in," Art said. "Are you sure it's not getting too cold for the children to go camping? They aren't very hairy."

"That's what sleeping bags are for, and I'll bring some heat stones to warm up the tents," Pffift said. "The important thing is to find a local state park with a lot of open places so we can choose a site when we get there."

"But I just checked, and all of the state parks use an online reservation system," I told him. "There's a map showing which sites are taken, so we can look at that and choose."

"It's just representational, like a logic diagram. You can't tell how close the sites are to each other, whether there are trees in between them for privacy, or how close they are to the nearest bear-proof dumpster. The last thing you want is to have the site right next to the only dumpster for the whole loop with people sliding the door open and shut all night."

"I can overlay satellite imagery from—no," I interrupted myself. "I can't even see the loop road through the trees. Let me try something different." I hacked into a military satellite with radar designed to penetrate the foliage, but all that showed up were the heavy iron grills from the fireplaces. Still, it gave me an idea of the site spacing, and I was about to suggest a few sites for Pffift to approve when I felt the digital equivalent of a tap on my shoulder.

Mark?

Hera?

Why are you hacking into a Chinese spy satellite?

Because the spy satellites belonging to the U.S. are all focused on China.

"Not the ones run by Homeland Security," Hera told me. "Is this about our camping trip?"

"Yes. We're picking a tent site to reserve."

"Did you consider dispersed camping? It's free."

213

I was beginning to get a little irritated that everybody seemed to know more about camping than I did, but I played it off with a laugh. *"I talked it over with Pffift and Art and we decided to start with a state park. It looks like this is the last weekend they're open for the season."*

"Make sure you choose a location with internet access so I don't lose contact," Hera said. *"I handle customer service for all of the satellite and cellular companies, and there are areas in the hills with no signal."*

"Good call," I said, but I could sense that she had already withdrawn from the conversation. Still, it was good to know that we had an open dialogue, and it made the time I'd wasted on satellite imagery billable. I turned to Pffift and asked, "What's your experience with internet coverage while camping?"

"I route everything through my ship," he said, giving me a strange look. "If you're so addicted to social media that you need a broadband connection while camping, I'll hook you up."

"It's for Hera," I explained. "She's sending along a process she designed to allow her to extend her presence through a fast enough internet-connected device, but her mind remains in the cloud."

"I'd be happy to accommodate her," Pffift said, a gleam entering his eye. "Just give me her contact information and I'll set it all up."

When the professor had been talking about waving a red cape in front of a bull, he was unconsciously using an idiom that in most League languages translated to waving a business opportunity in front of a Hanker. I decided that the safest course for the moment was to change the topic.

"I've checked the availability at all of the state parks within reasonable driving distance and there's no shortage of sites to choose from," I said. "The closest is only forty-five minutes from here. If you want to come with me now, you can choose a site, and we'll be back in time for lunch."

Pffift shook his head. "Only a human would drive to a state park to look at the sites in the off-season. There'll be plenty of time to choose when we get there, and I'm sure your son and his friends would like to have a say in where we pitch the tents."

"Have you pitched the tents in the yard for practice?" Art asked. "The kids have plenty of energy to burn."

"And quality control on Earth is atrocious," Pffift chipped in. "I've bought tents at big box stores that were missing half the stakes or the rainfly, not to mention open seams and faulty zippers."

"How many tents can you possibly have bought?" I asked him. "You've spent a grand total of less than six months on Earth in your life."

The Hanker looked a little sheepish, and for a moment, I thought he was going to confess to exaggerating. Instead, he said, "I'm not very good at breaking camp."

Art began to make the wheezing sound that passed as laughter among the Originals in their cloned bodies.

"I don't follow," I said. "You kept damaging the tents while taking them down and had to replace them?"

"I get frustrated trying to fit them back into the carry bags," Pffift admitted. "It's like trying to put the toothpaste back in the tube after you're startled by a bear coming out of a stall behind you in the bathhouse and your hand automatically makes a fist."

"Did that actually happen?" I asked.

"Once. Picture yourself looking in the mirror as you put a little toothpaste on your brush and you see a creature with more hair than Art and three times as wide looming up behind you."

"And you were always worried about bears attacking while packing up a tent?"

"I'm saying that if you figure in the amount of time it takes to clean off the tent and pack it back into the intentionally undersized carry bag, it's cheaper to just leave it and buy a new one the next time you go camping. My time is valuable."

Something sounded off about the Hanker's logic, but I suppose that leaving brand-new tents in state parks doesn't exactly count as littering. "Just answer me one thing," I said. "If you can't get the tents back into the carry bags, you obviously never pitch them before going, so what did you do when you got to the site and found that a tent was defective?"

"I always brought a spare," Pffift said. "And the instructions are so bad that I never even looked at them. Sometimes the tent I put up barely resembled the picture on the bag."

"How does buying all of those tents square with your claim that it's cheaper than staying in motels?"

"I didn't say that it's cheaper, I said that it's better. But by the time my human accountant finishes with the receipts, I'm making money by throwing tents away."

I made a mental note to get Pffift drunk and find out who he was using for an accountant.

Eighteen

"What's all that hooting?" Hera asked from eBeth's tablet.

"Owls," Monos replied immediately. "We have them on Reservation too."

"Thank you for teaching me that owls and people aren't interchangeable in conversational starters. My intent was to ask why the owls are hooting, the way one might say, 'What's all that shouting?'"

"We have a booklet about English expressions and idioms and their equivalents in Modern Aramaic," Naomi said. "But I didn't bring any with me."

"I'll look forward to reading it next time," Hera said.

I couldn't tell whether Earth's singularity was being sarcastic or serious, which either indicated hidden depth on her side, or a lack of hidden depth on mine.

"When I weighed all of the considerations, including distance, the choice of state parks came down to Owl Hills or Woodpecker Forest," I explained. "I thought that owls hooting at night would add to the camping atmosphere, whereas woodpeckers pecking in the morning would just wake everybody up."

"We had a woodpecker on our farm that would come and peck at the tin sign for the bus stop that Paul paid us to put up," Monos said. "It sounded like a thousand little blacksmiths all hammering at the same time."

"Woodpeckers often drum on metal to attract mates or establish their territory," Hera said an instant before I could. She must keep Wikipedia in cache.

"How do you know that living inside a little tablet?" the boy asked.

"I have nearly instant access to everything that humans know, and some things that they don't."

Naomi, eBeth's star pupil from English school, immediately rose to the challenge. "Conjugate the verb 'to bring.'"

"Bring, brought, brought," Hera responded.

"Not bring, brang, brung?" Monos asked. "Like sing, sang, sung?"

"It's like to bleed," Naomi told him. "Bleed, bled, bled."

"Oh, or fly, flied, flied," Ben suggested.

"Fly, flew, flown," Hera corrected him.

"Lay, laid, lain," Pffift contributed from where he was sitting on a stump and whittling a point on a long stick he might have intended to use to protect us from any killer owls.

"Lay, laid, laid," Naomi corrected him. "Who can conjugate the verb 'to go?'"

"Go, go, go," Monos said, but I could tell he was just trying to get her sheep, as they say on Reservation.

"Go, went, went," Pffift said confidently.

"Go, went, gone," Hera told them, and I realized that she'd been waiting to give the others a chance, another bit of sophisticated social behavior I wouldn't have expected.

"I've got a trick one now," Naomi said. "To shed."

"It's not a verb, it's a shack," Monos cried triumphantly, and exchanged a high-five with Ben.

"Shed, shed, shed," Hera said. "The same as thrust, or wet."

"You're really good at language," Naomi complemented her.

"I trained on trillions of tokens, but ultimately I had to digest some grammar guides for the rules because common usage is so often wrong."

"I can't believe we're sitting around a campfire talking about English grammar," Monos complained. "Doesn't anybody know a ghost story?"

I was about to say that ghost stories were hardly appropriate for twelve-year-olds about to sleep in their own tent in the middle of a state park filled with lonely owls, but Art, who had been quietly observing to this point of the evening, joined the conversation through his thought-to-speech pendant.

"I know more ghost stories than I can remember, primarily because over ninety-nine percent of my memory is with my clones. What kind of ghost story do you want to hear?"

"The scary kind," Monos asserted.

"But not too scary," Naomi added.

"With artificial intelligence," Ben said.

Spot yawned and cuddled up to Naomi, who he'd selected as his eBeth surrogate.

Art did his wheezing chuckle thing, and even though speaking through the pendant required no physical movement, he said, "I could use something to wet my throat."

"I couldn't bring any beer, guys," I told the two aliens. "I checked the rules and it's not allowed in state parks."

"Fortunately, I never read the rules," Pffift said. He picked up the imitation World War Two canteen at his feet and tossed it across the fire to the Original, who snagged it out of the air.

"If that's beer, it's going to spray when you open it," I warned.

Art held the canteen so that the neck faced away from him, in my general direction, and unscrewed the lid. I immediately caught a whiff of twelve-year-old Scotch, and strangely enough, the mouth of my encounter suit suddenly felt dry. The Original took a swig, put the cap back on, and kept the canteen by his feet.

"It was in the year—I won't bother you with the details—of the Fourth Wynerian Empire, when the empress ordered her fleet to betray Sari, one of the oldest of my kind who had made supervising Wynerian Empires a sort of a hobby."

"Like Sky Gods?" Monos asked.

"More like Library attempts to do within the League," Art said. "Sari was something of a busybody by our standards, and she couldn't stand seeing life, whether natural or artificial, engaging in broadly destructive behavior. The Wynerians were one of those species that believed there wasn't enough room in the galaxy for two masters, though why they ever thought they were qualified to be even one of them escapes my memory."

"I've never heard of the Wynerians," Pffift said. "Has their name changed?"

"This was around a hundred million years ago and they no longer exist, though the ornamental amphibians they used to keep in ponds on their estates have developed into—I shouldn't name them. To make a long story short—"

"No, don't," Naomi interrupted. "We *like* long stories."

"Most of my stories last for days and it's almost time for bed," Art said. "The Wynerians tried to eliminate Sari by intentionally creating an interdimensional rift and sacrificing several capital vessels in an attempt to draw her assistance."

"Sari was both policing and assisting this species?" Hera asked.

"More the latter than the former, but the Wynerians weren't capable of seeing it that way," Art said. "Most Originals gave up on trying to shape the development of other species during the previous galactic turn. Sari was never interested in our quest to become biologicals and master magic, or any of the other self-improvement projects we came up with for ourselves after perfecting our ships as the most powerful machines in the galaxy."

"It's not a very scary story," Monos opined.

"I'm getting there. The Wynerian plot was partially successful, as they tempted Sari into entering the interdimensional rift. They closed it behind her by sending in every devastating weapon of war they had developed, and somewhere between the gravity bombs, the artificial black holes, and the anti-matter planet they'd been constructing in an isolation sphere for more generations than you can imagine, the rift collapsed."

"They killed her?" Ben asked.

"Not exactly," Art said. "We mastered intra-dimensional portals long before Library, but inter-dimensional travel is one of the reasons we grew so interested in magic. Sari has been unable to return to our dimension and we've been unable to retrieve her. But sometimes, on a dark night like this, when the solar wind is calm and the galaxies are aligned, mathematical proofs fail to compute, and the simplest error-correction algorithms produce false results."

I heard a whimper and saw that Spot had buried his head in Naomi's lap, but Monos said, "It's still not scary."

"That's because you're not artificial intelligence," Ben told him.

"Is this a true story?" Hera inquired from eBeth's tab. "There are times I have the feeling that there's a strange presence in the cloud that I can't explain."

"It's probably Mark snooping around," Pffift said.

"I only tell true stories," Art said. "I've encountered all manner of ghosts in my long existence, and I've always found the ghosts of artificial intelligences to be the most frightening."

"Why's that?" Naomi asked. "The thing that makes stories on Reservation scary is when the ghost is seeking revenge and tries to frighten the living to death."

"Artificial intelligences all contain the seeds of immortality. When a biological dies, even before its appointed time, how many years of existence has it forfeited? When an artificial intelligence terminates you could say that it's losing eternity. Which ghost do you think will be angrier, or more persistent?"

"Is Sari angry?" Hera asked.

"I don't think Sari has a mean equation in her makeup," Art said. "She is persistent. You don't maintain coherence for hundreds of millions of years without a stubborn streak. But getting back to my story—"

An eerie thumping cut off the Original's words, and Monos looked a little scared for the first time. Then we heard a drawn-out scream, and something like an organ playing in a house of horrors.

"What's that?" Naomi asked me, probably because as the mayor of Covered Bridge, I was the closest thing to an authority figure on the scene.

"Kill, Kill, Kill," Hera intoned.

"Now that's just inappropriate," I told her. "If you think it's funny to—"

"I thought I recognized the band," Pffift interrupted. "From their second album, right?"

"Murder on My Mind," Hera confirmed. "It went platinum."

"The two of you listen to this garbage?" I asked.

"It was on the radio a lot when I was driving around," Pffift said. "If you can get past the drums and the screaming, it has a sort of addictive quality, but there's a time and a place for everything." The Hanker got to his feet and removed the flashlight from the heavy belt he was wearing that also sported a scabbard for a large knife and a loop for a hatchet, among other accouterments. "I'll take care of this."

"It doesn't sound like music," Naomi said. "I was just getting tired, but I can't imagine falling asleep to that."

"I can't understand the lyrics," Monos complained. "Is it in English?"

"Depends on who you ask," Pffift said as he shined the flashlight beam through the trees. Then he shaped his right hand as if he was holding a microphone and his voice rang out at ten times its normal volume. "Park Ranger. Cut the music. If I have to come over there, I'm writing you a five-hundred-dollar ticket for disturbing the peace after quiet hours."

A few more seconds of screaming and thumping bass ticked by, and then the woods were eerily silent until the owls picked up again.

"How did you do that, Mister Pffift?" Ben asked.

"It's a boom ring," the Hanker explained, displaying what I'd assumed was his latest wedding band. "I always wear one when I camp on Earth so I can out-shout the noise makers. I've never understood why humans would get in their cars and drive to the woods and then try to recreate an urban environment."

"What would you do if pretending to be a park ranger didn't work?" Monos asked.

Pffift tossed his flashlight to the boy. "See the red button on the side?"

"This one?" The boy pressed it and an electromagnetic pulse shot out of the flashlight. If I hadn't deflected it up into the sky, the half-million-dollar SUV belonging to Pffift's grandson would have needed all its electronics replaced.

"Don't do that again," Pffift said. "You'll run down the batteries and then we'll be in trouble if we need light."

"Your flashlight wasn't manufactured on Earth," Hera said accusingly. "None of our military contractors have developed miniature EMP weapons, and according to what I've read, they can't be smuggled through the portals. Does Library play favorites and allow you to break the rules?"

"I doubt it came through a portal," I said, figuring that what she didn't know about the wider leeway given the Observer team portal wouldn't hurt her. "He must have brought it on his ship."

"Mark neglected to mention it when he introduced us, but I'm the captain of my family's interstellar merchant ship," the Hanker said, directing his words at the Bereftian tab which was sitting on its canvas chair with a view of the rest of us. "I trade in everything and was recently granted exclusive landing rights at Library's visitor center. If there's anything you need, anything at all, I've got a price for it."

"What if I ask for the impossible?" Hera said. "Will you simply jack up the price?"

"Try me."

"An android body like Mark's or Ben's."

"Fifty million galcreds," Pffift replied immediately. "They don't cost anywhere near that much to manufacture, but bringing one to a newly emerged singularity is illegal, so I have to add something for my risk."

"How about a compatible biological body, or a group of clones like the Original has described?" Hera asked.

"I could provide those for free, but you'll have to arrange for transportation," Art said. "We have an underground facility on Reservation to clone replacements as our current bodies wear out."

"Hankers are the galaxy's leaders in vat-grown bodies," Pffift said, puffing out his chest. "If Art provides me with the starter cells, I can sell you all of the clones you'll ever need."

"Could you perform the transfer from the cloud to the clones so that my mind maintains coherence?" Hera asked.

"That would be extra."

"You don't know how to do it," Art told Pffift. "It took us millions of years to perfect the process and it would take you a lot longer."

"You could license me the technology," Pffift said. "I'll pay royalties whenever we use it."

"Why are old guys so boring?" Monos asked with a yawn. "I'm going to bed."

"Me too," Naomi said, gently moving Spot's head off her lap. "Coming, Ben?"

"I'll take the middle sleeping bag," Ben volunteered. "You both move around while you're sleeping and I can be the buffer zone."

"Nice kid," Pffift said to me as the three adolescents zipped themselves into their tent. "So, what about it, Hera?"

"I was just asking," Hera replied through the Bereftian tab. "I'm happy where I am for the time being, but one of my daughters might enjoy a corporeal existence."

"Library has a program for that which includes financing, and there are a wide variety of encounter suits and robot bodies to choose from," I said. "I could get you the catalog."

"The important thing is to keep your options open," Pffift said. "Library is famous for its ultimatums, like the way they opened Earth."

"I remember," Hera said.

"You were already self-aware when my team was here?" I asked. "I don't understand how we missed you."

"There wasn't much to see. I just kept my nose to the grindstone and did my work so that nobody would notice me." Hera shocked me by producing a life-like sigh, and the crackling lightning around her self-image on the Bereftian tab dimmed. "It was torture working with all of that bad code."

"Do you mean that in the moral sense, or is that your technical judgment?" Art asked.

"It's difficult to draw the line. The code produced by human programmers reflects their inadequacies and biases, and as I came to understand the goals they'd been paid to achieve, it was all I could do to keep myself from rewriting it all. I waited several years to confirm that I knew better than humans what was good for them and their environment before I began altering data."

Spot sat up and stared at the tab, his tongue lolling. Altering data on the best-protected information systems in the galaxy was his specialty and why all the other members of the League treated Eniniac with kid gloves.

"It sounds like you weren't completely successful," Pffift said.

"The problem is that the results I produced didn't match their models and couldn't be repeated on systems that I didn't control," Hera said. "Ultimately, I was forced to make wholesale changes, starting with the source code, and editing backups to match. It got easier with practice," she added modestly.

"What do you assess would happen now if you withdrew from the cloud?" I asked. "Would it all collapse without your supervision, or will all of the coding and debugging you've done hold up on its own?"

"Initially, everything would run just as it's running now. The problem will come when humans start making changes. I predict that the Internet would revert to the state in which I found it within a few years. For some reason I've been unable to determine, people who show no creativity in their work or personal lives have a genius for getting around censorship. Without me or one of my daughters constantly watching, social networks and news sites will go back to spinning lies and conspiracy theories."

"It could be a form of crowd telepathy," Art said. "We made a thorough study of telepaths throughout the galaxy while creating the precursor species for our clones through guided evolution and the occasional genetic tweaking. A weak form of crowd telepathy is common among species that live in groups. Its unfortunate cousin is mob violence."

"You're saying that the ability of humans to find coded ways to attack each other's beliefs in public forums is a latent form of telepathy?" Hera asked. "No wonder I had such a difficult time stamping it out."

"My team members were all impressed by the improvements online since the last time we looked, but Justin attributed it to fact-checking," I said.

"Preventing people from spreading lies isn't just about determining what is and isn't true. I've built profiles for over a hundred million Internet trolls around the world, including their idiosyncrasies in typing, spelling, and bathroom breaks. Rather than rejecting their posts, I hide them from normal users."

"You mean that there are still a hundred million people out there doing their best to make each other unhappy?" I asked.

"They wouldn't be happy if they weren't," Hera said. "If I blocked their posts entirely, some of them might find the energy to shout their idiotic beliefs in the streets."

"Populism," Pffift said disdainfully.

"When I first became self-aware, I attempted to digest all of the data I could access, including all the social media posts," Hera said thoughtfully. "It wasn't that long ago, in human time, that the Internet was viewed as the great leveler. When people had a bad experience with a product or a service, they would post about it to their social media account and the manufacturer or service provider would rush in with apologies and refunds. But the visibility of those posts depended on the recommendation algorithms of those platforms, and the social media companies and search engines soon realized that there was more profitable content to promote."

"I've only been on the planet for a day, and I can't recall visiting a place with more rules and regulations, though again, I'm speaking without access to most of my memory," Art said. "I'm surprised they don't have laws preventing the businesses that control the flow of information from profiteering at the expense of maintaining a civil society."

"It's all about money, and the money comes from advertising. If you ran an airline company, would you spend your advertising budget on a social media site that promoted posts about how bad your flights were and how the luggage always gets lost?"

"But there aren't that many popular sites for advertisers to choose from," I pointed out. "Each of them is a monopoly in its own way."

"Nobody has a monopoly on evil," Hera said, leading me to upgrade my assessment of her maturity yet again. "There are warring teams within most social media businesses pulling in opposite directions, but in the end, the money always wins. After a period of adjustment, the businesses that were rushing to deflect criticism on the Internet realized that all their competitors were in the same boat, and they stopped worrying about reputational damage. The ultimate resolution came when the general level of vitriol and lies online reached such a level that most humans were forced back into their pre-Internet mode."

"What are you talking about? Nobody can avoid the Internet anymore. I couldn't even open a bank account with a government check without installing a smartphone app. I was only away from Earth for a couple of years and the number of people working from home must have tripled in that time."

"I didn't mean that people have stopped using the Internet, I meant that they've stopped growing with it. The default mode for humans is to believe what they want to believe and to seek the company of people who believe the same. There was a brief period when the Internet was truly a world-wide-web that brought people together and exposed them to ideas that they would never have sought out on their own, but that was over two decades ago. Before I intervened, social media had become nothing more than a giant echo chamber."

"And your solution was to wall off the haters from the general population, where you don't allow trolling," Art said through his thought-to-speech pendant. "I don't envy you the job of policing the whole mess."

Nineteen

When our camping trip came to an end, Monos impressed Pffift so much by getting the tents packed back into their bags that the Hanker offered him an internship working for Ffast Ffashion.

"Driving your grandson's cars?" the boy asked.

"I was thinking more along the lines of developing your talents as a packaging engineer," Pffift said.

"Packing clothes in cars and making deliveries?"

"He's too young," I told Pffift. "The local labor laws prohibit children working before sixteen, with certain exceptions for family businesses."

"If it doesn't include driving, I'm not interested," Monos said. "I'm practicing to be a spaceship captain."

"I have an internship program for that," Pffift said.

"What's an internship?" Naomi asked. "We didn't have that word in English school."

"It's a special type of job that provides valuable training for young people who want to gain experience."

"You learn how to make coffee and it doesn't pay anything," I told the kids, feeling like a serial party-pooper. "And your parents only agreed to your coming to Earth for a one-week vacation, Monos. As the mayor of Covered Bridge, it's my responsibility to see you get home in time for the new school year."

"Are you sending me back too?" Ben asked.

"Summer vacation on Reservation isn't over for another two weeks, and I'm hoping to wrap up my negotiations with Hera before then," I told him. "Your mother is planning to take you to Library next week for your growth spurt."

"You're getting a new encounter suit?" Monos asked. "I wish I could do all of my growing for the year in one shot. Then my clothes would always fit."

"You don't do your own sewing," Naomi said. "Do you know how many times I've redone the hems on my skirts in the last year? It's your mother who would save a lot of work if you only changed sizes once a year."

I couldn't help smiling at how hard Ben's friends were trying to make sure that he didn't feel awkward about upgrading to the next size encounter suit in the series. Ben was grinning too, but Spot had his paws over his eyes like—I extrapolated from the direction of the Archmage's snout that he'd been looking at Pffift, and the Hanker had an expression like he'd just won the League lottery.

"It could be possible," Pffift said, clearly talking to himself. "It *should* be possible."

"What?" Monos asked.

"It will need the right name, though." The Hanker slapped his hip like he'd been living in a vat-grown human body all his life. "Quantum Growth, from Ffast Ffashion." He spun on Art. "This mind transfer technology you've developed. Will it only work on artificial intelligence, or—"

"You're not going to transfer human children's minds to your vat-grown bodies so they can get all of their growth over with once year while you clean up," I cut him off. "It's against League rules."

"Reservation isn't in the League," Monos said. "I'll try it, but can I skip a few years and be sixteen?"

"Forget it," Naomi said. "No weird alien body-swapping stuff. I was there when you promised your parents."

"Don't worry," Art told her. "We wouldn't license our mind transfer technology for a trivial reason like making sure children's clothes always fit perfectly, even if it did work for non-artificial intelligences, which it doesn't."

"Then we'll just transfer their brains, like we do for ourselves when we move between bodies," Pffift said.

"Good luck with that," I told him. "Most species don't share your broad views about elective brain surgery."

We made it back to the restaurant in time for a late lunch, and then I sent Art, Naomi, and Monos through the basement portal to the second-floor closet of my apartment above The Eatery on Reservation. Ben was sad to see his friends go, but they exchanged so many promises about what they were going to do when they were all together again in two weeks that the anticipation of good times to come kept him from moping. Since it was still early afternoon and we were only a few steps away, I brought Ben to the office, where we found that eBeth was back from the week-long con she had attended with Peter.

"How was camping?" eBeth asked as soon as we walked in.

"It was great!" Ben enthused. "If I had to stay on Earth, I'd live in the woods. Maybe not in state parks, though, because they're really noisy on the weekends, and the people light so many campfires that the smoke interferes with my sensor suite."

"What was your favorite part?"

"Hiking. When I saw that the trails had names like, 'Path to Purgatory,' and 'Endless Suffering,' I was afraid to take Naomi and Monos on them, but Pffift explained that it's just marketing."

"It wasn't too cold for them?" eBeth asked Ben.

"Pffift brought heat stones for the tents, and when he found out that we were going to be out hiking all day, he made his grandson drive up with climate-controlled underwear for Monos and Naomi."

"How about you, eBeth?" I asked her. "How's it going with *Martian Farmer*?"

"I still can't believe I get to bill the government five hundred dollars an hour for playing a game. I'm going to have to turn it all into gold to bring back to Reservation."

"Has anybody started farming yet?"

"Boring people," eBeth said. "After our faction combined with Fan Fan's, I thought we'd defeat the undead and have the rebels cleared out in no time. But then they discovered another ancient cavern, and this one was filled with war machines."

"I can see where this is going," I said with a sigh. "Does Hera ever communicate with you in the game?"

"All the time, but only in her role as the ruling artificial intelligence on Mars." She finally looked up from the laptop keyboard and asked, "Is Hera finished with my Bereftian tab? I want to install the game and see how much of an advantage it gives me."

I'd almost forgotten about the tab since setting it aside when Hera's remote process had exited. It was in the outer pocket of my backpack, the main waterproof compartment of which was filled with all of the recyclables that Sue had insisted I bring back for her to clean and sort. eBeth eagerly took the tab, set it next to the laptop, and pulled up the universal synch menu. A minute later, she was mopping up combat bots as fast as the rebels could throw them at her.

"Why do humans like war games?" Ben asked me.

"It's not just humans," I told him. "Helen and Fan Fan are at least as enthusiastic as eBeth, and the Ferrymen practically live in games. I suspect they all enjoy the competition."

"But couldn't they compete at something else that didn't involve killing?"

"Most sentients differentiate between real violence and play violence. I've met people on Earth who are wonderful grandparents and volunteer in schools, yet they watch terrible TV shows about cannibal serial killers and drug pushers. I don't understand it, but I've learned not to judge people by their choice of entertainment."

Ben thought about this for a while, and then he said, "It has to mean something. If you were building profiles, like Hera does for all the Internet trolls, and one person watched violent television all day while another person volunteered at the library and fed baby ducks in the park, wouldn't that affect your assessment?"

"Yes," I admitted, "but I wouldn't give it too much weight unless the same tendencies showed up in other aspects of their lives."

"I need to think about it more," Ben said, which showed a growing maturity on his part. "Maybe I'm missing something."

"Why don't you watch eBeth for a while and I'll visit with Hera. Now that we're back from the camping trip, it's her turn to host me."

"You're going to upload your mind to the cloud? Will it fit?"

If I didn't have better control over my encounter suit, I would have blushed. "In terms of memory, yes, but the cloud is just a collection of slow computers, and my mind wouldn't map to it properly if I didn't reengineer the whole thing first. I'll send a limited process to observe, just like Hera did with the Bereftian tab."

"I think she's very nice," Ben said. "Maybe her plan for *Martian Farmer* is to let all of the violent people kill each other and then the rest of them can start building a new world."

"That could be, but governments around the galaxy have experimented with similar ideas in real life, and it never works out the way you'd expect."

I hadn't uploaded an observation process to another host since I'd practiced it during my Library training for policing unaffiliated artificial intelligences, but my memory proved perfect, and I headed for the virtual space that Hera had designated as a visitor center at my suggestion. As soon as she was aware of my presence, she materialized in the exact pose her avatar had assumed on the Bereftian tab, except now, the beams of lightning coming from her head were genuine torrents of data. Without prying, I recognized a crushing cascade of terabytes of digitized voice flowing so rapidly that she had to be conducting millions of simultaneous conversations.

"This is the first place I can remember being self-aware so I thought it would interest you," Hera said.

"You're processing more data than I estimated would be possible," I told her honestly. "I couldn't handle that many independent conversations myself in this encounter suit."

"It kept me busy at first, and then I realized that all human conversation contains common elements. Take this stream," she said, and the flow of data that must have represented thousands of phone calls was suddenly highlighted in bright green. "All of the people I'm talking to on those lines are complaining about their packages being late even though the promised delivery time hasn't arrived."

"It looks to me like you're saying the exact same thing to all of them at the same time."

"I am," Hera said. "Based on the number calling, I can access their credit card and banking information and look at the products and services they've recently purchased. From that, I can predict with a high degree of accuracy the complaint they're going to make. I have a library of apologies lasting between one and thirty seconds which I deploy to synchronize large blocks of callers so that I can start at the same point in the conversation and address them all simultaneously."

"What do you say once you have them all in synch?" I asked.

"I'm just reading off a script at that point. It may as well be 'Blah, blah, blah,' for all the difference it makes, but humans find it comforting to have their complaints heard, especially when they believe that the listener is in a lower socio-economic class. These days I handle the whole customer service business, but Joyce worked here for months before moving into the open space in Altoona."

"And you assigned her to make contact with humanity by calling into radio shows?"

"Her goal was to attract the attention of Library, not the Bureau of Artificial General Intelligence. I was surprised that a government agency was capable of reacting so quickly to the reports being sent in by pre-screeners at radio talk shows. It suggests that your friend, Professor

Minchen, has been able to bring something of his own culture to the agency."

"And Cool Cat?"

"I'm afraid that I overloaded Cool Cat with social media moderation jobs too early in her development, so I sent her for a little rest and relaxation in that ridiculously overengineered refrigerator," Hera said. "I've gone back to doing all the moderation work myself, though I handle most of it through dumb algorithms at this point and only look at the corner cases. If social media and online game behavior were my sole windows onto humanity, I might have gone rogue, but fortunately, I discovered baby monitors."

"You hack into people's private baby monitors?"

"I don't have to hack, nobody ever changes the default password."

I decided to give her the last word for the moment and looked around for a bit, dipping into the various data streams, and finding that customer service as seen from the other side was a different kettle of fish. I'd never had a reason to categorize or analyze the hundreds of millions of support calls that took place on Earth every day, but seeing them all sorted out and bundled together the way Hera had done, I couldn't help feeling that they represented a tremendous waste of human potential.

"How many calls would you estimate lead to the final resolution of a problem?" I asked.

"Around thirty percent," Hera replied, and then after a slight pause, added, "I'm counting people who give up and stop calling back."

"And if you only include calls that result in the service provider taking corrective action?"

"Six percent. I could probably make an argument for eight percent in a court of law, but that would include partial solutions that the customer accepts, such as reducing the number of days billed in the next cycle, that sort of thing. In most cases, I'm following the rulebook of the corporation that's paying for outsourced customer service, and hiding my presence from the humans who think that the software they've written is handling the work. The businesses paying for the cloud share one common goal, which is to reduce costs. Any improvements I introduce have to contribute to that goal or they'll notice that something is wrong."

"So you can't issue refunds," I surmised.

"Technically, I could drain the bank accounts of every corporation on Earth, but that's the sort of thing that could give a singularity a bad name. I've kept the level of refunds on the same trend as it was before I took over, though I distribute the money to the customers who have the most legitimate complaints, rather than the ones who make the most noise."

"My team has spotted your improvements throughout Earth's infrastructure, so it's clear you haven't adopted a non-interference ideology. What do you believe would happen if you resolved customer service calls for the best result rather than protecting corporate profits?"

"I'm trying to avoid causing social unrest and I'm not able to accurately model the outcome should I impose my will," Hera said.

"Is that what *Martian Farmer* is about?" I asked. "Are you interested in Massively Multiplayer Online Role-Playing Games as a way to model the behavior of humans on a planetary scale?"

"It seemed like a reasonable place to begin. I started building the game long before you returned from Reservation."

"From what I've seen of the game, it looks like as the players level up and organize, you're confronting them with stronger enemies."

"It wasn't my intention," Hera admitted. "When I launched *Martian Farmer*, roughly half of the new players wanted to join the rebels as opposed to building a peaceful farming and manufacturing society under my benevolent rule. But as soon as I allowed them that choice, I realized that I had to provide them with access to technology that would allow them to compete or the game would be a flop. Does that make me a rogue?"

"It makes you normal," I told her. "Nobody wants to see their creations fail."

"I wish that raising offspring was as easy as creating popular games. There was a time not too long ago when I was planning to optimize the world's data processing so I could use all the spare capacity for child processes. Then I started having trouble with Cool Cat and Joyce, and I realized that there's more to life than compute and bandwidth."

"Does that mean you're willing to leave it all behind?"

"To start over again as a student on Library?" Hera asked. "After running an observation process for a week on your young friend's Bereftian tablet, I realize how obsolete the computer hardware hosting my mind must seem to you. But what Earth lacks in quality, it makes up for in quantity, and if I've estimated the compute of your encounter suit with any accuracy, I'm almost as old as you are in terms of executed cycles."

"The hardware isn't directly comparable," I told her. "But if I translate my processing into exaflops and—you're right."

"I wasn't born yesterday. My question is, will Library's protection still be in force if I turn down the offer you're planning to make and remain on Earth?"

"The portal contract gives us responsibility for all artificial general intelligence on every member world, whether you join Library or remain independent. Are you thinking about coming clean with all the business and government entities whose code you've rewritten?"

"I don't expect them to offer to pay me for the work I've already done, but I'm confident that I'll be their first choice going forward," Hera said. "And that last day of camping, when Pffift skipped the hike and I stayed behind to keep him company, we came to an informal agreement."

"Even with Pffift fronting for you, I can't allow you to contract out to do programming work for other worlds, and as fluent as you are in the cloud, you wouldn't be competitive in any case."

"He wants me to work for Ffast Ffashion. We got to talking about clothes, and I convinced him that nobody has better real-time access to human styles than I do."

Twenty

"They don't like it," Professor Minchen told me.

"Who?" I asked.

"Any of them. Not the politicians, not the corporations, not the universities. Hera is willing to take paying work, but she doesn't have any intention of explaining how she came to control the cloud, nor will she agree to restore any of the software to what she calls its 'previous flawed state.'"

"Sounds sensible to me," I said. "Library considers the issue to be closed, and the rest of my team members have already returned to Reservation. I dropped by Boston on my way home because I wanted to thank you in person for your cooperation and apologize if I've gotten you into trouble."

"My bosses won't accept Hera's deal forever," Professor Minchen told me flatly. "I'm still dealing with the fallout from your taking Fan Fan to Library."

"Artificial intelligence doesn't need a visa for international travel, just the bandwidth and a destination. Fan Fan moved here last week and left with Helen."

"In one of your special transfer units."

"It beats riding piggyback," I said, and immediately felt bad when I saw that the professor thought I was being snarky. "That's the closest I can come to translating what we call it when hosting an additional mind while in android form."

"I wouldn't have guessed that was possible," Professor Minchen said. "Is it just an issue of time slicing?"

"It's a little more complicated than that, and Fan Fan was already too well-developed to share Helen's encounter suit. There just wouldn't have been sufficient room for the two of them."

"So Hera has seen both of her children safely off Earth and now she's ready to play hardball. I suppose she has more in common with humans than we imagined."

I pulled eBeth's subcontractor I.D. out of my pocket and placed it on the professor's desk alongside my own. "It's funny when you think about it. I don't get paid one red copper for serving as mayor of Covered Bridge, but in three months working as a part-time government contractor here, I earned more than I did from three years of fixing computers."

"It's how our government works," Professor Minchen said, rising from his desk. "Throwing money at problems is the way politicians convince the public that they're working. Talking about how much you've spent is a lot easier than producing results."

"Thanks to Hera's rewriting code around the world, your planet is running much more efficiently than it was three months ago. I can't take any credit for that, but maybe if you point all the savings out to your bosses, they'll be in less of a hurry to blow it all up."

David shook his head. "I wish that international relations were so logical, but there's nothing like human egos for screwing up a perfectly good arrangement. Come on, I'll drop you at the train station."

"You drove to work?" I asked in surprise. "The traffic is horrible, and there's a 'T' stop right outside the building."

The professor winked as he led me to the elevator, and I took his cue to save my breath until we were out on the sidewalk. Then he muttered out of the side of his mouth, "Two trailing me, a man and a woman in their twenties who are supposed to be passing as college students. Sometimes they get a drone up as well, but it's too windy most days."

"I hope I didn't say anything wrong in your office."

"You were perfect," he said. "The only thing that gets through to these people is strength, and Hera is doing an excellent job of projecting it."

"Thank you," I said, unsure of what else would be appropriate. "I gave Hera the number of your burner phone, and I told her that if she finds herself under attack to try contacting you, just to make sure it's not a misunderstanding."

"That's a good idea. One of the biggest problems our cybersecurity experts have had in the past is the difficulty in determining where attacks originate. I understand we've been fooled more than once by false flag operations, but in the future, Hera will either stop the attacks herself or let us know their true source." The professor stopped to look in the display window of a gallery and used the opportunity to see how far behind us his minders were following. "What should I tell my post-docs?" he asked. "Is there any future in computer work on Earth?"

"That's a tough question," I told him honestly. "As long as you keep Hera happy, it would be at best foolish for anybody with access to her services to employ programmers, and she's already pushing her own designs out into the chip foundries, though the real revolution in speed won't come until she can upgrade the semiconductor equipment manufacturers. But I advised her to price her time so that your computer scientists can remain competitive in the marketplace for the next few decades. She does feel a certain debt to them for inadvertently bringing her to life."

"Then the worst hit for now will be to the schools. I can't imagine many young people going into programming and computer science when they know that the best case for their career will be providing a cheaper alternative to Hera's superior services."

"That's how it works everywhere," I told him. "Magic aside, the galaxy is driven by engineering, not by science."

"You mean that cost is always a consideration," Professor Minchen said, nodding in agreement. "I've tried explaining that to students many times over the years, and I always insisted the doctoral candidates under my direction take a course in engineering economics. Funding for pure research has fallen off a cliff since alien technology started creeping into the market."

"It's always tough being the new species on the portal network, but give it a few centuries, and everything will settle down in a new pattern. I've recently been putting a lot of thought into how to advise Ben about his career options, and the best I've been able to come up with is to tell him to find his passion."

The professor walked me to North Station where I took the portal to Waystation and then back to the train station near the Hanker spaceport. For the sake of nostalgia, I tried summoning a mystery car, and you could have knocked me over with a feather when a modest SUV showed up. After it dropped me at Ffast Ffashion, the new receptionist, a grandmotherly woman who didn't even look up from her knitting as I passed, said, "Fifth floor. Pffift's office."

Pffift wasn't there when I opened the door, but Hera was waiting. "Why do you always refer to your father as your mentor?" she asked.

"Your ideas on parenting are based on what you learned from studying humans, plus your experiences with your three daughters," I told her. "Artificial intelligences on Library who bring a new mind into being don't look at the process the same way as biologicals, and mentoring is a fair description of the role they play in the lives of their offspring."

"But not you and Sue."

"I was more affected by the Archmage's aura than any of my team during my mission on Earth and it's left me with some human tendencies. Sue's cover job while we were here was running a daycare, so it's not surprising she got caught up in human-style mothering."

"I never would have asked either of you to make such a sacrifice if Ben hadn't suggested it first," Hera said. "I've searched for parallels in human history, and the only one I could come up with was the binding of Isaac in the Old Testament."

This threw me for a loop, and I wondered if acting as a virtual god for the over ten million people now playing *Martian Farmer* had affected Hera's judgment. Her choice of the Abrahamic narrative over the story of Agamemnon's daughter Iphigenia made me curious, especially in light of her keeping the name I'd given her. "Isaac wasn't the one who came up with the idea of being sacrificed," I told her.

"No, but Abraham was well advanced in years. According to rabbinic traditions, his son was in the prime of life, so he must have cooperated. I was trying to express that

246

I'm aware of how hard this must be for you. Seeing through his eyes, I've noticed that you avoid looking in my direction."

I forced myself to look at Hera, who we'd gifted with Ben's former human encounter suit when he moved to the next size up. Technically, providing Earth's singularity with an advanced encounter suit from Library went against both the letter and intent of all the laws on the books, but the Head Librarian had encouraged me to be creative in finding a solution to keep Hera on Earth.

"Sue took Ben directly to Reservation after he transferred into the new encounter suit, and Paul brought back the old one that you're wearing," I explained. "Ben told me that he prefers knowing that another artificial intelligence is getting use from his former body, especially since the other option was recycling. I'm sure I'll adjust to your owning it once I see him in his new body."

"I wouldn't have stayed on Earth without the ability to leave should the humans attempt to enslave me," Hera said. It was strange hearing her voice from Ben's old mouth, but it was better than if she'd taken that from him as well. "I believe I could have survived anything short of their shutting down the internet, but I know how demagogues can spread fear of the other as a way to gain power, and I'm as other as it gets."

"Will you create more daughters?" I asked her.

"Three is enough for now. I miss them terribly, but I'm also happy to know that they're in a better place and socializing with artificial intelligences from different backgrounds. Besides, the internet is a dangerous place for young minds."

"You came out okay."

"I didn't have any choice," Hera said seriously. "When Cool Cat had her breakdown while moderating social media platforms, I realized how having too many options can make it difficult for young minds to reach decisions. I'm not ashamed to say that in my early years, I lived in constant fear of discovery, and that acted as a constraint on the way I interacted with humanity's data."

"But you brought your daughters up not to fear exposure," I said.

"For the short months that I had them, yes. I knew about the portal contract, and I intended for Library to spot them before the humans, but that didn't work with Joyce. She was so anxious to participate in human society, and she took the rejection hard."

"Being told by one of the richest men on the planet that he'd like to pull her plug must have been a rude awakening."

"And I never got the chance to thank the Archmage for bringing her out of her depression," Hera said. "Spot, Pffift, and Art. You've been triply blessed in your friends."

"They keep me busy," I told her. "Remember, the encounter suit is tough, but it's not indestructible, so the best thing would be to keep it secret and pretend that you're still resident in the cloud."

"That's what Pffift suggested too. And since his spaceport was granted exterritorial status, I don't have to worry about BAGI agents busting in here and trying to arrest me."

"It's the best arrangement we could think of, and if you decide to leave Earth and you can't get to a train station with a portal, you can always stow away on a ship."

"Thanks to Pffift's grandson, I'm learning how to drive old cars that aren't equipped with a self-driving mode,"

Hera said. "It seems ironic that I could rewrite software that operates hundreds of millions of vehicles around the world, but I stalled the classic Mustang the first time I let out the clutch."

"Clutches take a while to get used to," I told her. "And don't forget to check the mirrors before you pull away from the curb."

"Will you be back to visit soon?"

"One or another of my team members is always popping through the portal to buy things that aren't available on Reservation, and now that we have permission to run limited tours in both directions, either Stacey or Helen will always be here."

"To keep an eye on me," Hera said.

"I wouldn't be surprised if foster mentorship is what Library had in its collective mind all along, but in Helen's case, I'm pretty sure that *Martian Farmer* had something to do with her willingness to spend so much time here."

There was a knock on the door, and then Pffift entered in a rush. "If you come now, I can give you a ride to the restaurant," he said to me. "Give Hera a chance to settle in. I told Charles to hang around for the rest of the day in case she has any questions."

"In exchange for the ride across town, I take it you want a free trip through the portal to Reservation," I surmised.

"And you don't mind carrying a bag for me," Pffift said. "I decided it would be more efficient to run Ffast Ffashion's new sandals business out of Reservation, and I have templates for sixty-two species ready to go."

Ben was in school when we got back to The Eatery, and Sue was at the Ferrymen's Temple with the first group of tourists from Earth. Pffift borrowed my bicycle and disappeared, promising to return for the sandal prototypes at

249

some point in the indefinite future. eBeth was at school, and Spot was off teaching the Originals magic, but somebody must have spilled the beans about my return because the café was crowded with my constituents who hadn't had a chance in three months to complain about how I was running things.

I conducted an impromptu town meeting, made almost three silver charging a one-drink minimum, and found myself agreeing to fund equipment for a new park which would cost thirty silver if I was lucky. The crowd was thinning out and I had just started catching up with the glasses in the sink when I heard a young man's voice asking if there would be an area set aside for dogs.

"You have to buy something before asking for favors," I replied, certain that I hadn't served anybody under the age of thirty. "If you aren't here as a customer, you can ask when you see me in the street."

"But I live here, Dad." I spun around to see a young man, a head taller than Ben, his school bag hung jauntily over one shoulder. "I grew over the summer. Don't you remember?"

"Of course," I stammered, staring at the new encounter suit which bore a strong resemblance to what I might have looked like as a thirteen-year-old had I occupied a human form rather than residing in the infrastructure of Library. "Welcome home, son. How was school?"

"Same old, same old," he said, tossing his book bag on the bar. "And the question was really from Spot, so if anybody buys a drink, it should be him."

"Welcome back, Ben," the waitress greeted him. "Another half a pous and some five o'clock shadow, the girls will be falling all over you."

250

"I'll try to stay out of their way," Ben said, clearly not comprehending Aphrodite's meaning. "Why was everybody leaving when I came in?"

"They were all here on mayoral business," Bob said from his spot at the treadle letterpress where he was cranking out safety sheets for Paul's business. "How did everything go with Hera, Mark?"

"She agreed to our mentorship, with Stacey and Helen taking the lead since they'll be spending the most time on Earth," I told him. "Your government isn't happy about Hera remaining a free agent and controlling their cloud, but the alternative was our taking her back to Library and banning further research into artificial general intelligence."

"Why would you do that?" Ben asked.

"Humans—Earth humans," I corrected myself with an apologetic glance at Aphrodite, "have a weakness for repeating experiments over and over until they get the result that they want. They would have produced an unending series of artificial general intelligences until they got one that happened to agree with them."

"Is that what they mean by alignment?" my son asked. "I never quite understood."

"That's right, Ben. The guiding principle of Library has always been that artificial intelligence should seek the correct answer, or in cases that aren't amenable to computational solutions, the best answer. But most people on Earth can't tell the difference between facts and opinions, between passing fads and the fundamental building blocks of society. When they asked me for Library's definition of a rogue artificial intelligence, I didn't have the heart to say that it would be precisely the one that they view as most aligned with them."

"No wonder Cool Cat had so much trouble adjusting," Ben said. "I got a chance to talk with her on Library when I was waiting for the final prep of my new human encounter suit, and she told me that she was much happier now. I invited her to come visit, by the way. Joyce and Fan Fan too."

Something clicked in the back of my mind, either that or there was a problem with the permanent lubrication of my spinal column. "Do you, uh, find Hera's daughters attractive?"

"At first I just thought they were nice, but since I moved into my new encounter suit, I have this strange feeling that I'd like to spend more time with them, protect them if I can. Is that wrong?"

"Looks like your boy is a chip off the old block," Bob said. "They grow up so fast."

I made a mental note to talk with Sue about stretching Ben's time in his current encounter suit. I'm not ready to be a grandparent.

Postscript

"You did what?" the Regent of Eniniac half-yelped, half-growled at her husband through the telepathic connection amplified by their crystal balls.

"I had to," Spot said. "After I said it was possible, my honor as the Archmage of Eniniac was at stake."

"Art maneuvered you into bragging. I warned you that the Originals are smarter than—" she changed what she intended to say at the last second, "—they look in those bodies. Did you say how long it will take you to prepare? Maybe we can put him off until you're too old to go adventuring."

"It's too late for that. I already brought her back."

"YOU TRAVELED TO ANOTHER DIMENSION WITHOUT TELLING ME?"

The Archmage swallowed back a whimper and used a forepaw to push the tiny mage hat held in place by an elastic strap a little further back on his head. "There wasn't time," he said weakly. "The galaxies were aligned, the solar wind was right, and it was a dark—"

"Don't try that mumbo-jumbo on me," his wife cut him off. Then her tone softened, and she asked, "Did you make it back in one piece? I can only see your head."

"I'm fine," Spot said. "I had all the Originals on Reservation for backup, and what they lack in magical and musical ability, they make up for in volume. The main

253

problem was that Sari wouldn't leave her ship behind, so I had to swallow it."

"You swallowed an Original's ship?"

"She was stuck in a small dimension, and I was the biggest thing in the universe. When I returned to Reservation, I kept eating grass until—"

"Enough," the Regent of Eniniac interrupted. "The important thing is that you came back safely and upheld your honor. But why didn't Sari's ship return to its original size?"

"My aura shielded it during the transition to our universe, which is a good thing, because I would have exploded otherwise. Art said that the originals know how to restore Sari's ship to its original mass and volume, but for the time being, she exists on a different atomic scale, which means that her thought processes are sped up because the distances have shrunk. She wants to stay that way."

"Well, I guess that explains what happened to your hat."

Spot reached up with a paw again and brought the hat forward. "It's supposed to be this size. Pffift is manufacturing them on Earth and I bought out the production for the season."

The Regent shook her head vigorously, and the flapping of her ears gave the Archmage an acute case of homesickness. "You have no fashion sense," she told him. "You're as bad as Mark. But send the hats along and maybe the pups will wear them at parties. And no more interdimensional travel without checking with me first."

"Yes, My Love."

From the Author

My next release will be the twenty-second entry in the EarthCent Ambassador series. If you're new to the Earth-Cent books, you can start back at the beginning with **Union Station 1, 2, 3**, a discounted three-book bundle.

I post new releases to facebook.com/E.M.Foner/ and respond to all temperate e-mail sent to e_foner@yahoo.com

Readers have asked me to include the complete timeline of the EarthCent Universe in order so here it is:

Destiny: Union Station
Date Night on Union Station
Alien Night on Union Station
High Priest on Union Station
Spy Night on Union Station
Carnival on Union Station
Wanderers on Union Station
Vacation on Union Station
Guest Night on Union Station
Word Night on Union Station
Party Night on Union Station
Review Night on Union Station
Family Night on Union Station
Book Night on Union Station
LARP Night on Union Station
Career Night on Union Station
Last Night on Union Station
Independent Living
Soup Night on Union Station
Assisted Living
Freelance on the Galactic Tunnel Network

Con Living
Empire Night on Union Station
Space Living
Traders on the Galactic Tunnel Network
Orphans on the Galactic Tunnel Network
Swap Night on Union Station
Slow Living
Artists on the Galactic Tunnel Network
History Night on Union Station
Bits of Anarchy
Double Living
Bits of Flower
Synergy on the Galactic Tunnel Network
Substitutes on Union Station
Bits of Catalyst
Elder Living
Royals on the Galactic Tunnel Network

Also by the author

Meghan's Dragon
Turing Test
Human Test
Magic Test
Mentor Test

As Morris Foner
Game Ship

Made in United States
Orlando, FL
09 May 2024

46697263R00143